An Overriding Question

Merissa had her guard up as she faced Captain Alexandre Valmont. She would talk to him no more. But surely there was no danger in polite conversation?

Then out of the blue she heard him ask, "Is it not love that gives meaning to life?"

Merissa caught her breath. His question had caught her by surprise, with no response ready. Now as she opened her lips to attempt to answer, he just as suddenly put his arms around her and lowered his mouth to hers.

Merissa felt like a bonfire suddenly ignited. His kiss was seeking, testing. As she responded, it turned into another kiss, longer and more demanding. His arms pulled her closer, and her body fit against his as if it belonged there and there only.

"God help me, I cannot resist you. You are so beautiful, so alive," he whispered into her hair.

She did not have words to answer—only her lips . . . as she melted in the arms of this stranger who claimed to be a man of honor but who well might have none. . . .

The
Captain's
Dilemma

—⁂—

Gail Eastwood

◯

A SIGNET BOOK

SIGNET
Published by the Penguin Group
Penguin Books USA Inc., 375 Hudson Street,
New York, New York 10014, U.S.A.
Penguin Books Ltd, 27 Wrights Lane,
London W8 5TZ, England
Penguin Books Australia Ltd, Ringwood,
Victoria, Australia
Penguin Books Canada Ltd, 10 Alcorn Avenue,
Toronto, Ontario, Canada M4V 3B2
Penguin Books (N.Z.) Ltd, 182–190 Wairau Road,
Auckland 10, New Zealand

Penguin Books Ltd, Registered Offices:
Harmondsworth, Middlesex, England

First published by Signet, an imprint of Dutton Signet,
a division of Penguin Books USA Inc.

First Printing, November, 1995
10 9 8 7 6 5 4 3 2 1

To my mother and my sister Susan,
for getting me across the river;
to my sons and my husband, Ralph,
for their Herculean patience;
and to M. H., whose praise of my last book
fanned the fading embers of this one
back into a fire.

Chapter 1

In defiance of chilly evenings and ripe fields awaiting harvest, the September day had been a warm, bright imitation of summer. In the light of late afternoon, the colors of the countryside at the northernmost edge of Huntingdonshire showed a richness as lush and deep as the blue sky above. Cast against them like a bold stroke of white on a canvas filled with shades of green, Merissa Pritchard sat beside the River Nene, clad only in a thin muslin day dress.

"Why could I not have been born a duck?" she asked aloud, although there was no one with her to answer. She rested against the rough trunk of a willow tree, her long legs stretched out on the mossy bank before her. Her bonnet lay discarded in the grass nearby and her needlework lay untouched in her lap. A few feet away, the river eased past her with deceptive stillness, its mirror surface disturbed only by a few ripples of current and the wake from a pair of mallards swimming close to the bank.

Eyes as blue as the sky's reflection in the water followed the ducks' progress thoughtfully. Somewhere in the distance a dog was barking, threatening to disrupt the serenity of the scene like the ripples in the river's looking glass, but for the moment Merissa was utterly oblivious to the sound.

She cocked her head sideways to study the birds with one eye, the way they were studying her. "I don't suppose *you* waste months trying out dozens of different dance partners and playing foolish courtship games as I have been made to do."

How *did* ducks find their mates? She doubted that conscious choice or feelings played any part in the process at all. Yet they seemed content.

"You know, we humans make a terrible muddle of the whole thing. Terrible!"

The ducks did not appear surprised to hear this. The pair turned away, paddling slowly.

"I suppose it is foolish to envy a duck," Merissa said, giving herself a little shake. "Humans, after all, are seldom chased by dogs, shot for sport, or eaten for dinner. . . ."

Dogs. The faint but insistent sound of barking suddenly penetrated Merissa's consciousness.

"Good Lord—Polly!"

Minutes earlier, Merissa's brown and white spaniel had been snuffling in the grass and weeds close to the river. Now the dog was nowhere to be seen. No wonder the ducks had been so serene! Merissa scrambled to her feet, attempting to brush the dampness from her skirts as she did so.

She tossed her needlework into her basket and, without a thought for the bonnet still lying in the grass, hurried in the direction of the sound along the footpath that bordered the edge of the river. How could she ever catch up if Polly was pursuing some small creature?

With a twinge of guilt, Merissa admitted that she should have been paying attention. She was always woolgathering when she should not be. Thank heavens the barking seemed not to be moving from one stationary location up ahead.

Merissa stepped around a particularly muddy patch on the path, trying to think where Polly might be. Then in a sudden flash of intuition, she knew the answer.

Around the next bend in the river, blocked from her view by a clump of trees, the remains of an ancient windmill stood sentinel on the riverbank, at the edge of some pastureland owned by her father. Merissa knew it well. As children, she and her brother and sisters had always been warned not to play in it for safety reasons, although that, of course, had never stopped them.

"Polly, where are you?" Merissa called as she came within sight of the mill. "Come on, girl—it's past time to go home."

The young woman paused as she saw no sign of her dog outside the old building. She had always imagined the mill as a harmless old soldier, standing at attention from mere habit, growing increasingly tattered as the years passed.

The windowpanes were long gone and not a flapping shred of canvas still clung to the skeletal frames of the old sail arms, although the brick tower's sloping walls had gradually acquired a leafy covering of vines. Somehow it seemed less innocent now as the waning afternoon sun cast the ruin into deep shadow and gave it a slightly sinister air.

The barking continued without interruption.

"Polly, if you've managed to chase some poor animal in there, it surely deserves to be left alone," Merissa muttered, thinking of the surprising amount of damage a cornered rabbit could inflict upon a dog.

However, Polly's insistence had triggered Merissa's infamous curiosity, a force not to be taken lightly. She advanced through the long grass off the path and tried calling once more. This time the little dog bounded into sight from around the back of the abandoned building.

"There you are! What mischief have you been up to now?" Relief filled Merissa's voice, but only for a moment. The spaniel, having answered her mistress's call, ran back to the building and began to bark once again.

"Oh, botheration, Polly! This is no time to play games. What has gotten you so stirred up?"

A sound like a cough sent a sudden chill down Merissa's back. An inkling of caution tugged at her conscience, suggesting that she should grab Polly and simply go home. Her curiosity would be her undoing someday, she knew. Her mother had been predicting it since the day Merissa had first learned to crawl. Certainly Merissa's sensible, mature, securely married sister Francine would never do anything as foolish as investigating an old ruined mill when she ought to be heading home. But then, Francine would never have lost track of the dog in the first place, or have come out alone, or have stayed until so late in the day.

Merissa brushed all thoughts of Francine away in annoyance. Surely a single Season in London hadn't erased all her old sense of adventure. Had maturity suddenly made her a coward? Something had set Polly into a rare taking, and Merissa wanted to know what. She set down her basket.

"Polly, you stay right here," she said, trying to inject a note of firm authority into her voice. Clenching her fists, she stepped quietly up to the door entrance.

The old wooden door was half off its hinges and partly blocked the entrance, which was likely the reason Polly had not managed to get inside. The door had hung at its crazy angle for years, and Merissa knew she could not move it. The space beyond it was very dark. Vines had overgrown and filled in whatever window openings were not boarded over. The only light spilled in from the half-opened door. She gathered her skirts in one hand and carefully slid a leg over the barrier into the darkness beyond.

Precisely at the instant Merissa shifted her weight and eased her other leg in behind her, she felt a callused hand clamp over her mouth. An arm snaked around her waist. Caught utterly off balance, she was dragged backward into the deeper darkness away from the entrance. Only a muffled squeak of alarm managed to escape her lips.

Merissa was too stunned to react for a moment. Then she fought. She flailed her arms and tried to jab her unseen captor with her elbows. Only her back connected with anything solid, and that was unquestionably a man's hard-muscled body. When she realized that her attempts to kick him or step on his foot were having no effect whatsoever, she stopped struggling and tried instead to loosen his unshakable grip on her, prying in vain at his hand and arm.

It was then, when she realized how strong he was, that true fear seized her as surely as he had. A derisive little voice spiraled up out of her panic to tell her that the day of her long-predicted downfall had arrived. This was no jest. Polly stood outside, barking, but at this time of day there was not likely anyone within a quarter mile of the mill who would take any notice.

"You have made a mistake to come in here, mademoiselle," whispered a deep voice at her ear, speaking English with a heavy accent. "Most unfortunate. Now I do not know what we shall do with you."

The speaker paused, almost as if he expected her to offer some solution to his problem. That seemed to her more than ridiculous, since he was still holding her firmly against him with his hand over her mouth.

His words helped her begin to feel outrage instead of fear. How dare he handle her so? He was the one who had made a mistake; he was the one who was trespassing. She tried to jerk her head away from his hand, to no avail.

She stayed still then, realizing the need to cool her anger and keep her wits about her. His accent was French. What was he doing here? Where had he come from? He had said "we." How many others were with him, and were they French, too? If only she could see something in the darkness! Even with her eyes now adjusted, she could make out nothing beyond the shadowy forms of the huge wooden cogwheels and shaft that filled up the center of the room.

"If you will give your word not to make any sound, I will remove my hand," the man said softly.

Definitely French. Here was real trouble. Were they spies? Escaped prisoners?

Merissa nodded vigorously. As she did, a second man's harsh voice issued a quick stream of words out of the darkness nearby, ending in a fit of coughing. His dialect was so thick, she could only make out the words "dog" and "cut," but those were enough, given the heartless tone in which they were spoken.

"Taissez-vous, Guillaume," Merissa's captor commanded sharply, earning a grumbled reply.

She sensed a moment's hesitation in him, and jerked her head away from his hand. "Please! You must not harm Polly. She is only a dog."

The man moved his hand to her arm. *"Ah, vous comprenez le français."*

"Only a little. *Un peu seulement.*" She wondered whether she had made a mistake to let him know it.

"Do not be frightened," her captor whispered in English, as if he did not wish the other man to hear. Switching to French and speaking a little louder, he said, "You have more concern for your dog than for yourself, mademoiselle. That is not wise, but you will come to no harm as long as you do as we tell you."

The words came too fast. She shook her head, and felt his grip tighten.

"No? Do you understand?" He repeated the words for her in English. His voice had lost its gruffness, but now she thought a note of urgency had crept into it instead. "I do not wish to hurt you," he repeated in a whisper.

She nodded then, not trusting her own voice. Her throat seemed to have closed up after her initial outburst.

"Then at least you have a little sense." Loosening his hold on her, he set her firmly in front of him, putting some space between their bodies.

Shivering as the chilly air in the mill penetrated her thin dress, Merissa put a hand on the smooth wooden wheel in front of her to steady herself. She had sensed the Frenchman's apprehension as well as his relief during their brief exchange. Her own heart had been beating so wildly, she had not realized until he broke the contact between them that she had also been feeling his. Now she swallowed nervously and attempted a light tone. "My family would be surprised to hear you say that, monsieur. They suspect that I have no sense at all."

"None at all? But I suspect they would be surprised to hear me say anything," he answered.

She thought she actually heard him chuckle, although a second fit of coughing seized his companion at that moment.

"Your friend is ill," she noted with some anxiety. The coughing fit had ended in a moan.

"Do not concern yourself. If you will forget that you have ever seen us, perhaps we can let you go."

"That is easy—I have *not* seen you," she pointed out. She still faced the millworkings and the darkness beyond them. Even if she turned around, she doubted that she would be able to distinguish her captor's features in the shadows behind her.

This time he definitely chuckled. "*Vraiment*, and that is for the best. If you choose your words carefully you will not be forced to lie. You must forget, then, that you ever discovered us. You would not have, if you had not foolishly entered here. I must have your word that you will tell no one."

"But you are in trouble."

"Perhaps not so much as you, mademoiselle. Be sensible and look to your own safety."

He was right—she had been foolish. But there was no way she could possibly forget this encounter. How would she manage to say nothing of it?

His tone had softened as they spoke, and Merissa found that she did not feel threatened now, despite his words. "Your friend needs help," she observed quietly.

Quite abruptly, his tone hardened again. "Not of any sort that you could provide. Do as I say, mademoiselle, or you will regret it."

With courage she did not know she possessed, Merissa turned her head and glanced over her shoulder. She got an impression of a tall, well-built form in the shadows, one that belonged to a young man, but as she had guessed, she could not see him clearly. In her mind, she had already labeled him "her" Frenchman, as opposed to the gruff man who coughed.

She felt sure now that there were only two of them. They had to be escapees from the war prison at Norman Cross. In this year of 1813, with England still at war with France, how else would two such men come to be hiding in the middle of the countryside? How desperate they must feel!

"It is you who has made the mistake, monsieur," Merissa said carefully. "You must see now that this is not a good place for you to hide. You are not far from the village, and if I could stumble across you here, so could anyone else. You are foolish to think that you can escape. But there is at least another place you could go that would be safer than this."

"Oh, but of course, we should follow your recommendation, mademoiselle." His words were laced with sarcasm now. "That way we should be certain to be found when you direct the authorities there to trap us. *Merci, mais non.* I do not think so."

"I give you my word that I will say nothing to anyone," Merissa blurted indignantly, absurdly hurt to think that he would not trust her.

"I am certain you would not like to find your innocent pet with his throat cut in the night."

"*Her* throat. And I do not believe, now, that you would harm her. You are a gentleman."

"Do not underestimate us," he said harshly. "In any case, if you are foolish enough to alert the authorities, we will be gone from this place."

"Given such thanks for offering advice, I should say

nothing more," Merissa replied, trying vainly to rein in her impulsive urge. Truly, she should not help them. But the fellow's attempt to sound threatening now did not fool her. She imagined how hopeless the men must feel, and she felt sorry for them.

"If you cross the river, about a half mile east of here, you'll come to Landy's Woods, and if you keep going aways farther along the river path through the woods, you will come to Landy's Staunch, where there used to be an old lock. There is still an old lockkeeper's hut there, but it is out of the way. No one goes there. I think the roof might still keep out the rain."

"Someone goes there, mademoiselle, else how do you know so much about it?" Merissa's Frenchman put his hands on her shoulders and pushed her firmly toward the door. "Go, mademoiselle, and take your tricks and your dog with you. I suggest you get far away from here, and do it quickly, before I change my mind."

"All right, I'll go! I'm going." Merissa gathered her skirts and attempted to scramble back over the slanted bottom of the old door. Her hem caught and she found the whole effort more awkward than she expected. In the end, a pair of strong hands assisted her. When she glanced back to say her thanks, however, her Frenchman had already withdrawn again into the shadows.

Despite being thoroughly shaken, she felt a prick of disappointment when she got no glimpse of him. Barely remembering to retrieve her basket, she caught Polly and, dragging the dog by the collar, headed across the pasture toward the old mill lane that led to her home at Pie Hill. She never thought once of her bonnet until she arrived home and was about to enter the house.

Chapter 2

From the darkness inside the mill, two pair of eyes watched Merissa's retreat.

"I do not like it. She will tell," said Guillaume, the man who had been coughing.

"What did you want me to do, slit her throat as well as the dog's?" Captain Alexandre Valmont, the man who had spoken English to Merissa, turned away from watching with an impatient gesture.

"You should have silenced the dog—that way she would not have found us."

"Or I should have silenced *you*—that way she would not have come inside," Alexandre replied sharply.

He moved away from the shadows, ducking his head under a crossbeam and stopping by the giant wheels illumined in the fading light from the doorway. He ran a hand over the smooth old wood, thinking of how the girl had felt against him when he had first taken hold of her. He was hungry, but she had awakened a different kind of hunger in him, one for which he had not been at all prepared. The flower scent of her hair, the softness of her body, had rocked him with a force like the fire from an entire battery of twelve-pound guns. Long-buried emotions and craving need had rushed through him, taking him by surprise, as if the girl's mere presence had breached a dam somewhere within him.

How long had it been since he had touched, or even been close to, a woman? Especially a gentlewoman, someone of his own class, as he was certain this girl had been? In the brutal company of his fellow prisoners, and before that, in the hard company of his comrades-at-arms, such pleasure had become nothing more than a dim memory—a fleeting

haunt of night dreams that had so little bearing on the life
he faced every day that he had not even known how much
he had missed it. Until now. He cursed his own weakness.

"You should have had her," Guillaume said, as if he had
somehow followed Alex's thoughts.

The young officer knew what kind of sly look would be
on his companion's face if he could see it. The older man's
tone of envy, lust, and disappointment disturbed him as
much as the alarming weakness revealed in the fellow's
voice.

He ignored both the comment and the question implied
in it. "Please do not tell me you are too ill to move on," he
said brusquely. "I believe she will tell no one, but she was
right that others might stumble across us here as she did.
We must leave here and find another shelter. Not to mention food."

Guillaume began to laugh, but the effort dissolved into a
deep cough. When he was able, he replied, "She was a
pretty one. Do not pretend you did not like the feel of her in
your arms. Why did you let her go?"

"Did you rape women and loot farms on campaign, Guillaume? Did you?" Alex's voice hardened and he balled his
hands into fists as he spoke. "What do you think? That just
because we are considered the scum of the earth, we should
behave as such? No doubt that is exactly what these English expect escaped war prisoners will do."

He slammed his fist against the hard wood in front of
him. "We are not animals. We are Frenchmen. No matter
what happens we must hold fast to the tattered remains of
what that still means."

Silence followed this outburst.

Finally, Alex relented. "All right, Guillaume. Do not answer. Just do not ever ask me such a question again."

Alex hoped he had not betrayed himself in the other
man's eyes. The show of anger had been quite genuine, but
it also had been a way to cover his reactions to the girl.
Guillaume was not a gentleman, by class or by nature. Alex
had learned this quickly in the early stages of their acquain-
tanceship. Guillaume respected strength, skill, and cunning,
qualities which he seemed to believe Alexandre possessed.
Their escape from the prison at Norman Cross appeared to

have confirmed this assumption, but Alex knew that his authority over the other man was precarious and had nothing to do with his rank as a captain. A sign of weakness on his part could change the balance of their relationship quite unfavorably.

"I will be ready to go soon," Guillaume responded at length in a subdued voice. "I need to rest a few more minutes."

Alex kept his voice coldly controlled. "It will be dark soon. We will wait until then to make our move."

The dining room in the Pritchards' home was surprisingly large for such an unassuming country manor as Pie Hill. The ancient table itself could seat thirty people, so when the family took their evening meal together they customarily gathered at the far end nearest the fireplace. Merissa's father, known to most people as Sir Barry, had not yet departed for London, so on this particular evening he sat at the head as usual, with his lady wife on his right and Merissa, the eldest of the children still at home, on his left. Merissa's sisters, Juliana and Harriet, flanked the table just below them.

Merissa tucked a rebellious strand of honey-colored hair behind her ear with an unsteady hand and eyed the oyster soup being ladled into her bowl with suspicion. The Pritchards' cook had pretensions of far greater skill than he actually possessed, and frequently proved this with peculiar culinary experiments meant to be innovative. Eating at their table was as much of an adventure as anyone in her family usually experienced, she reflected, at least until today.

"You seem especially quiet this evening, Merissa," said her father. "Have you started to miss me before I have even left?" He smiled at her warmly, with a teasing twinkle in his eye. He was often called to London on business, and the family was used to his frequent, brief absences.

Merissa managed a smile, but she did not rise to the bait with a teasing remark as she normally would have. "I believe I walked a few miles too many this afternoon, Papa, that is all. I quite wore myself out." That much was certainly true.

"Whatever makes you think we would miss you, Papa?"

It was sixteen-year-old Harry, her youngest sister, who took up the challenge with an impish smile.

"Perhaps the way you leap upon me, demanding presents, each time I return?" their father quizzed back.

Listening to their normal banter, Merissa felt distinctly uncomfortable. She had told no one of her strange encounter that afternoon. After all, she had given her word, but she was not accustomed to holding back from her family. If only she had walked a few miles less! Polly might never have picked up the Frenchmen's scent, and she might never have made the mistake of entering the old mill.

Yet in truth, Merissa did not feel regretful. She did not know quite what she felt, besides uncomfortable. Stimulated, perhaps? Curious? Dissatisfied? She definitely felt relieved and grateful that no harm had come of the incident, but there was a strange mixture of other responses as well, including a vague sense of incompleteness.

Truly, nothing so exciting had happened to her all year, or perhaps ever, even though she had left the countryside for London to endure her first Season in the spring. London had been stimulating and exciting at first, although she had found it mortifying to be making her come-out at the ripe age of almost twenty. She had felt like an overaged horse on display among the younger girls.

It had all seemed so artificial, with everyone trying to impress everyone else. She had met great numbers of eligible men—some wealthy, some titled, handsome, quick-witted, exquisitely dressed, or courteous to a fault. She was well aware that she had not measured up to the requirements of many of them. But among those who had looked upon her favorably, she had found none with whom she thought she could bear to spend more than a few hours at a time, let alone an entire lifetime. The endless rounds of parties and balls had soon lost their charm.

She had held back her true feelings to spare her parents', and had felt almost as uncomfortable about it then as she did now, holding back from them again. Only this time she was holding back to spare someone else.

Lost in her thoughts, Merissa had not been following the conversation at the table. As she dipped her spoon into her soup, she heard her father mention Norman Cross, and she stiffened, suddenly very attentive.

"It is apparently more than a week now since they first escaped. I find it remarkable that they could have avoided recapture this long. At any rate, there seems to be some feeling that they could be in our area."

"But we are only five miles from Norman Cross!" protested Merissa's mother, Lady Pritchard. "After a week, why would they not be in Spaulding or beyond?" Blue eyes much like her daughter's reflected her distress.

"I suppose because that is the first direction the militia searches when prisoners escape, and this pair seem to be brighter than most. We forget that it is not easy for them to make their way. Most of them speak no English, and they have no knowledge of the countryside or roads. These two are rumored to have been sighted in areas all around Norman Cross, as if they have been traveling in a circle, and cannot get farther than five miles in any direction."

Lady Pritchard shivered. "I hope the rumors are not true. Perhaps they have been caught, and the word just has not reached us yet."

"Perhaps. Nevertheless, I want you to exercise due caution while I am away." Sir Barry looked pointedly at his daughters. "No going off alone or riding out without a groom, understood? Be sensible. They say these men are very dangerous."

Merissa was seized with a sudden fit of coughing, drawing all the eyes at the table. Harry jumped up to thump her on the back, while her mother commanded her to raise her arms. She waved her sister away as she recovered.

"Are you all right now, my dear?" asked Lady Pritchard.

Merissa nodded, although she was not at all certain it was true. "Horseradish," she managed to gasp, pointing her spoon at the soup. "Melders has put horseradish in the soup." Hadn't anyone else noticed?

"You must have gotten an extra piece in your dish," her mother said sympathetically. "I thought it was rather good, actually. An interesting combination."

Hopeless. Her family was hopeless, Merissa thought, at the same time feeling relieved that her explanation was accepted so easily. She was quite sure Melders would not have managed to keep his position in any other household, but at the moment she was grateful for his peculiarities.

Were the Frenchmen truly so dangerous? She had not sensed that—at least, not about *her* Frenchman. Had she had a narrower escape than she realized? Was she wrong to keep silent?

She had indeed been very frightened at first, but she had quickly come to believe that the men would not harm her. After she left them, she had not been able to put her Frenchman or their strange meeting out of her mind. Who was he? What was he like? How had he come to be in such a situation?

She had actually caught herself wishing that she might meet him again. She knew that was cork-brained—he was an enemy of her country. She knew nothing about him, not even what he looked like. Yet something about him fascinated her . . . Was it only the allure of the unknown? Of something that had been hidden in shadows, secret and forbidden? She had to admit she was prone to romanticize. She bit her lip and took up another spoonful of soup to sip cautiously.

"Most of these prisoners are rough soldiers and seamen, enlisted men, the very dregs of their kind," warned her father, retrieving the thread of his lecture. "Officers are usually exchanged or granted parole. These other Frenchmen have no sense of honor, and their escape attempts simply prove it. They are criminals, and it is an act of treason to render them any assistance. Not that that stops some people from doing it—not when there's money in it."

Merissa found it difficult to swallow her soup, and it was not only because of the horseradish. She pushed her bowl away in defeat. Had she committed treason this afternoon? She supposed that not telling anyone she had seen the French prisoners might be construed as assisting. Suggesting a better place to hide was probably assisting, even though she had not actually *done* anything to help them. She could not honestly pretend that she had not suspected their identity, even though she had not known then of any recent escape from the prison.

"People make money from helping them?" asked Harry, her eyes wide. "How?"

"Oh, Harry, really," said eighteen-year-old Juliana in disgust.

"Never you mind, young lady," said Sir Barry sternly. "I just want all of you to promise to remember what I have said, just in case the rumors are true. I don't want to have to worry while I am in London."

Merissa watched their footman clear the soup course and bring in mutton chops and stuffed onions. The young servant had large, strong hands, and as she watched him carry the dishes she could not help thinking again of her Frenchman. His hands had been strong, but not overlarge. The fingers had been long and tapered—refined, almost aristocratic, she would have thought, except that she remembered the feel of the rough, callused skin.

She knew he must be tall, for when he had held her against him, her head had been against his chin, and she was not considered exactly petite. He had been dressed in boots that resisted her efforts to kick him and tight breeches or pantaloons that had done nothing to disguise the feel of his muscled thighs against her. She had felt the hardness of his chest through the thin layers of her dress and his shirt—he had worn no waistcoat and his coat had been open. His arms had been like iron. Even though he had handled her in a way no man had a right to, his touch had been careful, not hurtful, despite his obvious strength. He had seemed a most reluctant villain, even a gentleman. He had spoken fluent English. He was not at all like what her father described!

Her thoughts were interrupted by Lady Pritchard. "You must indeed be tired, Merissa. I just told you that Harlan had been by to call on you this afternoon while you were gone, and you did not even hear me."

"She's always woolgathering, Mama," said Juliana. " 'Tis any wonder Harlan comes calling, for all the attention she pays to him."

"That is uncalled for, Juliana," reprimanded her mother.

Uncalled for, but probably true, Merissa reflected. She undoubtedly took Harlan Gatesby's interest for granted, if for no other reason than that they had known each other almost from birth. He was the son of the local squire, Timothy Gatesby, and they had grown up as playmates. But Harlan's interest in her now was matrimonial, and Merissa was not comfortable with it, despite her advancing age and her awareness of the fact that she must soon settle down with *someone* or be content to settle on the shelf. Since she had returned from London unattached, he had begun to press her for a decision.

The truth was, she had gone out and stayed out for most of the afternoon to avoid him. Harlan almost never let more than a day or two go by between his calls, and he had not come to see her the day before.

"I am sorry, Mama," she said, not quite knowing how else to respond. "Perhaps I should excuse myself and go up. I really am not feeling quite the thing tonight."

"Without finishing your dinner?"

"When is Rupert-Smoochert coming to call again on *you*, Juliana?" Harry asked with impeccable timing.

"Don't you dare to call him that!" snapped Juliana.

"Now, Harry, that is exceedingly rude," warned Lady Pritchard.

As Merissa rose from the table, she threw her youngest sister a look of gratitude for the distraction. Harry would be taken to task for her insolence, but then the conversation would move on to the fascinating subject of Juliana's newest beau, a viscount visiting in the neighborhood. Merissa's indisposition would, hopefully, be forgotten in the process.

At nightfall, the two Frenchmen emerged from their hiding place in the windmill and made their way cautiously across the open fields. Alexandre swore that there were as many crickets in those fields as stars in the sky above them; the insects' songs filled the night and seemed to throb in a rhythm that matched the racing of his heart.

He led the way toward a farm he had noticed in their predawn travels the previous morning. There was a sizable barn and other outbuildings that promised a henhouse among them. The rumbling of his stomach spurred him on and combined with Guillaume's noises to form a counterpoint to the quiet sounds of the night. The older man coughed at intervals and muttered curses when he stumbled in the dark.

It seemed to Alexandre that Guillaume moved like an ox.

That General Bonaparte had won so many victories with men like that seemed miraculous in some ways, but Alex knew such men were strong, stubborn fighters with the heart for battle. He slowed down and waited in the darkness for Guillaume to catch up.

"When we get nearer to the farm, I will have to go in alone," he said once the other man had found him. "One cough out of you could bring all the English down on our heads."

They slid down a small embankment and went along a road for a short distance before turning off into another field. In the distance a small cluster of lights showed the location of the farm.

"When it is time, wait for me here by this gate," Alex instructed. He knew that he could accomplish his task more easily alone. He was fast and agile, and he thought he was probably more used to executing missions in the dark than in the daylight. It would not be the first time he had had to steal to fill his belly, although that much could be said for any French soldier. "For now, we both wait."

He settled himself into the long grass close to the hedgerow and willed himself to relax, staring up at the wide, open sky. The canopy of stars overhead brought him no comfort. He thought of other nights spent under the stars—nightmarish nights with the stench of death in his nose and the echo of battle in his ears, and other nights too long-remembered to seem more than dreams from his childhood in France.

As he lay awake, he heard Guillaume begin to snore softly. He thought it an improvement over the coughing, so he let him be. Eventually, the lights at the farm were extinguished. The moon began to rise, warning him that it was time to make his move.

"I must go in now," he said, poking Guillaume awake. "Any later, the moon will be too bright." He hoped the farm people had had enough time to fall asleep.

As he slipped like a shadow across the field, he thought of the girl who had discovered them that afternoon. He hoped this was not her farm. He did not think it was, for it lay in a different direction than the way she had gone. But he was surprised that the thought should have occurred to him at all, and it annoyed him. He did not want these English to begin to have faces or to begin to matter to him. Too many already did—the agent at the prison, the baker's daughter, a few of the turnkeys and guards. It pained him to consider what they no doubt thought of him now. He was a fine one to have lectured Guillaume!

Speed was more essential than stealth once Alex located the chickens. He paused outside the coop just long enough to remove his ragged coat. He was struck by the warm, stale air and the smell as he eased inside the small entrance.

From that moment, everything seemed to go wrong, like dominoes toppling one after another. His foot slipped on some chicken droppings just inside the door. Trying to regain his balance, he staggered against a nesting box, making a noise and dislodging an overlooked egg which, of course, rolled under his other foot. Before he could prevent it, the shell was crushed beneath his boot, its contents released as a slippery mass. As surely as he felt the crunch, he sensed that he was headed for disaster.

He was too hungry and too close to his goal to give up. Awakened by his noise, the chickens were stirring, but he thought if he was quick enough, he could still capture one and beat a retreat before the others sounded an alarm.

The roosting pole was at his shoulder's height, the dark shapes of the hens lined up along it in a neat, close row. He flung his coat up over the nearest one and pulled her down, tucking the squirming bundle under his arm. The other chickens squawked and flapped away from him in distress. As he turned to duck through the door, the rooster came at him with a god-awful screech of attack.

Alex couldn't fling up an arm to defend himself without dropping the chicken, so he dodged as best he could. Sharp talons ripped his shirt and grazed his skin on the first pass, and then Alex was out the door.

That was when he heard the dog barking. *Damned Englishmen!* Did they *all* have dogs? A lamp had already been lit in the farmhouse, and he thought he heard a door slam. Alex ran.

Chapter 3

After her retreat from the dinner table, Merissa had sought refuge in her room. She sat in the cushioned window seat, staring out at the deepening colors of the evening sky. She always found solace there when she was troubled, and she was definitely troubled now. Polly had seemed to sense her distress, and laid her head in her mistress's lap.

Merissa had stroked the dog's silky head, drawing comfort from the action. She couldn't remember a time when her own head and heart seemed to be in such disagreement. She had been suffering only a mild tug of conscience until her father's remarks at dinner had fueled a full-scale conflict. A turbulent mix of feelings swirled through her now, and no matter how she wrestled with it or tried to reason, she could not seem to resolve it.

Her father's stern warning against the Frenchmen echoed in her mind. *These men are criminals. It is treason to assist them.*

Deep in her heart, Merissa could not accept it. Why were they criminals? Because they had fought for their country? Wasn't that their duty? They were not the ones who had decided to wage war. What crime had they committed besides wanting their freedom? Wasn't it natural that they should want to go home?

The men she had encountered had not harmed her or even Polly—indeed, the more she had thought about it afterward, the more she believed they had been more frightened of her than she had been of them. She believed their threats had been nothing more than a bluff. Yet, what if she was wrong?

Her father would say that she was not bound by a promise made to such men under such circumstances, she

was certain. Still, she felt honor bound to keep her word
that she would tell no one about them. But what if their fear
pushed them into something they never intended? She had
sensed desperation in her Frenchman as well as reluctance.
What if they did cause harm to someone? Her silence was
protecting them. Was it also treason?

Finally, she had gone to bed. She lay under the covers
unable to sleep, her eyes fixed on the patch of night she
could still see outside her window, her thoughts fixed on
two men in trouble who were out there in it somewhere.

She was still struggling with unanswerable questions
when, quite late, Polly stirred beside her on the bed.
Merissa stroked the dog soothingly. "Shh. What is it,
Polly?"

The spaniel growled and lifted her head, obviously aware
of some noise that human ears could not yet detect. Merissa
listened, but heard nothing. Polly barked once, twice, and
then Merissa did hear the sound of a dog—no, several
dogs—barking, quite far off but coming closer. " 'Tis nothing, Polly, just a—" she started to say, but before she could
finish she heard the sharp crack of gunfire. The sound traveled well in the clear, still night, sending a chill along her
spine.

There was only one kind of prey she could think of that
anyone would be hunting at such a late hour, and her stomach knotted at the thought. *Please, God, no. Not the
Frenchmen.* She lay absolutely still, not knowing whether
she hoped to hear the sound again or not. More shots would
tell her the first ones had missed, but then there would be
no such assurance for the next ones. *What could have happened? Where were they?*

The rising moon showed outside her window, unaffected
by any drama being played out below. Merissa waited, listening intently, keeping Polly quiet and hearing nothing but
crickets and the continued barking of the dogs in the distance. She knew what she had heard—there was no mistak-
ing it. She listened for a long time after that without hearing
it again.

Alex had heard the unmistakable sounds of discovery behind him when he fled the henhouse with his prize under

his arm. Hoping that the night's darkness would swallow him up before anyone actually caught sight of him, he had run straight for the gate where he had left Guillaume.

He had not even gotten halfway across the field before he heard the explosive report of a gun behind him. There had to have been a second gun, for another shot followed almost on top of the first. This time he felt the explosion in his arm, and he bit back a cry.

He was hit. Pain coursed up into his shoulder. He did not slacken his pace, however. Swearing softly, he shook the captured hen loose from the coat under his arm as he ran and clutched the fabric against his bleeding flesh instead.

Guillaume was not at the gate when Alex reached there. Undoubtedly, the older man had heard the commotion and decided to risk taking flight on his own, to gain a greater lead. The young captain did not have time to hesitate or wonder which way his comrade had gone, for he could hear the dogs barking and the men shouting in English behind him. They had found the chicken, but that had delayed them only a moment. Apparently they had not stopped to reload their weapons. Alex knew he could not outrun the dogs for long, especially with his arm bleeding, and the blood would make his trail easy to track. For him there was only one hope of escape, and that was the river.

Stumbling through rutted fields, scrambling over stiles, crashing through brush he could not take time to go around, Alex concentrated on one thing—speed. He knew he was headed in the right direction. He just was not certain how far he would have to go.

Miraculously, he reached the water ahead of his pursuers. His lungs hurt from want of breath nearly as much as his wound pained him. He welcomed the cold embrace of the river as he slipped into it and pushed off, holding his injured arm and his coat close to his body and using his other arm to stabilize himself. He thanked God that he could swim.

He let the gentle current carry him silently downstream in the darkness, away from the confused noise of the dogs and the Englishmen as they reached the riverbank. They would have to decide which way to search first. If he was very lucky, they would go the other way.

He had always been lucky during the war, until the day of his capture. Now his luck seemed to go by turns, more bad than good of late. Especially tonight. How ludicrous that he should be shot now, raiding an English henhouse, after escaping injury in so many Peninsula actions! His own men and even the Spanish had thought he was charmed. He had almost begun to believe it himself. Only pure chance could have guided this blasted farmer's ball to its target, in the dark or even in daylight. A common farmer would not have one of the rifle-bored muskets that the English soldiers had.

He closed his eyes, listening intently to the quiet sounds of the night, trying to hear whether he was safe for the moment or not. He could have wished for a faster current, but this English river was lazy and meandered slowly on its way. If he kicked his feet enough to speed his progress, the splash would make a noise he dared not risk. Besides, he was tired. So very tired. It felt good to let the water carry him.

He heard crickets and the gentle lap of the water against the riverbanks and among the reeds. Finally he heard the dogs begin to bark again, blessedly distant, it seemed to him, and moving farther away, unless his own growing weakness deceived him. He must not lose consciousness now, to drown in the river. He had already put so much effort into staying alive.

It was bright morning when Merissa awoke with a sudden jolt of uneasiness. What time was it? When had she fallen asleep? She dragged herself from the bed, feeling exhausted. The muscles in her shoulders, arms, and legs were tight, knotted and aching from tension. Polly had deserted her, probably in favor of breakfast.

She rang for her abigail and dropped wearily into the chair by the window. The sun poured down on the same peaceful fields that she saw every morning, but this morning the scene brought her no pleasure. Something terrible had happened during the night, and it seemed wrong that the world should reflect no hint of it. For a moment Merissa dreaded the thought of going downstairs, for surely there would be some word of what had happened, and a cowardly part of her wished fervently never to know.

The moment passed even before her maid arrived to help her dress. Merissa knew she could not bear the uncertainty of not learning the outcome of last night's disturbance. Maybe her assumptions were wrong, and the trouble had nothing to do with the Frenchmen. Besides, this morning her father was leaving for London. Would he have left already, while she was still abed? She did not like to miss the ritual of seeing him off. She decided to hurry.

When she at last descended, dressed in cheerful yellow muslin that did not at all reflect her mood, she discovered her family gathered outside in front of the house in a small knot around her father. The curricle in which he and his valet would drive to London stood ready, their luggage strapped on the back and Jackson, their groom, holding the horses, which stamped with impatience. The sober expressions on everyone's face rekindled the dread in Merissa's heart.

"Ah, here you are at last, Merissa dear," said her mother, detaching herself from the group and coming to meet her. Lady Pritchard was a tall, handsome woman with a dignified bearing and dark hair laced with silver. Her gifts were well represented in her daughters—Merissa had her eyes and height, Juliana her delicate features, Harry her lustrous dark hair.

"Are you feeling better this morning?" There was no way Merissa could escape her mother's sharp scrutiny. "You don't look at all well. Did you not sleep?"

Merissa shook her head. "Very little."

"Oh, dear," her mother answered, leading her by the hand to join the others. "I hope it wasn't all that talk at dinner about the escaped prisoners. I'm afraid your father is leaving us on the heels of some more distressing news. It seems that those men are indeed in our area. They were seen last night."

Seen, Merissa thought with a little spark of hope. *She did not say they were shot, or killed, or captured.* Perhaps the men had gotten away after all.

"Good morning, my sweet." Merissa's father took her hand and gave her a quick peck on the cheek. "I am pleased

that you're up in time to see me off. How could I survive
even a week in London without the adoring farewells from
each of the doves in my covey, eh?" He smiled at her en-
couragingly, and Merissa managed to find a passable smile
to answer him. He was balding, shorter than her mother,
and had become somewhat portly over the years, but she
believed he was the kindest father on earth.

"Now, now, don't you be worried about those Frenchies
at all," he continued smoothly. "I'm certain that they'll be
caught today. Tom Sibley came by this morning to tell me
that they tried to raid his henhouse last night. He and his
men went after them with dogs and guns, and he knows he
managed to hit one of them, for they found blood where the
fellow ran. But the dogs lost the trail at the river. Tom's or-
ganizing a search party this morning. The fellows won't get
far—not if one of them's wounded."

The sounds Merissa had heard in the night came back to
her with vivid clarity. She imagined her Frenchman running through the darkness, battling pain and panic as he left
a trail of blood. Her lip trembled, and she put a hand up to
cover it, closing her eyes at the same time.

Perhaps the wound was not bad, since he had managed
to elude his pursuers. Perhaps it was not he but the other
man who had been hit. Perhaps the thief had not been either of them at all. How could the neighbors have been so
sure in the dark? Even she did not really know what the
men looked like. . . .

Sir Barry patted her arm reassuringly, misjudging the
source of her distress. "There now, I know it is frightening.
Look at Juliana fidgeting, and Harriet looking about as if
the Frenchies might pop out of the hay field at any moment." He grinned at the denials this brought from his other
two daughters. Then he lowered his voice. "You are the
oldest, Merissa, without Francine or Rodney at home. I
must count on you to support your mother in this—see how
brave she is."

Merissa thought her mother seemed pale and more subdued than usual, but she said nothing to contradict her father. "Papa, how could—"

"I am certain there is nothing to fear, but even so, I have
asked Mr. Sibley to inform the rest of the neighbors that

I've gone to London leaving a house full of unprotected women," he resumed in a normal tone, hurrying on. "They will look out for you while I am gone, and I am sure you may rely on them if there is anything you need." He winked at Merissa. "I wouldn't be surprised if you suddenly find young Harlan coming around most every day, Merissa. I suspect he'll be glad for the excuse. Just you be sure to keep that young man in line!"

In line, or on one? Merissa thought uncharitably, swallowing the groan of protest that rose in her throat. She felt like a fisherman confronted with a fish he had no desire to catch. Her parents favored Harlan's suit, and she knew that she ought to. But every word her father spoke seemed designed to drive her deeper into despair. She didn't want to see Harlan every day or be watched over like a hatchling.

Perhaps if she crawled back to her bed, she could awaken all over again, and the morning would be different. While she was at it, perhaps she could change the whole night that had preceded it as well. Perhaps she should just wish to set the clock back weeks earlier, when life had been simpler, before two French prisoners had ever made their escape, or she had ever encountered them and somehow lost her reason.

The day threatened to crawl by in agonizingly drawn-out minutes once Merissa's father had departed for London. After a late breakfast, the four Pritchard women gathered in the family sitting room in the east wing, where they worked on embroidering new seat covers for St. Gilda's, the local parish church. Conversation did not seem to flow with its normal ease, and for the most part they labored in companionable silence.

Merissa was working a fanciful border around the Pritchard family's coat of arms and glanced up at her mother as she paused to change the color of her silk. Did her mother miss her father when he was called away on his frequent trips? Did she mind being left in charge of the family so often? Lady Pritchard's uncharacteristic silence communicated clearly that all was not well with her, but Merissa could not decide how much of it was due to her mother's fears about the escaped Frenchmen. Of one thing she was certain—she would never tell her mother that she had encountered the prisoners.

Merissa frowned at the half-finished design fastened tightly in her embroidery frame and continued to work, but after two more hours had passed, she jumped up restlessly.

"Please, Mother, may I not at least go for a short ride, if Jackson accompanies me? Father did not say we were forbidden to go out at all. I will go blind if I work on this any more today and am likely to go lame if I sit any longer."

Lady Pritchard sighed. "I am only asking you to stay in today, Merissa—just one day. Can you not pretend the weather is foul? Imagine that rain is sheeting down the windows as we speak, instead of the sun shining so beautifully. Is it such a sacrifice to satisfy my peace of mind? Once those men are caught, life will return to normal again. Today the fields are full of hunters and the hunted as well as harvest workers—it will not help to have you young ladies out there as well."

A thousand arguments presented themselves in Merissa's mind, but she did not voice them. She realized that it would not help her mother's state of mind to raise the possibility that the prisoners might not be caught, or that the searchers could be chasing the wrong culprits, and it did seem inevitable that life would eventually return to normal, for better or worse.

"Forgive me." Merissa crossed to her mother and kissed the top of Lady Pritchard's head. "I suppose it is a worry, and I am being selfish. I feel like a prisoner myself. I will take myself off into the library and find something absorbing to read for a while, or I'll fetch my sketchbook and draw. Perhaps later we three can entertain you by practicing our music together."

Merissa, Juliana, and Harriet were in the midst of just such a musical performance in the elegant gold and white salon in the late afternoon when the Pritchards' elderly butler announced Harlan Gatesby. Merissa, who had been accompanying her sisters on the flute, left off playing an intricate passage with a dreadful squeak and earned a critical look from the two of them seated at the pianoforte.

"Thank you, Backhouse," Lady Pritchard said. "You

may show Harlan up—" Before she had time to finish, the young gentleman himself appeared in the doorway.

"Good afternoon, Lady Pritchard, ladies." Harlan entered the room with a confident grin. His ruddy complexion and blond hair combined with his rugged build to suggest a strong line of Dutch blood in his pedigree. "I assured Bean that you wouldn't expect me to stand on ceremony and wait downstairs."

Bean was the Pritchards' footman. Merissa had always thought that the names of the two servants, Backhouse and Bean, sounded like a solicitor's firm. Looking at Harlan, she could well imagine that the servants might have wished to detain him, for he was hardly in a presentable state for a social call.

"You ladies look ravishing, as always," he said, including them all in the compliment but looking straight at Merissa. "I do hope you will forgive my ragged appearance. I thought you would be awaiting some news on the progress of our hunt, and I was loath to delay my visit."

That he had come straight to them from the fields was readily apparent. The smell of his horse had come into the room with him, and his boots and breeches showed streaks and splatters of mud. His dark blond hair appeared sweat-dampened and unruly, and his russet riding coat had a rumpled, wilted look about it. Merissa's feelings softened for a moment as she glimpsed in the husky man standing before her the boy who had been her childhood friend.

"Have you brought us news, then, Harlan?" Lady Pritchard's voice was full of hope.

"I'm afraid I cannot give you the reassuring report that we've caught those Frenchies," he said, "but I thought it would be at least some comfort to you to know that we think they are out of our area."

He went on to relate some details of the hunt, explaining how confused the dogs had been and how frustrated the searchers. "The bloody trail simply stopped—we could find no further trace of it. The dogs picked up a different trail that followed the river west, toward the Great North Road. We think now that both men must have gone that way and that they managed to find some conveyance on the highway. We have sent word both up and down the road to the

militias and the constabulary, and feel we can reasonably
leave the matter in their hands."

Merissa thought Harlan looked as pleased with himself
as if he had personally captured the culprits. She felt absurdly pleased to know that the searchers had failed. She
smiled with relief, trusting that her expression matched that
of her mother and sisters despite its different source.

Yet she was puzzled as well. Harlan's report raised un-
settling questions. How could the trackers know if the trails
they had followed were made by French feet? Could not the
chicken thief have been someone else? How could the
bloody trail simply stop?

Before she could voice any of these questions, Harlan
moved to her side, smiling broadly.

"I also found this down by the river, and thought I would
return it to you, Merissa. It is yours, is it not?"

Merissa swallowed nervously as Harlan brought his left
hand from behind his back to present the somewhat bedraggled confection of pale blue silk she had so carelessly left
behind on the riverbank the previous day. She took it from
him and dropped it on the floor beside her wooden music
stand.

What could she say? She was quite surprised that he
should have recognized it, and realized with a familiar sink-
ing feeling that it only proved how much more attention he
paid to her than she did to him. She could scarcely deny her
ownership in front of her sisters and mother, however.

"Why, yes, Harlan," she responded, letting her surprise
show in her face and hoping it might pass for gratitude.
"Imagine your recognizing it! When I was out yesterday, I
went part of the way along the river path. I feared I had lost
it when I had to chase after Polly and quite forgot to go
back for it."

She knew it was hardly a complete explanation, but how
could she say she'd spent her afternoon avoiding him, pre-
ferring the company of ducks or even escaped Frenchmen?
Why should she have to explain herself to him at all?

"If your maid had been with you, she would have retrieved it," Harlan said, his smile disappearing for a moment in a look of reproval. The look deepened into a

thoughtful frown. "Of course, I am assuming that you were alone."

Merrie was certain he could not suspect the truth, despite her suddenly fluttering pulse. What was he thinking? Who else could she have been with? She had never guessed that Harlan could be jealous or distrusting.

"It is a very bad habit of yours, going off by yourself. We must be grateful that you did not encounter those Frenchies, unprotected as you were," he continued quite ominously.

He paused, putting Merissa into a state close to panic, and then his smile reappeared with an impish twist. "You always have needed someone to look after you, Merrie."

How she hated that proprietary tone! It made him sound as if he thought he was the only one of them who had grown up.

"I gather that your father has left specific orders forbidding you to go out alone while he is away," he continued with obvious relish. "I must say I applaud his judgment. I am hoping you might like to go riding with me tomorrow, now that peace is restored to the neighborhood." He sought her hand at the same time he turned to gain her mother's approval.

"I'm sure she would be delighted," Lady Pritchard said. "Wouldn't you, Merissa, dear? She has been so restless today, after I asked the girls to stay in. I know she would be safe with you, Harlan."

Trapped, Merissa thought. There was no way for her to decline without being obviously rude. Harlan would expect her to ride decorously, at a proper lady's pace, when she would have liked nothing better than a wild gallop to release all the tensions that had been building in her.

But a ride with Harlan tomorrow would at least get her out of the house, and that would get her one step closer to resolving the terrible questions that were haunting her now. What had really become of her Frenchman? Was he out there somewhere, in desperate need of help? She would have to get away by herself to investigate, but a plan was already beginning to form in her mind. If only they could go now, today! But Harlan had clearly been in the saddle for many hours, and it was growing late. Someone might be suspicious if she suggested it.

She gave Harlan a brilliant smile, as if she found his offer highly amusing. In a voice everyone could hear, she said, "Shall we ride in the morning then, tomorrow? It is by far my most favorite time of the day."

Chapter 4

Merissa and Harriet stood in the terraced garden of Pie Hill very early the next morning, trying to keep their voices low.

"Two cushion covers! Harry, be reasonable."

Harriet's particular distaste for embroidering made the task a useful negotiating point when Merissa needed a favor from her youngest sister, as she did this morning. Merissa did not always have patience for the art herself, but sometimes sacrifices had to be made.

"I'm offering to do *one* for you, Harry. After all, am I asking so much of you? You want to go out riding anyway, and you can't go by yourself—Papa's orders."

"I don't have to go with you and Harlan and feel like a third wheel on a pony cart. Juliana and I could go out with Jackson or one of the other grooms."

Merissa glanced over the low garden wall to the fields beyond, noting how their gossamer blanket of dew sparkled in the brightening sunlight. She sighed, thinking of the squares of fabric and neatly bundled embroidery silks laid out in piles on the table beside their mother's sewing stand in the sitting room. Somehow she had never realized just how many cushions it took to fill the pews of St. Gilda's. And the covers were all to be finished before the Harvest Fair on Old Michaelmas! Perhaps the extra work was an appropriate penance for the deception she was planning.

She had slept fitfully during the night, haunted by the fear that her Frenchman might be slowly bleeding to death, lying in a hiding place where no one but she might think to look. The conclusions of the search party had in no way reassured her conscience. She had to know. She fervently wished she did not have to involve anyone else in what she needed to do, but every possibility of acting alone seemed to be closed to her.

"All right, Harry. I'll do two cushion covers. But you'll have to do something more than just keep company with Harlan and me. I need you to perform a bit of playacting."

Harriet was instantly suspicious, narrowing her eyes and frowning in a way that wrinkled her nose quite unbecomingly. "What sort of playacting? Merrie, what are you up to? I should have known you didn't need me just to play the chaperone."

Merissa could not help laughing at her sister's expression. "Harry, I think you have been practicing that face in the looking glass, figuring you can scare away any beaux who decide to come calling."

Harry struck a pose as if she were offended, but she could not sustain it. After a moment she lapsed into giggles, and Merissa joined in.

"Perhaps I should have tried that!" Merissa said with a wry grimace. "I'm afraid it is too late for me now, however. Harlan's interest seems quite fixed. Indeed, I think I do need a chaperone these days. He does not behave the same way he used to when we were just friends. I wish he would be content at that," she added soberly, as if talking to herself. She turned away to watch Polly sniff along a snail's trail, shiny in the sunlight where it crossed the flagstones of the terrace.

Harry had enough tact not pursue her sister's unthinking confidence. "About the playacting?" she prompted.

Merissa looked down at her clasped hands before she turned back to her sister. "Harry, I have something extremely important to do, but I can't explain anything about it. I have to get away by myself to do it. I won't be in any danger. You are my only hope of succeeding. Can I trust you, and will you trust me? Will you help me? Please?" She hoped she was right about not being in any danger.

Harry nodded very slowly. "If it is truly so important. But it sounds as if it might cost more than two cushion covers."

Later that morning the sound of a horse cantering up the drive at the front of the house drew Merissa to the sitting-room window. She watched Harlan dismount and hand his reins to the servant who came out to hold his horse. Harlan was a strong, solidly built man. Riding clothes suited him—he looked quite handsome, in fact. His dark blond head disappeared from Merissa's view as he headed for the front entry.

She sighed. Shouldn't she feel something? Anticipation, excitement, a quickening of her pulse at least? Merissa searched her heart, but found no reaction to his arrival except a feeling of resignation. There was also a tiny twinge of guilt, perhaps over the lack of other feelings, but most certainly because she was about to take unfair advantage of his honest interest in her.

"What if Juliana decides to come with us?" Harry whispered, coming up just as Merissa drew back from the window. Once Harry had agreed to the scheme, she adopted it with enthusiasm, treating it as a game and a challenge to her dramatic skills.

"She won't," Merissa replied with a confidence she wished she could feel about the rest of their plan. "All I had to do to discourage her was mention how wet everything still is outside this morning. The dampness has such a dramatic effect on her hair. I hinted that if a Certain Someone came calling later, she might not want to be seen with a mop of wild frizz sticking out beneath her cap."

Harry giggled. "You are too cruel, Merrie. Yet 'tis perfectly true."

Juliana's beautiful blond hair, pale as flax and the envy of many, was at times her greatest torment.

Merissa sighed a second time. "We'd best go down. I do wish we did not have to do this at all. Are you certain you can do it without injuring yourself, Harry?"

"Even in my sleep," her sister replied breezily, passing through the door ahead of her.

Harlan was waiting expectantly in the entry hall, holding his hat and twitching his riding crop rhythmically against his leg. Merissa knew him well enough not to mistake the gesture for impatience—for some reason, Harlan was nervous or anxious this morning. She hoped he had not quarreled with his father, as sometimes happened.

She gave him a warm smile as she descended the last

stair, and could not miss the look of admiration in his eyes as he regarded her. She was wearing the blue wool riding habit that had been especially made up for her come-out in London. It fit beautifully and was absolutely up to the crack of fashion with its military-style black velvet collar and black lacings. Its bright, rich color set off the honey tones of her hair and the blueness of her eyes. She had not worn it since her return home—the summer months had been too warm, and usually she preferred to wear her comfortable, old, rust-colored habit. But the mornings were cool now, and this particular occasion seemed to require that she look her best.

"Merissa, you look like a dream vision," Harlan said with the kind of ardent fervor that made Merissa uncomfortable.

"You are kind to say so," she replied, trying to keep her smile in place.

"Not kind at all," he protested, "just stating the obvious. Those bounders in London were fools to let you come home again to me. They must not a one of them had eyes in their heads. Lucky for me."

He talks as if we were already engaged, Merissa moaned inwardly. She never knew how to respond at the times when he began in this vein. She knew very well that she herself was responsible for her lack of success in London. She had made no effort to conform to people's expectations, or to charm those gentlemen who had found her face and fortune fair enough. Harlan's compliments were more sincere than any that she had heard there and she knew that they should please her, but instead they only filled her with dismay.

To her relief, her sister stepped forward.

"Ah, here is Harry," she said with perhaps a little too much enthusiasm. "I hope you don't mind her coming along with us this morning, Harlan. She, too, is feeling restless after being kept in, and you know that Papa does not wish us to go about unaccompanied quite so freely as we usually do. You are so kind to be our escort."

She hoped her choice of wording left Harlan no way to wriggle out of the arrangement. She could tell from the darkening of his expression that he was not pleased. That was certainly one thing that could be said about Harlan—he was easy to read. She doubted there was so much as a fraction of an ounce of subtlety in his nature.

"If it pleases you," he said with a quizzical lift of an eyebrow that clearly begged her to deny it. When she said nothing more he added, "I had thought you might like to ride out past the village and over to Dubro Vitae this morning."

The suggested route was one of her favorites, as Harlan knew well. The hilltop destination had once been the site of an ancient Roman settlement, and the grassy humps and bumps that remained in the ground teased her imagination. She was fascinated by the Romans; she prized the small collection of antiquities she and her father had accumulated over the years—bits and pieces of another age turned up by the plow or washed out by the river. Only today she wanted—*needed*—to go in quite the opposite direction.

That was part of the trouble with Harlan—he knew what she liked, and spent a good deal of his time trying to please her. It made her feel twice as guilty that his efforts ended up annoying her more often than they succeeded in their intended aim. Then the guilt made her feel even more annoyed. *Botheration!*

She exchanged a quick look with her sister and then fixed a bright smile upon Harlan. "I do enjoy that ride, Harlan, but this morning I thought we might head out the other way. The morning light is so beautiful on the fields, don't you agree? If we ride against the sun, it will seem as if we're riding through fields full of diamonds."

Harlan responded somewhat begrudgingly. "More likely we will all just hurt our eyes squinting, but I am here to oblige you, Merrie. We will go that way if that is what you want."

The three riders set off along the bridle path that edged the fields close to Pie Hill. The air was fresh and smelled of earth and grass. Merrie smiled and inhaled deeply, catching a good dose of horse scent as well for her effort. Riding close beside her, Harlan chuckled.

"Only you would see diamonds in fields full of harvest stubble, Merrie," he commented. Something in his warm tone caused Merissa to look at him, and she noted again the admiration in his expression.

Lowering his voice, he added, "I had particularly hoped we could ride out by ourselves this morning."

Oh, dear. What was she supposed to say? *I don't trust you anymore when you get that look? I wish we could go back to the way things used to be between us?*

She sighed. "Harlan, I . . ." *I asked my sister to come.* That was the truth, but she couldn't get the words out. "I'm sorry you are disappointed," she finally replied.

"There are things I'd like to discuss with you, but not in front of Harry."

"I'm sorry," she said again sincerely. "Did you have an argument with your father?" She suspected that even if he had, that was probably not what he would have discussed. She definitely needed to head off this conversation.

"Yes. How did you know?"

"You seemed a little agitated when you arrived."

Harlan gave a triumphant-sounding hoot of laughter. "You see? How well you know me! I swear we are meant to be mates, Merissa. Who else would have divined that?"

Aghast that her attempt to divert him had failed so utterly, Merissa tried to mask her reaction, but she must have been too late. Harlan reined in his horse, reaching for her reins to stop her progress as well.

"Merissa, I apologize. Please forgive me. That was thoughtlessly spoken. It's just that, well, you know how I feel, do you not? When we spoke of this once before, you asked for time to think. How much time do you need? Do you know how hard it is for a man to wait when he knows what he wants?"

The horses danced restlessly at the sudden change of pace and the tension between the two riders. Merissa glanced ahead and saw Harriet trying to turn her own mount back toward them. The animal seemed unwilling and did a little dance of its own.

"Oh, dear, Harry's having trouble," Merissa managed to say, giving silent thanks for the interruption. Just as Harlan turned to look, Harry's mare reared and then dashed off with the young girl clinging to its neck, crying pitifully in distress.

"He-l-l-p!"

"Oh dear Lord, what if she falls, or Genesis trips in a furrow?" Merrie exclaimed. She hardly needed to add, "I thought that mare seemed feisty this morning!" Harlan had already spurred his horse into a gallop on the instant, charging after the runaway.

Merissa permitted herself a small smile, thinking that Harlan had been very eager to play the hero in front of her. She waited until he was so far away that there was little chance he would look back at her. Harry's performance had been so convincing, she hesitated for another moment before going ahead with their plan. What if the horse had truly gotten out of control? But then, hadn't Harry done exactly what she had promised?

Merissa gave silent thanks for her sister's sense of timing as well as her acting talent. Praying that Harry could create enough delays to give her the time she needed, she struck out at a full gallop herself, heading for the cover of the trees along Robin's Green Lane. The ancient track led toward the river and the site of the old lock. Harry had agreed to say that Merrie must have gone for help if Harlan questioned her disappearance.

Chapter 5

Merissa did not begin to have second thoughts about her mission until she actually reached the river and sat upon her horse looking across at the abandoned lockkeeper's hut she had described to the French prisoners. She had spoken the truth about the isolation of the spot. Even in the bright sunshine, with the birds chirping cheerfully in the surrounding woods, the ruined cottage looked daunting. Half of the two-room stone structure had collapsed, no doubt from age and weather, although to Merissa it appeared rather as if a clumsy giant had simply stepped upon it. What remained still bore a roof and a door, partly festooned with blackberry creepers. There was not a sign that anyone was there, or had been.

What was I thinking, she asked herself, *coming here alone to investigate?* If a wounded man by some miracle had outrun dogs for miles to come here and hide, why would he still be here a day later? Now that she was here, it suddenly seemed a foolish notion indeed. Still, she had not come all this way not to make sure. All she had to do was cross the river, take a quick look in the cottage, and be on her way. Tonight her sleep would not be haunted.

She urged her mare along the river path, heading for the remains of an ancient stone bridge downstream that still spanned the Nene even though the roads it had once served were now buried in history. Few besides fishermen used the bridge now. As Merissa approached, she prayed that with the harvest in full sway no one would be there.

She halted Godiva at the bridge and dismounted. Her prayers were answered, for not a single soul was to be seen. Voicing soothing reassurances to the reluctant horse, she led the mare across the worn surface of the narrow bridge and continued on foot back along the little-used path on the opposite bank until she came to the lockkeeper's hut.

A handful of birds flew up out of the blackberry vines as she looped Godiva's reins around the branch of a nearby bush and stepped hesitantly closer to the entrance. She was always getting into situations when she should have thought before she acted. Was this to be one? What was she going to do if her Frenchman *had* come here? What if both prisoners had? What if the wounded one was not her man but the other one, the one who coughed and had spoken no English? She shivered as she remembered the cold tone of his words when he had threatened to harm Polly.

Merissa put her hand on the door, hoping it would not answer to her push. If the door was stuck fast, surely it would mean that no one had been there. The weathered wood was rough and warm under her fingers. At her touch it swung inward readily.

As light spilled into the space beyond, Merissa drew in her breath. A man in ragged clothes lay still on a pile of sacks just a few feet away.

"Oh, Lord," Merissa whispered. She looked about her quickly, but saw no sign of anyone else. What had been a doorway into the second room was mostly blocked by rubble and broken beams of wood.

She was aware that she had very little time before she would be missed, but she could not simply leave. Not yet. The man was lying face down, and she was not even certain if he was breathing. Jagged tears in his shirt revealed angry red scratches across his back and one shoulder. Dark-colored material was bunched around his upper arm, and she noticed that it was stained even darker with blood.

Flies buzzed about her as she approached him cautiously and crouched beside him, putting a tentative hand on his unscratched shoulder. The shoulder was cold, and the linen of his shirt felt damp to her touch. "What are you doing here all alone, poor fellow? Oh, please—don't be dead!"

Because of his injuries she was afraid to actually shake him by the shoulder, so she prodded at him rather ineffectually. "Sir! M'sieur?" She finally realized that she must use both hands and turn him onto his side. She was not certain how to achieve this with any delicacy. He was thinner than either her father or Harlan, but he was still a rather large man. Pressured by the urgency of her situation, she decided simply to lift and push.

The man flopped onto his back with an alarming abruptness that jarred his wounded arm and frightened Merissa even as it produced a most welcome, if agonized, groan. Then relief flooded through her and the tears that she had been suppressing welled into her eyes. "You *are* alive. Thank God."

For a moment, the man's eyes fluttered open, but so briefly that Merissa was not sure he could even have seen her kneeling by his side. "Let me be. I am dead," he murmured in French, and lapsed into unconsciousness again.

It was him—her Frenchman. The few syllables were enough for her to recognize the deep tone of his voice, although somehow she had already been certain. Even in his disheveled state, with ragged clothes, his brown hair in his face, and a stubbly beard of several days' growth, he was handsome. She studied his face, her curiosity satisfied at last. He had deep-set eyes under thick, dark eyebrows, and a straight, narrow nose. His jawline was strongly angled, with a well-defined chin. His full lips had sensuous curves.

There was no time to think now about who he was or what had driven him to flee the prison. She would have to leave and bring back help. She could not move him by herself, and there was no question that he could not remain here. He needed care. But could she leave him in such a state? He might be dead when she returned! *Perhaps if I can dress his wound, and get him to take a little water . . .*

Quickly she stood up. Turning her back to him modestly despite his unconscious state, she looped up the voluminous skirt of her riding habit over one arm. She struggled desperately to tear the fabric of her petticoat until finally it gave way along a seam. She divided a section into strips, which she took down to soak in the river. Stumbling in her haste, she returned to her patient and knelt beside him.

"Yes, perhaps it is better if you cannot feel this," she murmured aloud as she pried the wadded coat—for that is what she found it had been—from around his arm. It was stiff with blood, now dried and hardened. The linen shirt-sleeve beneath it was damp.

Taking hold of his arm gently, she could see that the musket ball had passed through, leaving two jagged holes. Apparently it had missed the bone. He was lucky in that, she thought. With shaking fingers she unfastened his cuff and pushed back the sleeve. Carefully she tried to clear away what she could of the dried blood with one of her moistened strips of lawn, and then wrapped the arm in a clean strip. She hoped the wound would not begin to bleed again.

Next she bathed his face, smoothing the hair from his brow, trying to coax him back to consciousness, if only for a moment. "M'sieur, m'sieur. You must take a little water. You must have been here like this for a day and a night. Where is your friend? I am so sorry. Oh, please, you *must* wake up—I cannot leave you like this, and I cannot stay longer!"

Something—the cool wet cloth, perhaps, or the urgent tone in her voice—stirred a response in the man. Consciousness flickered back to life in him and his eyes opened again. His eyes were brown—a rich brown like the color of sherry or warm, dark mahogany. They were beautiful eyes, Merissa thought, but at this moment they were full of agony and confusion.

"Pain," he muttered in French, choking on the word.

"Shh," she responded gently. "I know."

She squeezed some water into his mouth from the last clean cloth she had reserved for the purpose.

"My arm, my back."

"Yes, I know. I'll help you. Shh. Save your strength."

"So weak. No food."

Of course. He and his companion had been raiding Mr. Sibley's henhouse. She wondered when he had last eaten. "I'll bring food. I'll bring some salve for your wounds as well." She began to make a mental list of things she would need. "When I return—"

"No!" His hand shot out and grasped her wrist.

The vehemence of his sudden reaction took her by surprise. It was as if he saw her clearly now for the first time. There was strength in his grip despite his weakened state.

"But I must leave you," she insisted, feeling a little nervous with him now. "I promise I will return as soon as I can

possibly manage it. This afternoon. It may not be more than
just a few hours . . ."

"No." This time there was a note of desperation in his
voice. But Merissa had misunderstood his intent. "Do not
return," he said, speaking clearly in English, with visible
effort.

Merissa stared at him. "But of course I must!" she said in
astonishment. "I cannot leave you alone here to die."

He released her and closed his eyes wearily. "Please.
Leave me. I have tried . . . *Dieu connaît*, I did try . . . Perhaps it is best."

"You are weakened now from your wounds and lack of
food and water. Whatever it is you have tried to do must be
very important to you, to have gone through all this. You
must not give up! You must trust me." Merissa shook his
shoulder a little to rouse him again. "Would you just give
up so easily?" she asked, a note of challenge creeping into
her voice. "I would not."

He opened his eyes again and surprised her with a pained
half smile. "No? Perhaps, although you have no idea . . ."

She raised his head to give him more water, but holding
him so made it difficult to squeeze the rag. Finally she
repositioned herself and laid his head gently in her lap. His
hair was very thick and soft to her touch.

"*Ange*," he murmured faintly.

The weight of his head felt very disconcerting. "I am no
angel—I'm very much of this world," she said a little un-
steadily. "Here, take a bit more water."

"*Ange de la miséricorde*—angel of mercy." He sighed
deeply, then shook his head. "You must leave. You put
yourself at great risk. What becomes of me is no concern of
yours."

She looked down into his brown eyes to reply and discovered then that doing so destroyed whatever train of
thought had been in her mind. What strange power was
this? With a conscious effort she pulled her gaze away.
Looking down the length of his body only made her realize
how very long his legs were . . .

"I cannot leave you here to die, even if we are enemies.
You would not be here except for me," she said abruptly,
shocked by her reactions to him.

"I would be dead. So you see, you have already saved me. It is enough. I insist that you do not return." He paused, clearly struggling for the strength to finish. "You do not understand. You cannot save me, and to bring others means discovery—disaster. It would seal my fate. There is greater danger than you know."

"But—"

"Go. *Merci et adieu, mademoiselle.*"

Merissa knew a dismissal when she heard one. It was not the first time he had ordered her to go. Her Frenchman had closed his eyes, and if he was not already asleep or unconscious again now, he feigned it well. She realized suddenly that she had no idea how long she had been there. What if the others tried to look for her? She lifted his head and slid carefully out from under him. He winced as his shoulders once again touched the floor.

Stubborn Frenchman! she thought as she headed for the door. What right had he to dictate to her? Of course, she had already stayed much longer than she should have. But she *would* return—he was in no position to stop her. All she had to do was find a way.

Merissa faced a barrage of questions upon her return to Pie Hill. Harlan and her mother and sisters were gathered in the drawing room, an elegant, formal room swathed in pale gray-green damask. Polly was there also, and her exuberant greeting contrasted starkly with the reception from everyone else.

"Merissa! Where have you been?" Harlan was on his feet and coming toward her before anyone else could utter a word. "When I brought Harry back to the house and found that you were not here, I was all for going out to find you, but your mother bade me wait." He gave Merissa a reproachful look. "I was very concerned."

Merissa bent to scratch Polly's head. Helping the Frenchman seemed so clearly right! But life had suddenly become very complicated. She knew she would have to lie.

Lady Pritchard was sitting very erect in her favorite giltwood armchair, a sign that she was keeping her feelings under rigid control. Harlan was not family—not yet anyway—and Merissa's mother would not make a scene in front of him. Juliana sat on the settee across from her mother, and Harry was standing behind Lady Pritchard with one hand draped gracefully on the back of her chair.

"I am so sorry," Merissa said, deciding that contrite innocence was her best response. "As you can see, I am quite all right. Have you been waiting long?"

Harlan frowned. "No, we have not been here long. It took some time to get back . . ." He looked then at Harry, who met his gaze with an expression that more than matched Merissa's for innocence.

"I fell off Genesis when she suddenly stopped," the young woman explained with a shrug of her shoulders and a helpless wave of her hand. She cast a somewhat impish grin at her mother. "I think I may say—without being indelicate—that I was too sore to sit, so we had to walk the horses home."

"That was only after we waited quite some time for her ankle to feel better enough to walk on," Harlan added, rolling his eyes rather unsympathetically. "I was certain you would arrive with a groom and the pony cart, Merissa, but you never did."

"You must have had rather a long walk. Are you feeling more the thing now, Harry?"

"Oh, yes," Harry replied with a cheerfulness that reassured her sister that there had been no real fall and no genuine injury.

"So, where were you, Merrie?" Harlan was not to be deterred. He sounded more chagrined than worried.

Merissa had her story ready. It had occurred to her in a flash of inspiration, offering not only an explanation for her delayed arrival, but also the perfect excuse to go out again.

"I met Sally Whitcomb's husband along the way and stopped to speak with him," she said as evenly as she could. The Whitcombs were struggling tenants who had a number of wild children and lived on a conveniently faraway parcel. No one could easily check on her story.

"I'm sorry the conversation took so long. It seems that their youngest boy is homebound with an injured leg, and this has thrown quite a stick in their spokes, especially at harvest." Before the others could interrupt, she added, "I promised to call at their cottage this afternoon with some small provisions and things they might need."

"That was kind of you, Merissa, and you may do so," Lady Pritchard responded. "I am sorry to hear about young Whitcomb. But you should not be stopping to chat with men, tenants or not, when you are unaccompanied. A mere nod of acknowledgment would have been proper. Suppose the man had been poaching?" She sighed as if she knew quite well that her daughter was deaf to such corrective wisdom.

"I'm sorry, Mama. I apologize also to you, Harlan and Harry." Merissa could not possibly have looked more contrite.

"I still do not know why we didn't see you," Harlan grumbled in a quieter voice.

"Well, never mind, it is all over with now," Lady Pritchard said. "I'll ring for some tea."

The last thing Merissa wanted was a prolonged session with the Inquisition. Every fabrication she was forced to tell led only to more lies and deeper trouble. She held out the skirt of her riding habit. "Mama, none of the three of us are in a fit state to have tea, having just left our horses." She raised an eyebrow at Harlan and hoped fervently that he would catch the hint. He was not smiling. "Harry and I need to go up and change."

At least Harry knew a cue when she heard one and turned to gather up her gloves and riding hat. "Merrie is right, of course. I'm certain we must be making the drawing room smell like the stables!"

Harlan, for once, did take the hint and made his excuses. Before he left, however, he turned to Merissa, who was already edging toward the door.

"Perhaps we would have better luck riding tomorrow? Weather permitting, of course." If she had not known Harlan so well, Merissa would have sworn that his innocent tone sharpened slightly as he added, "We could try going in the other direction. Perhaps the horses will be less skittish if we are not making them head into the sun."

Lady Pritchard nodded with enthusiasm before her daughter could utter a word. "That sounds very sensible." To Merissa's dismay, she did not stop then. "I would also

like to invite you to come back to dine with us this evening,
if you are free, Harlan. Lord Rupert is coming, and with Sir
Barry absent, I thought another man at the table might be
appreciated."

Harlan's polite smile broadened into a grin as he accepted the invitation eagerly and then took his leave.

Merissa counted to ten before making her own exit. *Dinner! And a commitment to ride with him again tomorrow.*
What was she to do with the Frenchman in the meanwhile?
Things were turning up far worse than she could ever have
imagined upon her father's departure.

If Merissa thought that she was safe once she gained the
passage outside of the drawing room, she soon discovered
her mistake. Harry was not two steps behind her and confronted her as they made their way up the stairs.

"Clever, Merrie! Already you have managed an excuse
to go out again this afternoon. Only, I know you did not really meet with Mr. Whitcomb. At least, not by accident.
What are you up to? I want to go with you."

"Oh, dear, Harry. I thought you promised me no questions. I already told you, I cannot say anything."

"That was then. I did everything you asked me to, absolutely without questions. But if you can't explain now,
when are you going to? Is it something terribly shocking?"

Merissa shook her head as she turned the corner of the
landing and started up the next flight of steps. "I'm helping
someone. I gave my word that I'd say nothing."

Really, she did not dare to tell Harry now. If keeping
silent about the prisoners had not been quite treason, certainly what she was doing now must be. She did not want
Harry to join her in flaunting the law. She wished she did
not need to involve Jackson, either, but she had thought of
no way to move the Frenchman in his badly weakened condition without the groom's help. She would not tell him
who the injured man was, and she was resolved to take full
responsibility for involving him, a servant, if they should
ever be caught. She could not protect Harry the same way.

"Helping someone! But 'tisn't the Whitcombs, is it, Merrie?" Harry persisted. "Truly, I can't imagine what you can
have gotten into that must be such a deep secret. Why,

nothing remotely interesting has happened around here in ages except for . . ."

She came to a full stop and stared at Merissa with eyes suddenly round with astonishment. "Merissa Pritchard! 'Tis not the . . . I mean, you didn't . . . How could . . . ?" Astonishment gave way to excitement and Harry found her tongue again. "It *is* the prisoners! Small wonder you wished to say nothing!"

Chapter 6

Heat, darkness, pain, and confusion enveloped Alex like an impenetrable cocoon. *I must be in Hell,* he thought with a stinging sense of betrayal. He had always believed in a just and forgiving God. Was this all that awaited him, after twenty-seven years of honest faith and effort? He thought he had tried his best.

As he attempted to form the words of a prayer, he thought that he heard voices penetrating the mists of chaos in his brain.

"He's burning up!" exclaimed one of the voices, striking Alex with a burgeoning, ironic hope.

Surely such a voice did not come from within his own mind. It was decidedly female, for one thing. It spoke English, for another. So he was not crazed, and not alone.

He thought that the voice proved he was not in hell, either. Surely his burning up would occasion no special comment there. Besides, Spanish was the language of hell, he knew from prior experience. He had already been there, or as close to it as men on earth could come. Where was he, then—purgatory? He'd always thought the language of the afterlife would be his own native tongue.

He tried to rouse himself, to fight against the pressing confusion inside his pounding head.

"Drink," commanded a soft voice, and Alex obeyed, opening parched lips to accept a liquid he could not identify. His throat felt dry and raw. When he began to cough, the vessel against his lips moved away.

"Try a bit more," coaxed the same soothing voice.

He could not seem to focus—his awareness kept coming and going, as if the patches of fog obscuring his brain were being blown about by a fickle wind. He thought he had heard that voice somewhere before.

"His clothes are damp," came a different voice, also female.

"Like as not he come out of the river, miss." A male voice, this time. *How many were there?*

"He's very weak."

"How the devil are we going to get him to the pony cart?"

"Harry! Such language."

"I've heard you use it, Merrie."

"I should never have let you come with us."

Alex lost the thread again. He had no idea who these people were or where he could be. But the conversation did not sound like the sort you'd expect in the hereafter.

With a supreme effort of will, he opened his eyes. He saw a face like an angel's, with honey-colored hair; he smelled a scent like flowers. Recognition came to him like a sudden clearing in the clouds: the girl, the windmill! He remembered and groaned, for the memory of the windmill brought back everything else—who he was, where he was, where he had been, and the reasons behind it all.

She had told him to come to this place, a place she had promised would be safe. He had gambled on her word at the last minute, when there had been nowhere else to go and no other hope. But she had betrayed him. . . . She had come and brought these others with her. She had lied. . . .

"Look, he's stirring," said the other female voice, and for the first time he saw the dark-haired girl—younger, quite different from the first girl, yet both were pretty, and somehow similar.

Traitorous English! Why had he trusted the windmill girl? His head throbbed, and he felt so weak. It was so hard to think, to remember . . . Now he would not even die a free man amid the wreckage of his honor and his dreams. He would end his days on a prison hulk. He did not even have the strength to glare at them, let alone resist. He closed his eyes again.

"Easy now, fellow, here we go," said the male voice, and Alex sensed hands and arms supporting him, helping him to his feet. Did he have any choice? His limbs felt like melted butter. He did not think he could control them, any more than he could make sense out of what was happening. Nevertheless, by an intense, excruciating effort of concentration, he managed to put one foot forward and then the other, several times, until he was aware that the darkness around him brightened considerably. *Better this than landing face first in the dust.* He took a few more steps and then his knees gave way and the fog closed in once again.

When Alex next came to his senses, the confusion had returned. He was on a horse. Not riding it, exactly—he lay draped across the saddle on his stomach like a great sack, with his arms and head hanging down on one side and his legs dangling down the other. He recognized the smell first, then the horse's rocking motion.

He opened his eyes and discovered that doing so was a major mistake. The end of his nose was only inches from stirrup leather and the sweaty horse's belly. But that was not the most disconcerting. Straight below him were stones, and beyond them—some twelve or fifteen feet below, actually—was water. The sense of hanging over it head first was nearly as uncomfortable as the physical position of his body. Instinctively he tried to rectify that. Pain shot through his arm, his back, and his head, and he groaned once again.

"Oh, Lord! Don't try to move now!" called a female voice filled with anxiety. In his own language she said, *"Stay still, monsieur, until we get across the bridge!"*

So, it was a bridge. An old, narrow bridge, with worn stones and low sidewalls. . . . Roman? It was difficult to judge by what he could see of it, hanging upside down over the edge. *Roman, but ruined.* . . .

The two words seemed to knock together painfully inside his head. Crossing the river of life and death, an angel leading him. He squeezed his eyes shut, trying to clear his brain. Wasn't it supposed to be a ferry? That was what the Greeks had believed, wasn't it? But the Romans had built bridges—beautiful, damned near indestructible bridges—everywhere they went. And they had marched into eternity long before this. It made sense. The only part that didn't was, by God, when did he get to leave this bodily suffering behind? And was this any way to arrive?

The horse stopped when they reached the other side of

the bridge, and Alex felt hands lifting him, sliding him. He was shaky and hot, and he couldn't seem to help at all.

"Jackson, can you lift him?" said that same angel voice again, the one that seemed so familiar. "Harry, if you and I can get his feet, we'll lift him up into the cart. That's it. Steady now. Let's just ease him down onto the floor."

Alex forced his eyes open as they lifted him up and over. To his surprise he saw trees—trees and sky. Then he saw the slatted sides of the cart. He slumped wearily against the nearest support. He felt himself drifting away, but he resisted for a minute as a woman's dainty, slippered foot suddenly came into his view, followed by its mate. He saw slippers, trim ankles clothed in embroidered stockings, and a swirl of pale violet skirt that just as suddenly closed off his view.

"Harry, sit on the seat and see if you can get him to lie entirely on the floor," came the first woman's voice again. "He is too tall, and someone might see him. The blanket has got to cover him."

He sighed. The sound of her voice was very pleasant and somehow familiar. Maybe they did speak English in heaven. Would angels wear embroidered stockings?

Merissa had argued with Harry once the younger girl had guessed what Merissa was doing. She had pointed out the danger and difficulty of her task, but Harry had only insisted that such arguments proved the need for her help. With all the skill of a lawyer she had countered her sister's every objection, finally pointing out that if Merissa were caught, the scandal to the family would be equally disastrous no matter how many daughters were involved. Merissa had been forced to concede.

It had been Lady Pritchard's idea that they take the pony cart, although the good woman believed her daughters were calling on the Whitcombs. Harry was, after all, still supposedly suffering from her morning's bruises. Merissa had seized upon the suggestion eagerly, knowing how difficult it would be to move the injured Frenchman.

Even with Harry along, Merissa had known they would still need Jackson's help. When they had reached the abandoned hut, she had told the groom that the Frenchman was a Gypsy.

"We think someone took him for one of those escaped Frenchmen and shot him by mistake," she had said, rather unnerved at how smoothly and easily the lie had come out. "We'll tend to him until he is strong enough to rejoin his people. But my mother must not know. 'Twould only upset her."

The story was not the worst she could have used. At this time of year Gypsies who had not yet gone south often came down from the heath above Wittering and worked as day laborers helping with the harvest on the farms close to the Great North Road. If only the story were true! How much simpler everything would be. But she did not think her Frenchman could pass for a Gypsy under anyone's inspection except for the uneducated servants.

Jackson had a good heart and she thought his discretion could be relied upon, especially if she reinforced it by the judicious use of her pin money. If he had doubts, he was too respectful to question her.

Harry's voice interrupted her thoughts. "Do you think it too soon to start back, Merrie? And where are we going to put this fellow when we get to Pie Hill? Have you a plan?"

Indeed, Merissa had been giving the entire problem a great deal of consideration. "If we had truly gone to the Whitcombs', we would not have even started back yet. We mustn't return too soon, or our whole excuse for this excursion will be suspect. We will encounter fewer people in the yard as it gets later, and we will have less time to suffer idle questions and conversation if it is close to dinner, since we will still have to dress. Julie, in particular, should already be occupied with Lord Rupert by the time we arrive home."

"Julie does pose a problem."

Juliana had accosted her two sisters before they left, slipping into the little parlor off the hall where they had been awaiting Jackson's arrival with the horses and pony cart.

"I know you two are up to something," she had said boldly. "I think you are spiteful not to let me in on it." She had given Merissa a knowing look and added, "I think I know now why you seem so careless of Harlan's attentions to you, Merrie. You are seeing someone else on the sly."

The accusation was at once so pitifully ludicrous and yet so uncomfortably near to the truth that Merrie had been hard-pressed to stay perfectly cool.

"Of course, Julie. That is why I've been so eager to have Harry by my side," she had countered. "Would you not want Little Sister to tag along on *your* secret trysts?"

Juliana was momentarily flustered. "I—I have not been having secret trysts."

"Haven't you?" Merissa had been able to confuse and distract Julie by turning her accusation around and by reassuring her that she could accompany them to the Whitcombs' another time, when Lord Rupert was not expected. But she was still suspicious and the last thing they needed would be another confrontation with her upon their return home. At eighteen, Julie was at best unpredictable—as sweet as sugar sometimes and at other times as spiteful as an angry cat. Merissa dared not to trust her with something as dangerous as the truth.

"I am concerned about delaying," Merissa said, gesturing toward the blanket at Harry's feet in the cart, "but I'm afraid we have no choice. We may as well use the time to collect some of the vines and leaves and seedpods we'll be needing to make the decorations for the Harvest Fair. We can load them in the cart to help hide our Fre—uh, our friend. And I thought the barn would be the very place to work on them to keep the mess out of the house. Wouldn't you agree, Harry?"

"The barn?"

The corn barn used to store wheat and barley at Pie Hill was huge, with a pair of threshing floors and vast space that stood empty while the harvest was still underway. Like the house, it was ancient and sprouted additions of various ages. A cowshed had been added to it at one end and stables at the other, with separate haylofts above each of these sections.

"The stables are too busy, but the cowshed hayloft will be warm, and the corn barn has lots of space to work in until the harvest is finished."

Harry looked at her older sister with something like adoration. "'Tis positively brilliant, Merrie! Working on the decorations will give us abundant excuses to spend time in the barn without it being questioned, and the hayloft seems as safe a hiding place as any."

Merissa thought it less a matter of brilliance than simple deduction—she had considered and rejected every other possible place in Pie Hill. The dairy, the coach house, even the summer house in the garden were all too likely to have people about, yet she had to put the man near enough to the house to make it possible to tend him. There was only one immediate problem still to be solved—how to get their Frenchman up into the hayloft once they arrived there.

It was later than Merissa wanted when the little group finally did return home. She and Jackson led the way on their mounts, while Harry sat driving the pony cart with materials for the festival piled quite up to her knees. Coming from the east, they had no choice but to pass the house on their way to the barn and stables. As they approached, Bean's slight figure came out of the house at a trot and stopped them.

"Lady Pritchard would like the misses to hurry and come right in," he said apologetically. "Lord Rupert has been here this past hour, as expected, but Mr. Gatesby is also arrived early. I'm to help Jackson take the animals to the stables."

Merissa stifled the unladylike response that nearly jumped off her tongue and exchanged an uneasy glance with Harry. *Of all the wretched luck!*

Improvising quickly, she turned to Jackson, who was already dismounting to assist the two young women. "I'm afraid that means you will have to see to the delivery of *our materials* into the barn, Jackson," she said pointedly. "Bean, perhaps you would be kind enough to take Godiva and Persephone. Jackson can take care of Mignon once the pony cart is unloaded." She didn't dare to say anything more to the groom in front of the young footman.

A short time later, Merissa had changed her clothes and sat at the dressing table in her room, twiddling with her pearl necklace impatiently while her abigail added a spray of silk roses to her hair. Harry tapped at the door and came in, freshly gowned and coifed for dinner herself. She looked quite grown up in a simple dress of white *crepe lisse*, trimmed with pink rosettes and stripes of pink ribbon.

Merissa nodded to dismiss her little maid. "Thank you, Peggy. You did a fine job, especially in such a short time." Indeed, Merissa was handsomely clad in a dinner dress of pale blue Florence satin, ornamented with diagonal bands of sapphire blue satin on the bodice, sleeves, and hem. As the door closed behind her abigail, she turned to Harry.

"Harlan *would* have to come early! One might even think that he did so intentionally! What can we do? I hope Jackson was able to manage our friend all by himself. I suppose we shall have to endure the entire evening not knowing."

"Smile and be charming, Merrie. If Jackson did not manage, I think we would have known it by now. On the other hand, if anyone should see the black look that is on your face right now, we may be the ones who cannot manage. Juliana is already sniffing at our heels, and I do think Harlan may be harboring some unvoiced questions. Come, we had better go down. You look stunning."

Merissa sighed. She rose from the dressing stool and followed Harry. "Our Frenchman was so feverish, Harry. He needs to be tended. I cannot help worrying about him."

Harry stopped abruptly with her hand on the door handle. "*Merissa*. Did you hear anything of what I just said? How do you expect to get through this evening if you cannot get your mind off our friend in the barn?"

Merissa blanched. "Oh, Harry, how shall I? I'm not as good an actress as you."

"Well, you've fooled a good number of people lately. Listen, just focus your attention upon what is happening around you and under your nose," counseled her young sister. "Worry about what Melders has prepared for us to eat—Lord knows, that should be enough of a concern. Or worry about whether Lord Rupert is merely toying with Juliana, or whether we even wish him to do otherwise—anything that will keep your mind on the moment at hand."

"The man could still die if he doesn't get proper care, Harry. And there are things he will need, like a blanket and a chamber pot. Perhaps I could send Bean back out to the stables with a message for Jackson."

"Only if dinner isn't ready. If Bean isn't on hand in the

dining room to help serve, there'll be all sorts of questions
we can't afford. Trust Jackson, Merrie—you must trust
him, since you chose him to help us."

Dinner was indeed ready by the time the two sisters descended, affording Merissa no opportunity to send any
messages. Backhouse informed the young women that he
was ready to announce the meal as they entered the handsomely appointed salon. Lord Rupert and Harlan Gatesby
were standing near the fireplace, engaged in what seemed
to be a fairly heated discussion. Lady Pritchard appeared to
be observing them with mild concern, and Juliana looked
positively ready to throw daggers. She rushed to her sisters
as soon as they stepped into the room.

"Merrie, Harry! At last, thank goodness! All they've
done is argue about Wellington and the war since Harlan
first arrived and brought up the subject. And I haven't had
one word of conversation with Lord Rupert since Harlan
got here. Mama doesn't seem at all inclined to interfere.
Please, do something!"

Personally, Merissa thought any noninterference from
their mother ought to be applauded and encouraged, but she
felt pity for poor Juliana. "Hush, Julie, dinner is ready.
They'll be forced to stop in a moment when Backhouse
makes the announcement. You must appear as though you
did not mind in the least."

Juliana frowned rather comically and then assumed a
bright, false smile that did not match the frosty look in her
eyes. As Merissa had predicted, the men broke off their discussion and turned their attention to the ladies when the
butler made his announcement.

Not surprisingly, Merissa found herself seated next to
Harlan in the dining room. The soup course was already
laid out, an enticing aroma rising from the steaming bowls.
Melders's watercress soup was delicate and quite palatable.
So far, so good, Merissa thought.

She turned to Harlan. "What were you and Lord Rupert
so ardently discussing just when Harry and I arrived? You
both looked very intense. Juliana was a bit piqued."

Harlan regarded Merissa for a moment as if considering
whether or not to specify. "Why was Juliana piqued? It was

nothing to interest you ladies. We were just talking about the war."

"Why should the war be of no interest to ladies?" She, for one, was more interested in the war now than ever before.

Harlan groaned. "Are you going to be argumentative, too, Merrie? I'll tell you. Lord Rupert believes now that Austria has switched to our side, Denmark and Saxony will do so as well. I say just because a handful of high-ranking officers have done so doesn't mean their governments will prove so sensible.

"Then, he thinks a strong blow against the French at Dresden will finish the war. I think it could prove a very costly mistake! We even argued over whether or not Wellington should invade France from the south. It's like having a conversation with my father! The only thing we agree on is that the tide of the war has turned in our favor. You see? Boring, and a most indelicate topic for ladies' ears."

How could such favorable news be boring? What if the war did end soon? Her Frenchman would no longer be a fugitive.

"I suppose we are meant to confine our conversation to the new shipment of muslin that has arrived at Hingham's shop in the village, the weather, and the preparations for the Harvest Fair," Merissa said dryly. "In truth, Harlan, *that* could prove to be truly boring."

She would have liked to hear the details of the two men's differing opinions, but she did not think anyone would appreciate her restarting their argument. Instead, Merissa bent her head to the task of eating her soup, thinking that this dinner might prove to be the longest one she had ever endured.

For the most part, the meal was unexceptional. The gentlemen managed not to argue further with each other, and the food was quite good. Melders had added nuts to the fenland cranberry stuffing in the roast duck, but after the first surprising crunch, no one seemed to mind. No one was impolite enough to mention the unusual seasonings in the fish soufflé.

The gentlemen—wisely, no doubt—declined to separate

from the ladies to indulge in the ritual of after-dinner port. At Lady Pritchard's suggestion, the young people gathered around the pianoforte in the salon and Juliana sang, accompanied by Harry on the keyboard and Merissa on her flute.

Unfortunately, Juliana chose "Moscow, or Bonaparte's Retreat" among other pieces about the war in what was undoubtedly an effort to show Lord Rupert that she was musically *au courant*. Merissa concentrated hard on the black notes wavering in front of her on the pages; part of the war was so much closer than any of them realized—just outside in the barn.

Eventually the little party settled down to play cards. Loo was suggested since there would be six players. Merissa was pleased, as she had no doubt with whom she would have been partnered if they had played whist. She thought the choice diplomatic as well, for Harlan was not a particularly skilled card-player, and a game depending less on luck would certainly have placed him at a disadvantage to Lord Rupert.

As it happened, she had too much difficulty keeping her mind on the game to play well herself. More than four hours had passed since she and Harry had been forced to leave the Frenchman hidden in the pony cart. What if Jackson had decided the safest course was to leave the man hidden in the cart all this time? What if he had been unable to get the man up into the hayloft by himself? Twice she played out of turn and had to forfeit a loo, and once she quite unforgivably failed to follow suit when she should have, forfeiting a double loo as well as her share in the stake.

A branch of candles had been placed on the table to supplement the light from the chandelier, and Merissa watched the slow, deliberate progress of a drip of melted wax down the side of one candle. How could time pass so agonizingly slowly? Harlan was dealing, and next it would be her turn to lead.

"Play your hand, take Miss, or decline?" he asked.

She had not evaluated her cards and did not know what she wanted to do. She winced—actually, she knew very well what she wanted: to jump up from the table and go running out to the barn. As she opened her mouth to answer, however, Backhouse suddenly materialized by her elbow, clearing his throat discreetly.

"Excuse me, Miss Merissa. Young Collins just came over from the stables with a message for you from Jackson. He says to tell you that Godiva seems unusually restless from that stone she picked up this afternoon, and perhaps it might help to settle her if you could only come out for just a few minutes."

"Goodness, I'll go at once," Merissa answered, her eyes meeting Harry's across the table. She tried to show just the right amount of regret and concern as she handed her cards back to Harlan. "Clearly, I must decline. How fortunate that we had not yet begun! Please forgive me."

"I'll go with you," Harlan offered, standing up as Merissa rose from her chair.

"No, stay," Harry said rather forcefully. "You are the dealer, after all. And you would leave us with only four players."

For once, Lady Pritchard's response was all that Merissa could have wished. "Do stay, Harlan. Merissa, I am sure, will be back long before we can empty this pool."

It was all Merissa could do not to fly from the room. She forced herself to walk calmly all the way to the front entrance, and hoped her hand did not shake noticeably as she fastened the frog closings on the lightweight wool cloak Bean had ready for her when she got there. Backhouse was lighting a lantern, which he then handed to her. For the sake of appearances, she headed for the stables as she crossed the yard.

Godiva, of course, was perfectly settled in for the night. After a quick glance at her, Merissa slipped through the side door and as quietly as a shadow crossed the cavernous darkness of the corn barn. Her lantern showed the pony cart standing empty and the various branches, vines, and seedheads she and Harry had collected heaped in piles on the floor near the cowshed. At least her Frenchman was not still in the cart.

She stepped quietly into the cow barn, hoping her pres-

ence would not disturb the animals. She also hoped no one
would notice her light.

"Jackson?" she whispered, peering into the inky upper
recesses of the shed. Her light threw grotesquely giant
shadows that moved as she did. She saw the ladder to the
hayloft and moved uncertainly to the foot of it. "Jackson?"

A face appeared at the top of the ladder. "Up here, miss.
Do you need a hand?"

Merissa shook her head. "I'll just leave the lantern." She
would not be able to climb the ladder with any sort of
grace, encumbered as she was by her skirts and cloak, but
she thought she could do it. She hung the lantern on a peg
and started up.

Jackson assisted her when she reached the top, and then
led her around some substantial piles of hay to a space he
had made at the back of the loft. Her Frenchman lay on a
soft bed of hay, sweating and restless with fever, but what
shocked Merissa most was that someone else was with him,
kneeling in the hay beside him, wiping the sweat from his
face. The young woman turned as Merissa approached.

"I hope we done right, miss."

"I didn't know what else to do," Jackson apologized.
"He needed to be tended. I made him some tea on the grate
in my quarters, but I had my own duties to get the stables
straight and the horses bedded down for the night and all. I
asked my Bessie here to come out once she could get free
from the kitchen. I didn't tell no one else, and neither did
she."

Relief washed through Merissa, despite her dismay that
yet another person was now in on her secret. Jackson's wife
Bessie, would be an invaluable aide—she could be in the
barn at times when Merissa could not, and she would be
able to smuggle much-needed nourishment from the
kitchen besides.

Unfortunately, Merissa's relief was short lived.

"There's somewhat else we've got to tell you, though,
Miss Merissa," Jackson continued very soberly. "This fella
beain't no Gypsy." He paused, either to let this sink into
her mind or to find the words he needed to finish. "There

was French maids at the last place where Bessie worked, miss. She says that gibberish he keeps talking is French, pure and simple."

Pure and simple? Merissa sighed. Apparently there was not going to be anything about this that would be pure and simple.

Chapter 7

Merissa looked at the servants' concerned faces. What should she say? Trust and respect were so precious, and so irreplaceable! She felt she had been testing and treading on everyone's. She had only lied to Jackson to protect him, but how was she to explain that now?

"I had truly hoped he could pass for a Gypsy," she confessed finally, looking down at her clasped hands. "This would be so much less complicated if only he were one. I am sorry to have involved you in this. Jackson, Bessie, I want you to know that no matter what happens, I will bear the full responsibility."

"Miss, what are you going to do with him?"

She looked at his form, lying in the shadows. "I'm going to help him. How can I not? Look at him—he's not a monster, he's just a man. Just an ordinary man like anyone else. He probably has a wife and a family. Who knows what he has been through?"

Merissa hoped the servants would be moved to feel the same degree of sympathy that she felt, rather than fear and suspicion.

"He's very handsome, ain't he, miss?" Bessie wiped a trickle of sweat from the Frenchman's temple.

"Yes, Bessie, he is, even in this sorry state." Merissa thought he was, in fact, not at all ordinary; something about him affected her every time she looked at him. The dim light cast by Jackson's small lantern did nothing to lessen the effect. "I'm not sure that we dare to clean him up," she added with a smile. "We might be struck blind by his brilliant good looks."

Bessie giggled, and Merissa breathed a little easier. If only Jackson would make some comment now.

The groom removed his cap and scratched his head thoughtfully. "This be a risky business, miss, helping a Frenchie. A serious, risky business. But seein' as how I've already carried him up here on my own back and made him tea on my own hearth, reckon I'll stick by you for the long run."

Thank heaven! Merissa renewed her resolution to pay Jackson a hefty bonus out of her pin money.

Crouching down next to Bessie, she studied the unconscious Frenchman. His deep-set eyes were fringed with long lashes that fanned against his cheeks. How unfair for a man to have such lashes! Quietly she reviewed what Jackson and Bessie had already done for him, and concluded that they were doing a better job of nursing him than she might have done herself. Their conversation was only interrupted once when their patient became restless, thrashing about and muttering French words in his delirium.

"I wish we could send for Dr. Haddleston, but I do not dare," Merissa whispered. "He would surely report him." She also wished she could obtain some laudanum to help fight the pain he must be suffering. "Can you stay with him? Perhaps in turns? I know you both have your duties to do tomorrow and need your sleep, but he shouldn't be left alone. If I can find a way, I will come back to stay with him later tonight. We must keep trying to give him liquids and applying the wet cloths to keep down the fever. You have been doing a splendid job. Right now I must go back in before someone comes looking for me."

"Miss, you leave him to us. You mustn't be leaving your own bed to do sick duty in an old barn."

"Jackson, I cannot ask you and Bessie to do more than I am willing to do myself. Just asking for your help and your secrecy is already asking a great deal. Thank you."

The valiant Frenchman fought the fever through the night and by morning slept more peacefully. Merissa and Harry took turns sitting with him as much as they could, knowing that neither Jackson nor Bessie could afford to leave their work.

The two young women were forced to leave him unattended, however, while they spent part of the morning working on the dratted cushion covers with their mother. Then at midday Lady Pritchard developed a notion about going into Eastholme to view the new muslins Merissa had mentioned at dinner, the very last thing Merissa wanted to do. She fretted and worried while they did this errand, straining herself with the effort not to show that anything was amiss. What if the poor man awoke while he was alone?

She was nearly frantic by the time she returned to the barn in the afternoon, using the excuse that she would work on the decorations for the upcoming festival. Polly had wanted to accompany her, of course, and Merissa had had to trick the poor dog in order to get out to the barn without her.

Climbing the ladder to the hayloft was difficult in a dress, as she had discovered the previous evening. She had donned an old pale blue muslin upon her return from the village. Her skirts seemed to be more in the way than ever as she struggled up the rungs, trying not to step on the fabric or misplace her feet.

She sensed that something was different even before she reached the back of the loft and saw her Frenchman. He had obviously tried to move. He lay sprawled against the hay, propped to a half-upright position, about four feet away from the matted hay where he had last been sleeping. His eyes were open. She felt him watching her as she approached—watching not with appreciation or gratitude but more like a trapped animal that was wary and ready to flee. She thought it was tension she had sensed in the air.

"You are awake, monsieur."

He did not reply.

She sighed as she knelt beside him to feel his forehead. The fever was gone, but she was not sure what were left in its place.

He pulled away from her touch as if she were the one burning up. "Why have you brought me here?"

"I want to help you."

"Why? What are you planning to do?"

The fact that he was addressing her in English did not necessarily mean that he remembered meeting her before. If he remembered, would he still be so hostile? Merissa could not begin to guess. All she knew was that she hadn't expected this reaction from him.

"You've moved from your bed," she said softly, giving him what she hoped was a reassuring smile. "Are you more comfortable? Where did you think you would go?"

"I meant to leave while I had the chance. *Quelle erreur!*" He snorted in disgust. "I did not know I would be *si faible*—so weak, or that my arm would be so useless."

"You should not sound so surprised. You are wounded and went without food or drink for two days that I know of. Who knows how long before that? You have been ill with a fever. Do you remember anything of what happened?"

He leaned his head back wearily against the soft hay behind him and closed his eyes. "I do not know how I came here. I remember being shot, and swimming in the river to get away. Before that . . ." He opened his eyes again and looked at her. "You. I remember you, mademoiselle—at the windmill. I told you then not to help us." He sat up, suddenly agitated. "What of Guillaume? Where is he? Do you know anything of the other man who was with me?"

"Shh. Do not excite yourself." Without thinking she put her hand on his chest to push him gently back against the hay. The hardness of his muscles beneath her palm and the soft tickle of hair brushing her fingertips at the open neck of his shirt sent strange messages racing up her arm. She snatched her hand away and wondered if she had in any way betrayed her reaction. His eyes met hers for an instant so brief she decided it meant nothing.

"By all reports, your friend got away," she said hastily. She was surprised to see him frown.

"I do not claim him as a friend. He is a dangerous man, mademoiselle."

"And you are not? That is not what you wished me to believe when we met in the windmill."

"If you were not frightened, you should have been. You know nothing of him or me. We could be murderers or thieves, escaped from the prison to avoid a trial. . . . You had a narrow escape. If Guillaume is still free, others may not be so lucky. There will be trouble."

"I believe he must be far away from here by now. And I

do not believe you are so dangerous. It is too late to try to frighten me now. You would not even harm my dog."

For the first time, he smiled, and for a moment Merissa quite forgot to breathe. "Never underestimate the power of a man, mademoiselle."

Merissa did not know how to answer. Certainly he was right. No smile from Harlan or any other man she'd ever met had affected her like that! She thought her heart had stopped. Her Frenchman seemed to be studying her in the silence that fell between them. Her awareness of his gaze made her feel exceedingly awkward.

"I do not even know your name, monsieur," she said finally.

"Nor I yours."

Should she tell him? She felt far less in control with him watching her and asking questions. "I need to check your arm and back," she said briskly, removing her gloves. After a pause she added, "I am Merissa Pritchard." She began carefully to roll up his sleeve.

He repeated her name, rolling the r's in typically French fashion, drawing out the syllables and placing special emphasis on the last one. His pronunciation made her name sound musical and exotic, almost seductive. "It is a very lovely name, Merissa."

Instinctively she glanced around, although of course there was no one there to overhear them. "Please! You must call me Miss Pritchard."

"How shall you punish me if I do not obey you, Miss prim and proper Englishwoman? I am already your prisoner, am I not?"

Merissa pulled back from him. She was shocked—by both his forwardness and his perception. Had she been so mistaken in taking him for a gentleman? And did he really believe that she was holding him prisoner?

"You are not my prisoner," she declared loftily. "The only thing keeping you here is the state of your bo—, uh, health. You will be free to leave whenever you wish, once you are strong enough to do so."

"*Miss* Pritchard. So, this is not your husband's farm."

Merissa blushed without quite knowing why. "No, it is my father's."

"Now why would such a beautiful woman not be married? A husband would keep you out of such trouble as this. Does your father know his foolish daughter is sheltering an enemy in his barn? Will he be so quick to let me go? Why wait for me to get stronger? Why does he not turn me over to your authorities now?"

"He is not here," confessed Merissa, her voice reduced now to a whisper by the intensity of his questioning. When she risked a glance at him she saw that his brown eyes seemed to blaze. The fire there kindled an answering flame deep inside her.

"Not here! She allows me to know he is not here! *Ma chère*, your naïveté is beyond belief. Who will protect you from me? Do you expect me to wait here patiently until he comes? I assure you, I will not. Where will that leave you when he learns that you let the escaped French prisoner slip through your hands?"

"I hope to God he never learns of this at all."

Something of the urgency in her tone must have reached through to the Frenchman, for suddenly he slumped back against the hay, quiet again. "So. What do you plan to do with me, then?"

"I told you before, I will help you."

"Mademoiselle, we are enemies, you and I."

"No. We are only strangers. It is your Bonaparte who makes the war."

"You do not care about the bounty for my recapture? Why break your laws to help me? You know nothing of me."

How could she put into words something she did not fully understand herself? Still, she had to say something.

"I did not know about the bounty."

"*Que je suis l'imbécile!* Now I have told you."

"I have no need of any bounty. It just seems right to help you. You seem to me an honorable man."

He startled her by bursting into laughter, although there was no amusement in his face. "Honor! Such a precious concept. I was an honorable man once, but circumstances have forced me to discover that I can be otherwise."

The bitterness in his voice betrayed pain that went far deeper than his physical ailments.

"I am sorry," Merissa said, somewhat shaken by his response. She was curious to know his story, but this was clearly not the time to ask.

"I do not want your pity. But now that I am trapped here, I see no choice but to accept your help."

He paused as Merissa examined his bandaged arm. "Perhaps there is something I can offer you in return," he added, his voice soft and very low.

"What would that be?"

"A little insight into the nature of men. Frenchwomen seem to be born with such knowledge, but you English seem utterly unschooled." He caught her hand and raised it to his lips. In the brief second before contact, he turned her hand deftly and brushed the kiss on the inside of her wrist.

Merissa recoiled in shocked surprise, her eyes locked on his. She felt a blush burn her face all the way to the roots of her hair.

"You see?" said her Frenchman, laughing merrily. "Perhaps we see now why you have not yet a husband."

Watching Merissa Pritchard blush was quite enjoyable, Alex decided. The effect was subtle, but if one looked closely, you could see how the soft color stole up her neck and spread out into pink roses in her cheeks. He found it very charming. She was very much an English beauty, and he thought it puzzling that she was not wed.

She opened her mouth to reply to his impertinence, but the rebuke he expected never came. Instead a voice came up from the floor below them, cutting off her words.

"Merrie? Is that Jackson with you? I'm coming up."

Who the devil would that be? Alex tensed and flashed a wary look at Merissa. He should have known better than to let down his guard for even a moment. He was dealing with the English, after all. He was in a very dangerous position.

"It is all right," the girl said softly. "It is only my sister. She knows—she has been helping me care for you."

"So, you did not keep your word after all. You agreed to tell no one."

"Did you think I got you up here by myself? I had to have help," she said, glaring at him in obvious exasperation. She rose and left him to meet whoever it was.

"He's awake," he heard her say. "I've been trying to convince him that we are friends."

"Well, it certainly sounds as though you succeeded. I could hear the laughter down below. Really, Merrie! You must be more careful. Suppose it had been someone else coming into the barn?"

There were rustling noises and then the squeak of a rope and pulley. A few moments later Alex watched the two young women coming toward him, carrying a basket.

The sight of Merissa together with the dark-haired sprite beside her jiggled clear a little more of his memory. He had seen them both somewhere—was it at the ruined hut? There had been a man with them, too. Not their father, and clearly not Merissa's husband, either. Who had it been then? A brother? Alex instinctively sensed he had less to fear from the women, but he must not forget for a moment who and where he was. How many people knew he was there?

"Awake at last, monsieur?" said the dark-haired miss. "You had a long sleep." She turned to her sister. "Are we finally to be introduced, Merrie?"

Merissa blushed, for the third time since he had awakened. Before he realized what he was doing, he decided to spare her the embarrassment of admitting she still did not know his name.

"Mademoiselle, I am Alexandre Valmont, captain of engineers in the emperor's *Grande Armée*. I am afraid I cannot say that I am exactly at your service."

Now why had he done that? He had resolved not to give his name, or any particulars of his situation. Somehow he thought that the less the women knew of him, the safer they might be from the consequences of their rash action. He had meant to give a false name if he had been forced to give any.

The younger girl smiled at him and dipped a quick curtsy. Merissa said, "This is my sister, Harriet Pritchard."

Reluctantly, he nodded his acknowledgment.

"You can see he is growing tired again already," Merissa noted. "We must feed him and let him rest."

Food! Alex felt as if his entire being lurched at the suggestion. When was the last time he had eaten? He remembered eating some blackberries outside the abandoned lock-keeper's hut. They had not even taken the smallest edge off his hunger then. How many days had passed since then? He realized with surprise that he had no idea.

"Bessie gave me a small kettle of soup and some bread," the one called Harriet said.

Bessie? Did yet someone else know about him? "Who is Bessie?" he asked in fading tones.

"Oh, Bessie and Jackson have been helping us, too."

Alex slid a hand down one side of his face, feeling the rough growth along his cheek and jaw. *Bessie and Jackson.* That made four people who knew he was here, or possibly five, counting the unidentified man. How soon before the secret became common knowledge?

He knew all too well how quickly a sanctuary could prove to be a trap. The sooner he was gone from here, the better. Despite all the careful planning he had done, the plotting of possible impediments and the calculating of odds, he had never anticipated something like his current predicament.

Suddenly one impulsive, foolish, beautiful young English woman with sky-blue eyes seemed to loom larger than any of the other obstacles he had tried to imagine.

Chapter 8

Merissa found the Frenchman still asleep upon her arrival in the loft the following morning. She shook his shoulder gently.

"Monsieur? Capitaine Valmont."

She was quite unprepared for his abrupt and violent reaction. "*Quel diable! Qu'est-ce que c'est?*" he shouted, swinging up wildly and grabbing her by the arm.

"Oh!" Merissa squeaked as she tried to pull back.

The brown eyes opened, seemed not to focus for a moment, and then sharpened. Alex groaned as he released her and flopped back onto the soft hay. "Mademoiselle, never, never do that to someone who has lived as I have."

Merissa rubbed her arm. "That is undoubtedly good advice. I would follow it gladly except for one small detail. I know nothing at all about the kind of life you have lived. I was only trying to wake you."

Alex did not reply but lay back in the hay, moaning. His eyes were closed again.

"I'm sorry. Have you hurt your arm?" The indignation in Merissa's voice gave way to anxiety. "Here, let me look." She got up to move around him, crouching under the roof rafters that came down to the floor of the loft. "That dressing needs to be changed, anyway," she added, kneeling down beside him.

Alex moved so quickly that she hardly knew what happened. One moment she was beside him, and the next he had pushed her over into the hay and pinned her beneath him. As she gasped in outrage, he brought his mouth over hers.

The crushing kiss she expected with pounding heart never came, however. The kiss he offered was as light and gentle as a butterfly's tickle, only greatly prolonged. She was dismayed to discover that her urge to fight evaporated in the heat he generated and a slow, languorous fire ignited inside her instead. Just as it did, he stopped and flopped back into the hay next to her.

"Yes, I did hurt my arm," he said with a wicked chuckle, "but it feels immeasurably better now."

"How dare you!" she sputtered.

"I much prefer to wake up with you like this. Consider it a second lesson. But I have barely begun to even the score between us. I am still greatly in your debt."

"This is hardly the way to show it, sir!" She sat up, brushing the hay from her shoulders. She stopped when she realized that he was enjoying watching her.

"We could continue the lesson, if it upset you to stop," he said innocently.

"You know very well that is not why I am upset! I never accepted this offer of yours. My help is given freely and does not need to be bargained for. The only insight your lessons are giving me is the certain knowledge that you are as devious and dishonorable as my father said escaped Frenchmen would be."

He stiffened under the lash of her words, as if she had actually slapped him.

"But of course," he said, the bitterness back in his voice. "Why would you think otherwise? I asked you before why you thought to help me. But wait! It is not too late to regret it. You could still turn me in." He narrowed his eyes. "Perhaps that is what you have planned all along."

In her heart Merissa knew she did not mean what she had said. She did not think those things about him, but he confused her. In some deep and very secret corner of her soul she had to admit not only that his kiss had been pleasurable and exciting, but that it had left her desiring more. What she knew he meant as a harmless flirtation was awakening her to a passion that she had never known was part of her nature. But was such knowledge a gift or a curse? No other man had ever created such reactions in her. Shackled to Harlan or some stranger in the future, would not this new awareness bring only misery?

She looked at the captain, whose face now bore only a

hard, mocking expression. "No, I will not turn you in. I apologize. I did not mean what I said."

"No? But perhaps I deserved it. Perhaps you should have listened to your father. He is obviously a man of far more experience in the world. You will remember, I warned you."

"People are not all the same, despite what he said. I will still help you. Perhaps we should just forget that this happened." She rose and went to get the basket she had brought up with her.

"I'm afraid your breakfast is only a sausage and a piece of Stilton cheese this morning," she said, fishing in the basket as she returned to him. She set the basket down in the hay beside him and handed him the food.

"Ah, yes," he said, "the infamous Stilton." He bit into it hungrily. "An excellent cheese. Too bad it will always taste like Norman Cross to me."

He made short work of the meal, leaving not a crumb. "A soldier learns to feast while he can, for the chance he counts on in the future may never come."

Merissa hoped he was only talking about food. She took out bandages while he ate. "If you are finished, I need to look at your arm. I have brought fresh dressings and also salve for your back."

"Belle mademoiselle," he answered with another sudden, wicked smile, "you may look at any part of me at all that you desire. With such a beautiful lady to attend me, I shall think perhaps I am in heaven."

"Need and *desire* are not the same thing," Merissa said crossly, wondering if she should not give up her task in light of how he was behaving.

"Oh, but they can be," came his quick reply.

The only possible response to such a mixture of blatant flattery and shocking impudence was to ignore it, Merissa decided. She proceeded to roll up his sleeve. "Does your arm pain you greatly?" she asked him.

"Only when I try to use it."

It seemed an obvious and very intentional reference to his earlier actions. "We will have to fashion you a sling."

"To prevent me from using it."

"Precisely."

Sitting so close to him, she could not help being aware of his body. She could feel the heat that radiated from him, although she suspected that she was the one who felt feverish. He said nothing, seeming only to be watching her with his intensely brown eyes.

She checked his arm and carefully removed the old dressing. His arm seemed large and powerful to her. The hair that covered it was dark and wiry, yet it felt as soft as down to her touch.

As quickly as she could, she redressed his wound, placing clean linen over a pad and wrapping it around his upper arm. He did not flinch or show any sign of discomfort. She hoped he did not notice that her hands were unsteady. Truly, the prospect of tending him now that he was improving seemed much more daunting than it had when he had been feverish or asleep.

"So. Is a Frenchman made any differently than an Englishman?"

Merissa started. "Why, what do you mean?" Unfortunately, a traitorous blush proved that she knew very well what he meant.

"I mean, you have been studying me with interest. I'm curious to know your conclusions."

She turned away to hide the blush, too late, of course. "I have not been, but even if I had, it would not be very gentlemanly of you to remark upon it."

He chuckled. "*Ma chère*, it is only you who seems to think that I am a gentleman. I have never claimed to be one."

"I am not your '*chère*,'" she said stiffly. Truly, the man was impossible! She gathered up the remaining strips of linen and stuffed them hastily back into her basket.

"On further consideration," she said, "I think perhaps your back is a job we had best leave to Jackson. I can leave the salve here for him." She paused, sitting back on her heels to look at him. "How did you get those nasty scratches?"

"Male possessive instinct," he replied evenly, tilting his head a little and returning her gaze. "The rooster in your neighbor's henhouse."

She wanted to ask more questions, dozens more, but she

held off. Instead she only asked, "Do you have everything that you need?"

"What I need most is to be gone from here, as quickly as may be."

"I meant for your comfort while you are here. I can be so forgetful sometimes, I might have overlooked—"

"You have provided for me handsomely. I do not wish for more than I can hide under the hay should someone come. But one thing that would be worth more than its weight in gold to me is clothing. I am not likely to get very far dressed as I am now."

She could not help glancing again at his body, noting the way his broad shoulders stretched the fabric of his torn, bedraggled shirt and the way his long legs stretched out in the straw.

A deep chuckle was Valmont's response. "You must admit that these have been rather sadly used. And they have not even been mine for very long."

Merissa got up. "I thought at first that I would like to know the details of how you have come to be in these circumstances, Captain. But I think now perhaps I would rather not. However, I will see what can be done for you."

She glanced down, brushing some remaining bits of hay from her pale green muslin gown. Looking up again, she realized that the Frenchman's glance had followed hers and still lingered. Without another word, she gathered up the basket and left him. As she started down the ladder, she heard him chuckle. "Deserted by my angel," he said with a melodramatic sigh. "I must not be in heaven, after all."

Alex did not see either Merissa or her sister for the better part of the next two days. The empty hours crept by slowly as he sat alone, resting and thinking. He listened to the noises of the busy farmyard all around him, feeling very vulnerable.

He knew he should not have kissed Merissa. He tried to focus his mind on what he should do once he left the questionable safety of the Pritchards' barn. Instead, he would catch himself recalling the flowery scent of Merissa's hair, or imagining the gentle touch of her hands. His response to her had only grown more intense since their first encounter at the windmill, and the kiss had only fueled it further. He had been both disappointed and relieved when she had decided not to put the salve on his back.

What was keeping her away? Had he pushed her too far? Had he intended to shock her? He hardly knew. The spark of interest in her blue eyes had made him think she would not be truly offended by his outrageous behavior, but perhaps he had misjudged her.

Such an error could have dangerous consequences. What if she decided that her father's assessment of his character was right? What would stop her from betraying him? He thought of Guillaume, and wondered if the fellow had been caught. If so, would he tell the authorities where he had last seen Alex? Would the citizens, or the militia, come searching in this area again? If they did, would Merissa reveal him?

Alex tested the muscles of his arm, but pain and weakness were the only rewards for his efforts. The arm was not strong enough to take him down the hayloft ladder yet. Until he had two arms to use, he was virtually a prisoner in this barn—Merissa's prisoner.

At least he was not entirely abandoned. The faithful Bessie and Jackson came to tend him when they could, bringing food and checking his wound. Bessie fitted him with a muslin sling, which allowed his arm some much-needed rest. Jackson managed to procure a basin and razor for his use. Also, most blessedly of all, the groom conjured up a shirt from somewhere that was clean and intact and also came close to fitting Alex.

It was not until late in the afternoon of the second day that Merissa came out to the barn again. By this time sheer boredom had prompted Alex to discover that he could at least use all of his fingers and he had begun to amuse himself in the fashion of his fellow prisoners at Norman Cross.

"What in heaven's name are you doing?" Merissa cried as she came upon him in the hayloft.

He was kneeling in the hay, busily laying cross-pieces to form the roadbed of a tiny model bridge made from hay he had soaked in his shaving basin. His sling hung empty around his neck and he was quite oblivious to the picture he must have presented as Merissa approached.

He looked up at her with a grin that hardly did justice to how glad he was to see her. "*Bienvenue, mademoiselle.* Welcome." He scrambled to his feet, struggling a little because of his injured arm and because he could not stand entirely upright under the rafters. "Come into my parlor and be seated, will you not?" With a bow and a sweeping gesture of his good arm, he indicated a mound of hay shaped more or less like a settee.

Merissa did not move. She stared.

He advanced a step toward her, his smile fading. "What is it? What is the matter?" Then, suddenly guessing, he ran a hand along his jaw. "Ah, this. I had forgotten. I am now a bit more *convenable*—respectable, *n'est-ce pas?*"

"Yes," Merissa said woodenly, seeming almost embarrassed.

He plucked at his shirtsleeve. "It is amazing what wonders a shave and a shirt can do, mademoiselle. I feel like a new man, and perhaps for a moment, you thought I was, eh?" He tried to give her his most winning smile, for she still seemed ill at ease. After his behavior the last time, he supposed he should not be surprised.

"Come, let us cry peace, even if our governments will not do so. I will endeavor to behave like a new man, to please you. Allow me to apologize for my behavior when you were here last. I was unpardonably rude."

"Outrageously insolent is more like." Merissa sat down cautiously, as if the mound of hay might be full of sharp needles. Her blue eyes were full of wariness, but she looked more beautiful to him than ever. "Is that how you set out to charm all young foreign ladies?"

He laughed. "No, only those who risk their pretty necks by helping evil escaped war prisoners despite being warned against them." The captain deposited himself on a mound of hay opposite her. "Let us begin again. I missed you and your sister very much these two days. Am I duly punished for my bad behavior? You see I have been reduced to making fribbles to pass the time." He waved toward the little grass model at his feet.

Merissa gave a cry of protest. "We were not punishing

you. And how can you call that a 'fribble'? May I see it? It is a little bridge, is it not? However did you make this? It is more like a—a clever work of art."

He handed her the bridge, surprised by her interest.

"*Pas du tout,* Mademoiselle Pritchard. Not art at all—merely the product of unrestricted time and a small measure of patience. I have had an abundance of the one, and I have learned the other in the course of my work. Many of the prisoners make such things."

"It is beautiful." She paused, then added, "I'm sorry that you were left alone so long. Our absence was not meant as a punishment. We went to visit my sister Francine who lives in Marholme."

"She is married?"

"Oh, yes, very much so. She has been Lady Chetwood for more than a year, and now she is increasing."

"My congratulations. You will make a charming aunt."

She looked down, running her fingers over the surfaces of the little bridge. "Condolences might be more in order. You must understand, this all reflects very badly upon me. Francine is only two years older than I, and my parents' expectations weigh very heavily on me at times."

"Of course. They are disappointed that you are not yet married." He could sympathize; the grandparents who had raised him had not understood his own decision not to marry. "Is there no man whom you find interesting?"

There was a long pause before she answered. *Yes,* she wanted to say. *You.* But of course, she could not say that. She should not even have been thinking that.

Who else was there? Only Harlan, but she was increasingly impatient with his company. He had accompanied the Pritchards to visit Francine, rather as if he were already a part of their family. He had seemed pleased when heavy rain had kept them at Chetwood Hall overnight. Merissa had been quite put out.

There was no one else.

"Perhaps I need to learn patience, as you say you have done," she replied at last.

"Perhaps you simply have not yet met the right man."

She sighed. "You are kind to say so. My parents think I am too choosy, or that I have not tried hard enough to change the situation. Soon I will be old enough to sit among the chaperones instead of the eligibles when we go to a ball." She shifted her position in the hay, and balanced the little bridge on the upturned palm of her hand. "Sometimes I think I should listen to them, and that there is no such thing as 'the right man.' "

"You do not believe that."

She looked at him to see if he was mocking her and found herself caught up by his intense brown eyes. He appeared to be perfectly serious.

"You should listen to what is in your heart, Miss Pritchard."

"Do you?"

"Oh, yes. Always. I do not always choose to follow what mine says, but at least I always listen."

How do you hear what it is trying to tell you? Merissa wanted to ask. She wished her heart would send louder messages. If her attraction to him was a message from her heart, she would be foolish indeed to listen.

"It sounds to me as if your parents are the ones who need to learn patience, *ma chère*. I'm sorry I cannot offer to teach them."

She heard his deep chuckle and was amazed at how easily he had managed to lighten her mood. Surely it was dangerous to be so much in his power!

"So. My drawing room may not be elegant, but you must admit that my furnishings are comfortable," Alex said, steering the conversation in a safely neutral direction.

Merissa relaxed a little. He was being so charming now—perhaps he really meant to behave himself. "I hope so," she replied. "I mean, I hope you are comfortable enough here, and that you do not find the smell of the cows too offensive."

"Mademoiselle Pritchard," he began, looking at her very intently. "You cannot begin to know how to appreciate a sanctuary that is soft to sleep in, warm at night and protected from the rain. I do, for I have done without such many a time. If I have not seemed very appreciative of all you have done for me, it is because part of me is appalled by the risk you have undertaken to help me. I wish you to know that I am grateful. If I could leave today, I would do so."

Merissa understood what he was saying. He was right, of course—the sooner he left, the sooner she and her assistant conspirators would be out of danger. But surely this was much too soon.

"I grow stronger each day," he continued. "My arm is not yet healed, but I am beginning to manage with it. However, without passable clothes my chances of getting away are next to nothing. Your Jackson thinks that given more time he can procure another shirt, some breeches, and even a respectable waistcoat and coat."

"And then what will you do?"

He sighed. "My plan is the same as every French prisoner's—to get to the coast and, with the precious ten pounds I have preserved to pay my passage, find a fishing boat to take me home before the winter storms begin. It is very inconvenient of you English to live on an island."

"I'm sorry," she said sincerely, making him laugh. She did not join in. His plan sounded very dangerous to her. What would drive a man to take such risks? After a slight pause she asked, "Was it so terrible in the prison?"

He sobered, staring down at his boots thoughtfully. Then he looked up and caught her gaze. "What you want to know is why I could not stay there, waiting, like so many others. Do you know, mademoiselle, some men have been in there for ten years or even more? Do you think their children will know them if they live long enough to ever go home? And how do you think their families fare, while they rot here in prison because our countries are at war?"

Suddenly he reached over and snatched the little bridge from her hand. "This, this is how they spend their endless days, making toys to sell in the prison market, hoarding up money to take home with them if they should ever get to go. Foolish hopes!" With a single quick motion of his large hand, he crushed the bridge, dropping the bits of hay at his feet.

Merissa was shocked by the vehemence of his outburst. Her soft heart felt his passion and pain. But he was not finished.

"I thank God I am not burdened with the responsibility

of a family depending upon me. I had other reasons that forced me to choose this course."

Merissa waited but he showed no inclination to say more. She was frightened by the dark expression that had come over his face. Should she press him to go on? She hesitated, glancing down at the crumpled remains of what had been the little bridge. What did she really know of him? What if there was a violent side to his temperament? She had tapped into passions and bitterness whose depths she could not know.

She decided she would be wise to leave him for now—it must be time to change for dinner anyway. But she was determined that she would ferret out what had happened to him.

Chapter 9

Merissa felt weary as she struggled up the ladder to the hayloft the following morning. Her night had been troubled with dreams of Alex—not idyllic dreams of being in his arms for another kiss, but frightening dreams of a beach that turned into a cliff under his feet and a ship that was always just beyond reach as he tried to swim to it. She had awakened pondering for surely the hundredth time all the questions that filled her head about the handsome stranger hidden in her father's barn.

She could hardly believe that such a handsome man was not married. No wife, and no family? And apparently no wish to change that. If it was not love, what force was it then that drove him so strongly to return to his country?

"Good morning," he said as she joined him. "I hoped it was you coming up."

"Have you eaten?" She looked around for signs that someone had already brought him some food.

"Yes, I've had a fine breakfast delivered by Bessie. I wanted to apologize for frightening you with my outburst yesterday."

"What makes you think I was frightened?"

He chuckled. "Weren't you? You flew away like a little bird, but you were right. I wasn't fit company."

"I did not mean to upset you," Merissa said. "My curiosity is a curse. I just would like to understand you, and how you have come to such a state as this. I have so many questions! Why is it that you were in the prison at Norman Cross at all? My father said it is usual for officers to be granted parole, or even to be exchanged."

He sighed. "Let it be enough simply to say that my parole was withdrawn."

"But why? I cannot believe you deserved it. I would like to know your story," Merissa replied. "Is it too much to ask in return for the help I am giving you? Surely—."

She was interrupted by a voice coming from the base of the ladder to the hayloft. "Merrie, is that you up there? I thought you would be working on the fair decorations, but obviously you are not. Who on earth are you talking to?"

Both Alex and Merissa froze in position for the full length of a heartbeat, blue eyes staring into brown ones.

"Not again!" Alex groaned.

Merissa jumped to her feet, heading for the ladder.

"No, Julie! I mean—you needn't come up, I was just coming down. There's no one up here but me."

Unfortunately, Juliana was already on the ladder and was not so easily hoodwinked. "Nonsense, Merrie," she said, her voice coming louder as she climbed. "I distinctly heard two voices, and one of them was male."

When Juliana reached the top, Merissa said hopefully, "You see, Julie? There's no one else up here."

Juliana gave Merissa a crafty sidelong glance and looked about. "Yes, I see. There's no one right here, at the top of the ladder. But 'tis a large hayloft." She attempted to push past Merissa, who blocked the way around the largest pile of hay. "There's no use in trying to fool me, Merrie. I heard two voices."

"All right, Julie, suppose there is someone up here with me? Are you certain you really want to know who it is? I warn you in all honesty, if you are as smart as you think you are, you will turn around and go back down, right now."

Juliana's tone was scornful. "Who are you to be claiming honesty, Miss Merissa Pritchard? You have been up to some scheme ever since Papa left for London, and I doubt that you have been honest with anybody." She narrowed her eyes. "As for regrets, perhaps the only one who will have them is you, or your gentleman friend. Get out of my way, Merrie, or I will push you right down."

Merissa did not budge. "It isn't anyone you know, and the situation is not what you think. What a high opinion you have of me, Julie!"

Juliana laughed. "Isn't the man supposed to protect the woman? I'm warning you, move out of my way, Merrie."

The confrontation was interrupted by the captain's low voice. "Let her come through, Miss Pritchard. It is already too late to do otherwise."

Merissa watched the expression on her sister's face change from suspicion to incredulity as she heard the accent that inevitably colored Alex's fluent English. Merissa stepped silently aside to let Juliana pass.

Juliana went around the hay pile and stopped short when she saw Alex. "Merrie, who *is* this? Where has he come from? What is he doing here?"

Coming up behind her, Merissa answered quietly. "I told you before, Julie, you don't want to know. I beg you not to get involved. Harry already has, much against my wishes and my better judgment."

"If you are both involved, why should I not be?"

Merissa could not simply say, *Because you are too mercurial, too undependable. Because we do not trust you.* But before she could find a response that she felt would not be cruel, Alex levered himself up from the hay using his good arm and stepped forward.

"I believe you are the one your sister wishes to protect, Miss Pritchard," he said gallantly, making a graceful bow to Juliana. "She has undertaken a great risk to give me shelter, and wishes to —what is that word? implicate?—as few others as possible. I am *Capitaine* Alexandre Valmont. I have come here by a very long route: Spain, Portugal, Portsmouth, Bristol, Yarmouth, Norman Cross. What I am doing here is hiding."

He very charmingly raised Juliana's gloved hand to his lips and kissed it, as if they had just been introduced at a ball. Juliana appeared to be transfixed, but whether it was from enchantment or shock Merissa could not tell. She herself was flustered by the oddest mixture of feelings she had ever experienced.

"Captain Valmont, may I present my sister Juliana."

As if the sound of her name had brought her back to reality, Juliana snatched her hand out of Alex's. "Merrie, he's a *Frenchman*! He is one of the escaped prisoners, isn't he?

But—how did you meet him? Where did you find him? How could—?"

Merissa could almost see the wheels turning in her sister's mind.

"Merissa Pritchard. What do you think you are doing helping him—and especially hiding him here? Do you not remember what Papa said about people who aid the escaped prisoners? They—you—are committing treason!"

"Now do you understand why I did not want you to become involved?"

"I'm already involved just by the fact that he is in our hayloft!" There was an edge of panic in Juliana's voice. "We can't keep him. Think of the scandal, if anyone found out! Think of Papa's position!" The pitch of her voice crept upward a note. "Who would marry us if they knew we'd been involved in such a thing as this! We'll have to turn him in, Merrie, and pretend that had been your plan all along."

Merissa sighed. *Trust Julie to react in the most conventional manner.* "I can't do that," she said quietly.

Juliana stared. "Can't? You mean you won't."

"All right, I won't. But I assure you I wasn't planning to keep him."

"Mesdemoiselles, s'il vous plaît! I am greatly distressed to be the source of a quarrel between two sisters."

At this moment, Juliana was as great a threat to Alex as the searchers with their guns and dogs had been. Her tone told him that like so many of the English, she thought the French prisoners would murder them all in their beds if given the chance.

"I assure you, mademoiselle, I shall not linger here a moment more than is necessary. I never wished to put you and your family at risk. But who will know if you say nothing?"

Alex hated having to beg, but he was in no position to use threats or force. He was far too practical to let his pride overturn his priorities, and staying alive was high on his list. But the pretty blond sister did not appear convinced.

He had never used sympathy as a ploy to gain Merissa's help—he had never sought her help. But the situation had changed now. He had no choice but to change his tactics as well.

He sighed and gestured to the mound of hay where Merissa had been sitting earlier. "Perhaps you should take seats, *belles mesdemoiselles,* if you would hear even a part of my tale." Wearily he lowered his own long frame back onto the hay opposite them.

"Am I too late to join the party?"

Harry's voice froze them. Unnoticed by anyone, she had climbed up the ladder and come around to the back of the loft.

"Harry! Thank goodness it is only you! We did not even hear you," Merissa exclaimed, her voice reflecting the same relief and dismay that Alex felt himself. How could he become so careless, so distracted by these young women?

He looked now at the three sisters, neatly arranged in front of him like a grouping of pretty porcelain figures. Honey-haired Merissa, the tallest, sat in the middle with her arms wrapped around her drawn-up knees, looking everywhere but at him. Flanking her to her right was dark-haired Harry, who sat with her legs curled up beneath her. Flaxen-haired Juliana perched to Merissa's left, looking as stiffly uncomfortable and out of place in the hayloft as if she had indeed been made of fine porcelain.

Alex closed his eyes for a moment to compose his mind. "I was captured in Portugal three years ago, at the battle of Busaco and Alcoba, a tragic slaughter that should never have happened," he began. "But that is beside the point."

What *was* the point? So much of what he had been through was not fit for young women to hear. "After months in Portugal awaiting transport, I was shipped here and held briefly at Portsmouth until I received my parole. I was supposedly high on the list for exchange. Engineers are valued, you see—our work puts us at high risk."

He looked at Merissa. "You asked me what happened. I lived quietly in Bristol until a year ago, when I was accused of a crime and my parole was revoked. I was arrested and sent to the prison at Norman Cross." What had been devastating to him then now sounded so simple.

Merissa looked down and fidgeted with her skirt, obviously uncomfortable. Were his words of warning finally taking root in her mind?

"Of wh—what crime were you accused? she asked, raising her eyes to meet his.

He looked away and gave a bitter laugh. "Of not being myself—can you believe it? They charged me with being an impostor—claimed I had taken the identity of Alexandre Valmont in order to get parole and perhaps be exchanged. It is as serious a crime as attempting to escape—which of course I have now added to my case."

"But why? Why did you escape? The charges against you are not true, are they?"

"Is it not a bit late to wonder now, Mademoiselle Merissa, after you have already broken your laws to help me? But no, they are not true. I asked them who I was supposed to be instead, but all they would tell me was that their information had come through official channels from France. Nothing I could say made any difference."

"That is not fair!" cried Merissa. She look utterly incensed, her cheeks flushed with becoming color. Alex marveled that she would react so strongly over what had happened to him. Harriet, too, looked suitably shocked. Juliana said nothing but nodded for him to continue.

"I began a letter campaign, seeking an investigation. I wrote to your Transport Board, your Admiralty, and to the French agent in London who handles the affairs of my fellow countrymen who are prisoners here. Above all I wanted to know where this information against me had come from!

"At the prison I was billeted among the regular men, but as the agent, Captain Draper, came to know me, he said it was plain to him that I was an officer. He began to believe I was who I claimed to be. He moved me into the officers' section of the prison and he, too, wrote letters."

"And nothing came of it? Did neither of you get any response?"

"Captain Draper died in February. Since then I have had many interviews with his replacement, Captain Hansell. But the wheels of government move very slowly, when they move at all. Our small lives get buried under piles of paper. I realized that I would have to contact friends in

France, to see if I could investigate for myself. I sent many letters through the agent in London.

"Still, it was only when a new batch of prisoners taken at Vittoria arrived this summer that I learned anything at all. I knew a man among the new arrivals. He became very excited when he recognized me. 'Everyone thinks that you are dead,' he told me. It seems that my cousin so informed my government and anyone and everyone to whom it might matter. Why? I still did not know until I received word from a friend that my grandfather had died. My cousin has laid claim to his estate. I am his heir, you see, but my cousin is next in line. He has found a coward's way to rob me—a paper murder made possible by the war. He has destroyed me in every way but life itself, by leaving me stranded in the midst of a strange country with no name and no honor. It would have been kinder to kill me."

Alex struggled to his feet. Kicking hay out of his way, he moved restlessly to the end of the little space that had been cleared for his accommodation. How could he expect these young Englishwomen to understand? He had no choice but to try to go home; it was the only way he could clear himself. Time was his enemy. If he survived the wait for warring governments to straighten out the mess or end the war, it might still be too late to undo his cousin's treachery.

He turned back to Merissa and her sisters. "I have no choice," he said simply, gesturing with his free hand. "In France I can prove my identity and stop this grave injustice. Here I am helpless."

"It is so important that you risk your life for it?" asked Merissa.

"Shame eats away a man's heart. You cannot imagine how it feels to be denied your own name and stand accused of stealing another man's. The dishonor is far worse than the stain on those who simply break their parole. And in wartime, a soldier's future is always at risk, Mademoiselle Pritchard."

In the sober silence that followed this pronouncement, Alex studied the faces of the three sisters. What did they think of him now?

He was not to know. Before another word was spoken, a

dog began to bark from the barn floor below them. Alex's gaze met Merissa's in a shared moment of horror.

" 'Tis Polly," she whispered. "How she—"

"Merissa?" called a voice.

"Oh, no," whispered Harry. " 'Tis Mama."

Chapter 10

Alex held his breath, wondering if Juliana would betray him. Merissa must have felt the same, for her gaze broke from his and her eyes turned toward her sister.

"Shh. Say nothing," Juliana whispered, giving them the answer. "Pretend that we are not here. She'd never climb up."

The four conspirators sat utterly motionless as long seconds ticked past, measured by their heartbeats.

"She is clearly not here, Polly," Lady Pritchard was heard to say. "It does not look as though she has been, either. I do not know what has been wrong with her these recent days, but something is most assuredly amiss. No, girl, I do not think it likely that she would be up there."

The sound of Polly's barking indicated that she had entered the cowshed and stationed herself at the foot of the hayloft ladder.

"There shouldn't be anything up there but mice. Come here, Polly. We will have to seek out the other girls and see if Merrie is with them. Polydora, come!"

Only with a great deal of effort did Lady Pritchard coax the steadfast spaniel away from the ladder. When they had left the barn, the sisters turned to one another in consternation.

"She is looking for all of us! What shall we do?" asked Harry.

"We must go down right now and split up," Merissa said. "Where did each of you say you would be this morning?"

"I said I would be writing letters in the garden," Juliana said in a subdued voice.

"I said I was going out to ride with Collins, but if she checks in the stables, she'll know I did not go," said Harry.

"And she knows now that I was not here in the barn working on the fair decorations," Merissa lamented.

"So. None of you did what you originally planned—it must be plain that you changed your minds, *n'est-ce pas?* It must be that you decided to go do something together instead."

"Of course! Captain Valmont is right. If we hurry down right now, we can say that we decided to go for a walk in the orchard together, and can pretend that we are just coming back!" Merissa scrambled to her feet, brushing the hay from her skirt.

Ever courteous, Alex rose with her and, as he did, managed to catch her eye. "Polydora?" he queried with a sardonic lift of an eyebrow.

Harry and Juliana had also arisen and were already headed for the ladder.

Merissa shrugged and gave Alex a sheepish smile. "I named her after Polydorus, the Greek sculptor."

She turned quickly to follow after her sisters, and in what seemed like only an instant, Alex was left alone. He was astonished that a young English miss would know anything about Greek sculptors. Astonished, and also intrigued. Merissa Pritchard was a most unusual young woman, he was coming to realize. If only their circumstances were different!

Of course, such thinking led nowhere. He chastised himself for losing sight of his goal for even one moment. His risk of discovery was becoming greater every day.

Ducking his head to avoid the roof beams, he paced in the confines of his hiding space like a caged animal. He could not put the Pritchards to any further risk. He would willingly face whatever consequences might come to him because of his actions, but he could not bear to see Merissa and her family ruined if their own actions were discovered.

He flexed the fingers of the hand that was held up by his sling. He was recovering from the traumas his body had suffered. Soon he would begin to weaken from lack of activity. Surely he could leave tonight, once it was dark.

He would have given almost anything to obtain the clothes Jackson had hoped to get for him—anything short of his freedom and that of the Pritchards'. He would have to find another way to procure clothes. At least Bessie might slip him some extra food from the kitchen to see him through the next few days. He would only have to climb down the ladder once, just once. His injured arm would not have to sustain his full weight as long as his feet did not slip off the rungs.

So resolved, Alex composed himself to take a nap. He would need all the rest he could get.

It hardly seemed as if he had been asleep for any time at all when a rough voice and a booted foot nudging his legs awakened him rudely.

"All right, you! Wake up here, and get up, only do it slowly."

For a moment Alex did not know where he was. He opened his eyes and saw a spindly young man in livery standing over him nervously, clutching a pistol in his hand. Hovering behind him was Jackson, looking exceedingly anxious. Alex assessed the situation, weighing his own disability against the advantage of surprise, and the insignificant body weight of his immediate opponent against the fact that the young fellow was armed.

If he could have moved with his normal speed and grace, it might have been worth a try to leap up suddenly, knocking the first fellow back into Jackson and slipping past them while they disentangled themselves. With any luck, the pistol would have discharged into the hay and Jackson might even have been deliberately slow to move.

In his present condition, Alex knew it would be foolish to risk it. Perhaps some other chance would present itself. He nodded his head and rose slowly.

"He looks like some Gypsy fella to me, Bean," Jackson suggested helpfully. "Might be he doesn't speak English." Standing behind Bean, Jackson rolled his eyes and put a finger to his lips, sending Alex a clear message.

"Well, I'll leave that up to her ladyship," Bean replied. "She's the one who'll have to ask the questions, not me. I just have to deliver him."

"He's got a bum arm. It'll be some trick getting him down that ladder."

"Aye. We'll have to help him, is all, and watch out for any tricks of his."

Merissa was in the salon practicing her flute, postponing another inevitable session of working on the cushion covers for St. Gilda's. She had just achieved a particularly satisfactory E, sending the high note soaring gracefully, when the mahogany doors burst open and a breathless Harry rushed in.

"Merissa! Bean and Jackson—they have the captain," she gasped.

Merissa set down her instrument. "Harry, what are you talking about?"

"Mama—she sent Bean out to the barn." Harry gulped for breath. "Bean found the captain. He went and got Jackson, and Mama gave him Papa's pistol from the study, and now they've just brought him into the house!"

Disjointed though it was, Harry's account made some sense to Merissa, none of it good. "Oh, dear Lord."

"What should we do?"

"I don't know, Harry. I truly don't. Wait and see what happens next, I suppose." Merissa sank down slowly onto the nearby bench of the pianoforte. "Mama must have been more suspicious when she came out to the barn than we thought."

They did not have to wait long. A few agonizing minutes later, Backhouse presented himself at the door.

"Miss Merissa, your mother wishes you to join her in the drawing room," he announced. His curiosity, held in check by his professional reserve, was betrayed by an unusually bright gleam in his old eyes.

Merissa rose to follow him like one summoned to her execution.

Harry reached out to give her hand a reassuring squeeze. "I'll go find Juliana," she offered softly.

As Merissa approached the drawing room, she noted Bean and Jackson stationed like guards outside the door. Bean held himself stiffly erect, still armed with Sir Barry's pistol, while Jackson stood with hunched shoulders, staring down at the cap in his hands. The groom looked up at Merissa as she passed him, his eyes full of apology.

She nodded in acknowledgment and gave him a brave little smile. Then she entered the drawing room and quietly closed the door behind her.

The click of the door sounded loud in the unnatural stillness of the room. For a moment the only sound was the ticking of the longcase clock in the corner. The afternoon sun poured into the room, illumining the soft gray-green fabric on the walls, warm and incongruously soothing in view of the tension that permeated every corner.

Predictably, Lady Pritchard sat in her giltwood armchair, her spine as straight as a poker. The captain stood near the carved marble fireplace, his hands behind his back and his sling hanging empty.

Had they bound his hands, then? The position of his arms pulled back his strong shoulders and drew the shirt fabric taut across his chest. Merissa's gaze lingered on him for a moment. He stood at his full height, dominating the room with his presence. Truly, he was a magnificent man.

Was he in pain? She could not read the expression on his face. Better to let Mama make the first move, she thought.

"Well, Merissa," said her mother. "This fellow was found sleeping in our barn. Bean and Jackson are of the opinion that he must be one of the local Gypsies, but I have serious questions about that. He has had nothing at all to say for himself. Would you like to offer me some help?"

"Help, Mama?"

"Yes, help, as in information, my dear. It seems to me you have been spending an unusual amount of time in the barn these last few days, working on the fair decorations that seem not to have made much progress. Or did you think I would not notice?"

"You think this man has been in our barn for several days, Mama?" Merissa tried to make it sound ridiculous.

"He seems to have been made quite comfortable, I would say. According to Bean, he had a blanket, a chamber pot, dishes he had apparently been eating from . . . and with that injured arm, I don't believe he carried all that up by himself. I don't even see how he got up there in the first place."

Merissa cast about frantically for something to say. As she hesitated, her mother went on.

"He might very well be a Gypsy, but if that is so, why

did he not go back to his caravan when he injured his arm? Why hide in our barn?"

"Perhaps he was too ill!" Merissa blurted out. "Uh, perhaps the constable was after him, or something like that. You know how quick people are sometimes to accuse them of stealing, even when they've done nothing wrong."

"Is that what happened, Merissa? Why has he not told me this himself? Most of our Gypsies are not so disrespectful that they refuse to speak. If he is innocent and in need, he has nothing to fear from us. Why would you keep him hidden, when perhaps we could help him?"

Merissa's fertile brain failed her for the moment. She glanced at Alex, but his eyes were fixed on her mother.

"I hoped that you would give me some other explanation for your odd behavior, Merissa. I hope that we had raised you properly enough for you to know better than to spend time alone with a strange man in a hayloft, no matter what the circumstances!"

I was not alone with him—not all of the time, thought Merissa, but she managed to clamp her lips over the words before they slipped out.

Lady Pritchard sighed and rose from her chair. "We are not making much progress. I shall have to question Bean and Jackson further. *Someone* has been providing for this fellow."

She actually got as far as opening the door before Merissa confessed, "No, Mama. It was I."

Jackson and Bean had turned curiously as the door opened. "Never mind," said Lady Pritchard, closing it again.

She walked with great dignity back to her chair. The effect was spoiled before she could sit down, however, by a commotion in the passage outside, which culminated in the opening of the door and the breathless arrival of Harry and Juliana.

"Ladies?" said their mother with great surprise. "I thought I was conducting a private interview."

"Mama, we believe the subject involves us," Juliana said, holding her head high with dignity that mirrored her mother's.

"Oh, ho! So, has it been all three of you, then? I had no

idea my daughters were such deceivers! What am I to do with you?"

"Jackson and Bessie were helping us, too," blurted Harry, earning a murderous stare from Merissa.

At that, Lady Pritchard sat down. "Jackson and Bessie, too? What about Bean? Anyone else? Or has it been everyone in Pie Hill except for me? I can hardly credit this." Her composure weakened, she waved faintly in the direction of the door. "Please have Jackson come in."

As the groom joined them, Merissa thought she would try to intervene on Alex's behalf. "Mama, does he have to have his hands tied? His poor arm, you know. I'm sure he must be in pain."

"Merissa, the only thing I shall do is send for the constable unless someone in this room tells me what is going on."

Merissa felt emboldened by the increased numbers in the room. Her mother was suddenly very much a minority among the little group of conspirators.

"Well, Mama, I think you should not do that unless you want to see us all hauled away to the county lockup," she said quietly. "Captain Valmont is not a Gypsy. He is a French officer, escaped from Norman Cross."

It was quite fortunate that Lady Pritchard was already seated. The good lady closed her eyes for a moment, leading everyone to believe she had swooned. Before any of her daughters could rush off to find her *sal volatile*—her smelling salts—however, she opened her eyes again.

"Perhaps Madame would be restored by a glass of sherry?" Alex's deep voice drew all eyes. He nodded his head toward the decanter and glasses displayed on a tray on the mantel. Merissa hurried to pour a glass for her mother.

Alex waited until Lady Pritchard sipped from her drink, then he stepped before her, bowing gracefully despite his tied hands.

"Madame Pritchard, je vous prie donnez-moi votre pardon. Je suis responsable pour tout cet embrouillement."

How handsome and dignified he looked! Merissa could not help admiring the fine figure he cut as he spoke to her mother. She also admired his wisdom in addressing her mother in French; the choice at once acknowledged Lady Pritchard's status and education as a gentlewoman, and

opened communications with her in the universally accepted language of diplomacy.

However, Merissa was not about to allow Alex to shoulder all the blame for what had happened, which was obviously his intent. She stepped up beside him.

"Mama, I would like to present Captain Alexandre Valmont. He may claim that all of this is his fault, but I have to
tell you that is not true—not in the least. In fact, everything
that has happened occurred precisely against his wishes."

She was standing very close to him—close enough to
hear him exhale. She didn't dare to look at him.

"Merissa, do you expect me to believe that you forced
this man here against his will?"

"Well, in a manner of speaking, yes." She had not
thought of it in exactly those terms until now. She glanced
hesitantly at Harry and Jackson. "He was mostly unconscious. He did not want me to help him, but Mama, he
might have died! We couldn't leave him there!"

"And where exactly was he, Merissa, when you found
him 'mostly unconscious'? I assume that you had no idea
who he was until later."

Merissa looked up at the delicate plaster garlands that ornamented the ceiling. *Dear Lord, this was going to be hard
to explain!* "Not exactly, Mama."

Neither Jackson nor Juliana knew the full story of how
Merissa had happened to find the injured Frenchman.
Would they be so shocked when they heard that they would
no longer be willing to help? Then again, would that matter
if Mama could not be convinced to save him?

Merissa took a deep breath and plunged into a full reve-
lation of all that had occurred. She did not look at Alex or
anyone else while she spoke, staring down instead at the
floral patterns on the French carpet. The design seemed to
burn into her brain as she fought to keep her emotions
under control.

"So you never did meet Mr. Whitcomb that day, or go to
see his family, did you?" Juliana interrupted at one point.
No one else spoke.

When Merissa finished, Lady Pritchard rose and poured
herself two more glasses of sherry. No one said a word as

she drank them. When she had set her glass carefully back on the tray, she turned to Merissa.

"Well, my dear, it seems you did all but abduct this young man, after all. We may thank you for bringing trouble right to our doorstep—there's no justification for blaming Trouble himself, much as I might like to."

Merissa was appalled to feel tears spring into her eyes. "Mama, if you could have seen him, you'd understand. He was so ill, and weak—he'd had nothing to eat or drink . . ." She looked toward Harry and Jackson for support.

"Mama, he looked as though he were dead already," Harry declared passionately.

"And do you think it was fair to involve Jackson and Bessie in this with you, Merrie? Do you realize the serious consequences this could bring down on all of us?"

"No, Mama. Yes, Mama." *Maybe Australia wouldn't be so bad—if only it weren't full of convicts!* Merissa closed her eyes for a moment, trying to get her tears under control. "I just didn't feel there was any choice! It wouldn't have been right to leave him there to die like that. It wouldn't have been right not to go and see if he was there, either— not after I had suggested it! What are you supposed to do when what the law tells you goes against what you know in your heart is right?"

"I suppose we must all answer to our own consciences," Lady Pritchard conceded.

"If you only knew, Mama. He has been made the victim of a terrible injustice!"

"I am certain that every prisoner who has ever escaped from anywhere thinks that, my dear. But I suppose I can at least listen to his story."

Before Alex began, Merissa made another plea for his comfort. "Please, Mama, can we not untie his hands? He never harmed me or Polly when we had no one to protect us; what do you think he would try to do in a room full of people, with Jackson among us and Bean outside the door?"

"It is against my better judgment, but—very well."

Merissa darted behind Alex and began to work on the knotted rope that bound his hands as he began a second recital of the tale he had told in the barn. All the while he talked, Merissa pried and pulled on the strands of rope, easing the knots loose until at last the captain was free. If only she could free him from the rest of his problems so simply!

Alex rubbed his wrists as he came to the end of his narrative.

"Here let me see," Merissa demanded, taking hold of his hands. His wrists were chafed and red, but the rope had not broken his skin. "Are you all right?" She made the mistake of looking up into his dark eyes. They seemed a darker brown than she had ever noticed, but in their depths a fire burned.

"Mademoiselle, I do not know how to answer that," he murmured so softly that only she could hear him.

"Captain Valmont," said Lady Pritchard, "I have a few questions."

Chapter 11

Merissa noted that Lady Pritchard had more than a few questions.

"I'm not sure we wish to know, monsieur, how you managed to escape from Norman Cross," she said, "but there is something you must clarify."

Alex stared into Merissa's eyes for another moment, as if he wanted to be certain that she believed him. "I assure you, no one was hurt."

"I believe it was said there were two escapees, and you have said nothing concerning the other prisoner who escaped with you."

"Ah, that is simple, madame," he said, breaking off the exchange and turning to the older woman with utmost courtesy. "Guillaume had no part in my plan. It was my misfortune that he was clever and observant and suspected that I was preparing to make an attempt. I had resisted pressure to help other prisoners make their escapes, but with my own arrangements already set and the time so close at hand, I could not ignore his threat to expose me if I refused to allow him to come along."

"You were not partners, then?"

The captain shook his head.

"Where is he now?"

"That I do not know. I have neither seen nor heard anything of him since the night I tried to steal your neighbor's chicken. I believe he must be far from here by now, unless he has been recaptured."

"I see. Well then, tell me about your grandfather. Who was he? It seems his estate must have some value, to have pushed your cousin to such extreme measures."

The captain moved to the window, gazing out thoughtfully. "My grandfather was the Comte de Montiere, an honored general who retired to the mountains when the Revolution came. He and my grandmother took me in after my parents were killed during the Terror. We went into Switzerland for a time, but we did not stay there very long, for the revolutionary fever came there, too. Eventually there was an amnesty, and we returned to my grandfather's estates in the Isère. His title was abolished along with all the others for the sake of the Republic. It means nothing."

"You are his heir," Lady Pritchard pronounced with confidence. "When the monarchy is restored in France, as we know it shall be, the old titles will be valid once more, and you will be the Comte de Montiere, whether you approve or not."

Merissa looked at Alex accusingly. "You said you were Captain Valmont. Are you an impostor after all?"

He turned back from the window with a shrug. His full lips showed a hint of a rueful smile.

"Valmont is our family name. It is all I have ever used since I was old enough to go away to school and then enter into the military. My full name is Alexandre Christiane Armand Valmont de Montiere."

He opened his hands outward and encompassed all the occupants of the room with a sweeping gaze that ended at Merissa. "I deeply regret that my problems have come to involve you all. You are good people. I know you, Miss Pritchard, meant well when you disregarded my warnings. Perhaps I would indeed be dead now if you had not done so. But my presence here imperils you all. I had resolved to leave tonight. Do you think, Lady Pritchard, that you might be willing to allow me still to do so?"

Tonight? Merissa felt the words stab at her heart like knife blades. *No!* she thought. *Not yet!*

She did not realize that she had spoken aloud until she saw everyone staring at her.

"I mean, his arm—it is not yet healed. He has no clothes. . . ." She turned to glare at Alex. "What did you intend to do, if you left tonight? You have no money, no food, not even a coat to cover yourself. How far did you think you would get? Did you even know in which direction you would go?" Her chin rose a trifle as the words came pouring out of her. "Did you not berate me for rescuing you without any thought for the consequences? Do not tell me now that *you* would also be so foolish."

"Alas for me, I can give no other answer," he responded, flashing her the devastating grin he seemed to reserve just for her.

For a moment, they stood regarding each other as if there were no one else in the room.

"I confess, I wish your father was here," Lady Pritchard said. "I hardly know what to do. I shudder to think that the best we could give the rightful Comte de Montiere, recognized or not, has been a bed of hay in our barn during his stay here. On the other hand, *Monsieur le Comte* is a fugitive, and we are breaking our own laws by assisting him."

She paused, and it seemed to Merissa as if everyone held their breath along with her, waiting for her mother's decision.

When finally Lady Pritchard gave her answer, it was as if she were speaking to herself. "No, I don't believe we can let the comte leave tonight."

Merissa glanced at Alex and saw the muscles move in his neck as he clenched his jaw. As she regarded his stoic expression, she knew she would defy even her own mother if she must, as she had already defied the law, to help this man. Even at the cost of her heart!

But Lady Pritchard was not finished. "As it happens, we have already broken the law, have we not? What would be the point of all our efforts, then, if his escape attempt should fail? If we are going to do this at all, let us do it thoughtfully and thoroughly. We will pray that no one ever learns of it, including Francine or Rodney. What we need is a plan."

Merissa wanted to jump and cheer. Instead, she settled for hugging her mother, saying, "Oh, Mama. Thank you."

Harry and Juliana joined in the hugging. Jackson stood awkwardly near the door, turning his cap round and round in his hands while he smiled.

The plan was that Alex should become an ailing Gypsy once again. "We will put it about that his arm was injured while he was helping work in the fields on another farm," Lady Pritchard explained. "A missed stroke with a sickle could easily have hurt him. Why make all our servants test their loyalty to us against their loyalty to the law? This way they will be entirely innocent of any wrongdoing.

"This way, too, should there be any talk, it will not be dangerous at least. Better a Gypsy than a Frenchman! Perhaps it is scandalous, with your father absent, but at least it is not illegal. I'm sorry, Jackson, that you and Bessie could not be spared in this way. Do you think you or she will have trouble keeping up the pretense?"

"No, ma'am, your ladyship," Jackson answered deferentially. "We'll do all right."

"I'm afraid that he must stay in the barn for now, to lend credence to our story. No one would expect a Gypsy to be given shelter in the house! This way he will also remain out of sight most effectively. In the meantime, we will try to devise some method to get him safely away from here. Perhaps Sir Barry will have some suggestion when he gets home."

"Papa! Does he have to know?" The thought made Merissa very nervous.

"My dear, I would never keep anything from your papa. He is a kind, wise, and well-connected man who can very likely help your friend. Do not worry. How can he go against his own family? And now we will all be in this soup together."

Merissa slipped out of the house alone and hurried to catch up to Alex in the barn as he returned to the loft.

"I wanted to congratulate you," she explained. "My mother is not charmed and impressed by everyone, you know. But I'm sorry you were subjected to such indignities!"

"Do not apologize," he said, smiling. "It could hardly have been pleasant for you to have to face all those difficult questions." He found her hand and took it into both of his. "You were a wonderful champion—thank you."

Merissa could feel a current running from his warm, dry hands to hers—she felt it with her whole body. His eyes seemed alight with it. To say that they were brown was wholly inadequate. His dark pupils were surrounded by a warm pool of brown the color of French brandy, surrounded by an outer ring of even darker, richer brown. She felt she might easily fall into their depths, with no hope of being saved and no desire to be so. She knew she should look away, but she felt utterly powerless to do so. She struggled to remember the other things she had wanted to say to him.

"I'm sorry about your grandfather. Did you love him?"

"Yes, in my way. I had not seen him for several years. The war made it difficult to get away."

She could sense his sadness and regret, and wished that she could comfort him. "How unfortunate to have to learn of his death the way you did."

"It explained why I heard nothing from him after I wrote to him of my difficulties. I chose to believe that my letters were not reaching him rather than accept any of the other possibilities. I always believed that we would be reunited one day."

Hesitantly she brought up her other hand and placed it over his. "How terrible," she whispered. "You must have felt so forsaken."

He did not answer. With the gentlest of tugs he brought her against his chest and bent his head down to rest against hers. *Ma chère Merissa, vous étes si sensible et si belle.* He drew back just enough to brush a light kiss across her forehead. Then he released her and Merissa realized that she had been holding her breath.

"Someone will see us standing like this, *ma chère*, and it will not do," he said. "You must go back before you are missed."

The advantage of the new ruse was that, although Alex still slept in the cramped hayloft of the cow barn, during the day he had the freedom to come down. The ladder still caused him pain, but he claimed that the exercise helped to strengthen his arm.

Merissa and her sisters all found time to keep him company working on projects in the spacious corn barn.

"When the sheaves are dry, they will be collected and stored in the center of the barn to await threshing," Merissa explained one day when Alex expressed his wonderment that they could work there undisturbed. "The space for the threshed straw will not be needed until after the harvest. Threshing goes on all through the winter months."

Alex was impressed. "I must admit, we did not grow grains—what you call corn—on my grandfather's estate. We had mostly orchards and pastures. I was free to roam, to fish, and to steal apples from the orchard. The running of the farm was not my concern."

Merissa was pleased whenever he revealed such glimpses of his past. She treasured up the bits of personal information that he dropped in this way, collecting and hoarding them much like the fragments of Roman antiquities she kept in her straw box in her room. Slowly she was coming to know him.

Polly, too, had come to accept him. Merissa's spaniel had been suspicious at first, but over the course of several visits to the barn she and Alex had become friends. He knew exactly how to scratch behind her ears in the way she liked best. He always called her by her full name, as if the idea amused him.

"How did you come to name this shameless hussy after Polydorus?" Alex asked one day. He was relaxed, his long frame stretched out on what was left of the old straw, his hand stroking Polly's underbelly while the dog basked in ecstasy.

Merissa was trying to tuck some bright scarlet rose hips into a wreath she had made from strands of bittersweet. When she looked up, she was momentarily transfixed by the image of Alex caressing the dog. She hastily pulled her gaze back to the task in her lap, before she became mesmerized by the rhythmic movements of his hand.

"My father introduced me to some of the ancients through books in his library. I was very taken with the idea of learning about the Greeks and Romans after I found my first shard of Roman pottery in one of our fields. I must have been seven or eight," she added, "about the same age you were when you lost your parents and went to Switzerland."

She paused, uncertain how to express what she wanted to say. "It seems so unfair. My life has been so idyllic, by most standards. At the age when I was happily dreaming of Romans and looking for coins in the plough furrows and on the banks of the river with my father, you must have been grieving for yours. Those years must have been a painful, terrible time for you."

She felt a deep sadness, and her hand shook as she tried to fasten the rose hip into place without breaking the stem. There was a rustle of movement in the straw as Alex rose and came beside her. He crouched down and placed a hand lightly on her shoulder.

"You are too softhearted, Miss Merissa Pritchard. Do you not know any better than to compare one person's life to another's? I believe God places each of us on our own path, to do the best we can. Imagine being moved to tears by some young boy who lived a long time ago!"

His hand moved from her shoulder to her chin, and he turned her face toward his. "Yes, I thought so," he said softly.

She had not been able to banish the tears that had started to collect in her eyes. Annoyed and embarrassed, she pulled her head away. "That young boy still lives inside you. I think who we are changes a little every day, as we add to what we have already experienced. But we build on what was already there. Your life has been so different from mine! I can hardly conceive of what yours must have been like. It makes me feel ashamed that I am not content with my lot."

Dear Lord, he was so close to her! She felt as though she was trembling all over. She was awash in a flood of feelings—she was drowning in them. Her heart was full of pain for the life he had known—so much lost! Mixed with her sympathy was a tender yearning and admiration for the man he had nonetheless become.

How unfair that this man should come into her life, raise these feelings in her, and then—nothing would come of it! She felt cheated and angered. But the worst feeling of all was that she desperately, passionately, wished he would kiss her. Very slowly, deliberately, she made herself ease away from him.

"We are not as different as you might think," he said, getting up and walking back over to the corner where he had been petting Polly. He stooped down and picked up something from the straw, stopping to pat the dog's head in passing. When he walked back to Merissa, he was smiling.

"*Voilà*," he said, thrusting a small object into her hands. "You see, I, too, have always had a fascination with the Romans. You were distressed the other day when I destroyed the little bridge I had made. This is a better one—it is sturdier, made of straw instead of hay. You can pretend it is a model of a Roman bridge, although the resemblance is only one of shape. I have not found a way to make straw resemble stones."

"It is wonderful!" She accepted the little bridge with delight. It was beautifully crafted, but most especially she liked it because he had made it for her.

"The Romans were brilliant engineers. Living with my grandparents so near to the Alps, I found the story of Hannibal and his elephants most impressive when I heard it. To see the challenges of building roads and bridges in those mountains—that is inspiring! The Romans were the true artists. The works they built had permanence; no one knows better how beautifully made those were than we who, thanks to the war, have had the task of trying to destroy them."

He waved a hand at the model in her hand. "This is not art. I do not make things that are meant to have permanence. My bridges and barracks are dismantled as soon as they are used; my tunnels lead only to the destruction of walls. A bridge of straw—it is a small thing."

He stopped suddenly, as if he had only then become aware of how much he was talking. The small puckers of concentration between his dark eyebrows smoothed out, and the smile returned to his eyes. "So. I hope this bridge will last a little while at least. May it be a bridge of friendship between us, two people who have led different lives, but share a common love for history."

She smiled up at him. "I will treasure it always. It can last a long time with reasonable care. Someday you will build something permanent, when you wish to do so. You are a skilled craftsman, it is plain to see."

She was afraid of intruding, afraid of saying the wrong thing. He had bared a little more of his soul, and she did not want shutters to slam shut over the window. She veered away from the sensitive subject of permanence.

"This makes me think of the corn dollies the harvest workers make out of the last sheaves. They are very superstitious about how those sheaves should be handled." She set down the little bridge and pushed aside the wreath she had been working on. Rising, she went to Alex and took his hand, a dangerous thing to do given the way she was feeling. But she only led him to the pile of vines and leaves and seedpods.

"Here," she said. "You have made the mistake of showing me how skilled and clever you are. You can help us to make wreaths and garlands and ornaments to decorate for the fair."

He chuckled. "I led myself into this, did I not? I suppose I cannot refuse."

She showed him some of the decorations that she and her sisters had managed to finish, to give him ideas, and she talked a little bit about the fair—how it combined the traditional goose festival celebrating Michaelmas, the hiring fair that followed the harvest, and the individual harvest home dinners that some of the outlying farms still put on for the workers when the harvest was complete. After that, they sat and worked in silence.

Merissa tried to settle her mind to simply enjoy the peace and companionship. Polly came to lie down beside her with a great sigh of contentment that Merissa could not share. It was quite amazing, however, to see that the captain could take odd bits of vines and leaves and work them into a garland in half the time she could, and that he even had some new ideas. She caught herself watching his nimble hands, and forced herself to focus on her own work instead.

"Tell me about your collection of Roman artifacts," he said a short time later. "It must feel special to live on the same land where they once lived."

She nodded, less surprised that he should understand her feeling about it now that he had revealed his own interest. How different he was from Harlan! Harlan did not have the imagination to understand the romance of riding through Robin's Green Lane thinking about the Romans who had ridden there centuries before, or the excitement of finding a

Roman coin turned up by the plough. She was certain that all Harlan saw when they rode out to Dubro Vitae was a grassy hilltop pasture with curious humps in it. Her Frenchman would see walls where the embankments ran along, and probably streets and buildings besides. How she wished she could show it to him!

He was hunched over his creation, frowning a little. As she looked at the way his waves of brown hair fell forward over his forehead, she felt a surge of resentment wash through her. Why must he have been a Frenchman? Why a fugitive? Why had God thrown them together, when they would only be wrenched apart?

She sighed. "Most of the pieces I have found are very ordinary. I have a number of coins, and many pottery shards, mostly Castorware, which they made in this area. There are some fragments of old glass, too, and bits of broken bracelets. But I have been given some pieces that I particularly prize—one is a bone gaming piece, and another is a little brooch made of bronze . . . Then there are some small buckles that my father says came from the armor they wore."

"That sounds to me like a most remarkable assemblement. How does it happen that there is so much to be found here?"

She did not correct his word. "Just across the river, not far from here, there was a Roman town, Dubro Vitae, along the main road. Our Great North Road was once their Ermine Street."

"I wish that I could see your Dubro Vitae," he said. The wistful look on his face made her wonder if any of the feelings that were torturing her might not also have even briefly touched him.

Chapter 12

Merissa, Harry, and Juliana were all in the barn with Alex a few days later when they heard a carriage drive through the yard and pull up in front of the house.

Curious, Merissa rose and went to see who had arrived. Sunlight poured in across the huge threshold where the barn doors had been opened to let in the air, and she blinked in the brightness for a moment as her eyes adjusted. She saw her father's curricle, with Jackson and Collins already in busy attendance, and Bean carrying luggage up to the front door of the house. Bessie was coming toward her, carrying a heavily laden tea tray.

"Good Lord, 'tis Papa!"

" 'Tis your father, miss," announced the breathless kitchen maid at the same time. "I hurried across the yard—I didn't know what he'd say if he saw me," she added in a worried tone.

"Julie, Harry! Papa has come home! I think we had better hurry in. He will be expecting to greet us in the house, and I think it best to let Mama introduce what has happened here in the way she thinks is best."

Merissa glanced reluctantly at the tea tray. "Run along back to the kitchen, Bessie, thank you. We will have to leave all those delicious-looking cakes for Captain Valmont." She looked at Alex. "I hope you will excuse us?"

He grinned. "I suspect Mademoiselle Polydora would be delighted to assist me in eating them."

"Don't you dare feed them to her!" Merissa exclaimed. "You pamper her too much. She will soon be as fat as Annie, our prize pig!" Hurrying her sisters, she added, "Papa should have gone in by now, so he will not see where we are coming from. Go now, quickly!"

The three young women hastened across the yard and up to the house. After cautiously opening the unattended front door, they piled through in an undignified scramble. Backhouse was probably seeing to their father. They stopped abruptly as they discovered their parents standing between the columns separating the hall from the great stairs, just breaking off an embrace.

Sir Barry and Lady Pritchard turned to them.

"Ah, there you are, girls. Here is Papa."

"What handsome young women!" said their father, beaming. "I saw not a single young woman in London to compare with my three." He opened his arms and the sisters flew into them.

"Of course, you are not the slightest bit biased, Papa," said Merissa, hugging him.

"No doubt you had your eyes closed the whole time you were there," Harry chimed in.

"The sight of us has simply banished the memory of all others from his mind," Juliana teased.

"Well, perhaps not quite all others," Sir Barry admitted reluctantly, releasing them. "I believe I saw Bessie carrying a tea tray out to the barn as I arrived. It did strike me as rather irregular. May I ask what . . . ?"

Lady Pritchard linked her arm through his and patted his shoulder comfortingly with her other hand. She turned and began to walk with him in the direction of his library. "Now, now, I shall tell you all about it after you've had a chance to relax and clear the dust of your journey out of your throat."

She waggled her fingers over her shoulders at her daughters, a clear signal that they should leave this matter to her for now. "So tell me how you found London, besides dreadfully thin of company at this time of year . . ." she said as she disappeared with him down the corridor.

"I wonder how long she can put this off," Merissa said morosely to her sisters.

They had not long to wait. They had retired to the sitting room upstairs, where they could look out onto the yard. In less than half an hour they saw Backhouse walking stiffly out to the barn. He returned to the house with Alex. Polly trotted along dutifully behind them, looking quite as if she belonged there and rather more cheerful than either of her human companions.

Merissa got up and began to pace. "Now how long, I wonder?"

What would her father say? She expected that at the very least, he would be angry with her, something that happened so rarely that she was not sure whether the prospect should frighten her or not. It pained her to cause him any grief, but she could survive it. Far more important than that question was, would he agree to help the French captain? If he agreed, would he have any idea what to do?"

"I believe I'll go downstairs and find Polly," she said at last, too restless to stay still.

"We'll come down with you," Harry replied quickly with a glance at Juliana. "They are likely in the library or the drawing room. Either way, we can wait in the passage outside the door."

They found both their mother and Polly in the passage outside the library. There was a niche containing a bust of Constantine on a fluted pedestal flanked by two lyre-backed chairs, and Lady Pritchard was seated in one of them.

"I was banished," she said ruefully. "Your father wanted a private interview."

Merissa stroked Polly's head absently, and then took up pacing as she had done upstairs. Harry, Julie, and Lady Pritchard looked at one another and fidgeted.

Merissa bit her lip and said nothing. She needed every ounce of effort to maintain her control over her feelings. How could she care so deeply about what became of this foreigner, who was little more than a stranger to her? In truth she was frantic to know what was happening beyond the closed doors of the library, and if she ventured too close she was certain she would try to break them down.

Finally, Lady Pritchard called to her. "Come and sit down, my dear. You will wear the polish right off the floor, and to no purpose."

"It gives me something to do," replied Merissa, reluctantly complying with her mother's request.

"Perhaps we should have brought down our needlework," Harry said with a mischievous gleam in her eye. "We still have cushion covers to finish, and time is getting short."

"Every one of mine would wind up embroidered solid black," Merissa growled, glowering at her youngest sister.

Harry answered with a grin.

The walls of the library were thick, and not a sound came through them to the women waiting outside. The faint chiming of the longcase clock in the drawing room on the hour, and the thumping of Polly scratching herself only served to accentuate the silence.

"Merrie, dear, I'm worried that you are taking this young man's fate too much to heart," Lady Pritchard said after a few minutes. "I know you could not help wishing to help him—it is natural to your sweet, impractical temperament. And I must admit that he is very handsome and dashing! I might have been tempted myself. But . . ."

There is always a "but," thought Merissa. Just now the last thing she wished to hear was a lecture, although she knew her mother meant well.

Lady Pritchard had paused, but now she went on. "You know that your captain will soon be gone, whether he manages to successfully escape or not. We will put this episode behind us, and things will go back to the way they have been." She lowered her voice. "I just don't want to see you break your heart, my dear."

Too late, thought Merissa. *It will break into a thousand tiny pieces the day he leaves, and there is nothing I can do about it*. Things would never go back to the way they had been before, not for her.

"I know, Mama. Don't worry," she said, summoning a brittle little smile she hoped would serve in the dim light of the passage. She was determined not to have regrets. Coming to know Captain Valmont had allowed her to know how different it was possible to feel about a man. She might be heartbroken when he left, but she was determined to be grateful as well.

She was certain she had memorized every stroke of color in the design of the hand-painted wallpaper and every scuff mark on the floor in the passage by the time the mahogany double doors to the library opened, and Sir Barry stepped

out. He was clearly surprised to find his daughters waiting
there as well as his wife.

"Well, well. I see the *comte's* admirers have been assem-
bling." He nodded. "Very well, since I have no need to
send Bean or Backhouse to find you, come in, ladies, come
in."

The library at Pie Hill was a long room with a gallery
along one side and windows only at one end. Alex stood at
that end of the room looking out, the bright light from the
windows throwing him into partial silhouette. To Merissa
he seemed very remote

The women selected seats and settled themselves.

"What we have here is a most delicate situation," Sir
Barry began. "I might, through my contacts in our government, be in a position to help expedite the investigation of
the claims against the captain. I believe his story, and agree
that his cousin must be exposed.

"However, I am not at all certain whether it would be
better to have him return to custody and wait while we
work this through official channels, or to help him reach
France, where he can hopefully expedite matters by simply
appearing where he is known. No matter which course we
choose to pursue, it is essential that no hint of our personal
involvement should ever leak out. Which in itself creates
another problem—how can I intervene in his case without
having to explain how it came to my notice in the first
place?" He sighed, and rubbed his hands together as if they
were cold.

Merissa did not know whether or not she should speak. If
her father was angry with her, it might only make matters
worse by calling his attention to her presence. On the other
hand, it was essential that he be persuaded to help Alex—
Captain Valmont—get to France. Further imprisonment
after what the captain had already suffered was beyond
considering, and the risk that he would be condemned to a
prison hulk was very real.

"Papa," she said cautiously. "I know you have every reason to be angry with me. I would do anything to gain your
forgiveness. But please, first, may I say something?"

Sir Barry looked surprised. Lady Pritchard bit her lip.
For an instant, Merissa wondered what they thought she

would say. Then she drew in her breath and plunged ahead, making a passionate case for her Frenchman's freedom.

"Until Captain Valmont is cleared of the charges against him, is it not true that those in authority over him have no choice by the law but to treat him accordingly?" she concluded. "What good will an official resolution to his problem do if it comes too late to do him any good?"

Alex cleared his throat. Turning, he walked back to the center of the room. "Monsieur, your daughter pleads my case well. I very much appreciate your willingness to intervene with your government on my behalf, but I'm afraid it will not help in time. Neither do I know how you could effect it without jeopardizing yourself and your family. Someone would be bound to ask how you came to know of my case. I would not want you to take such a risk."

"What can we do then?" Lady Pritchard spoke what was in everyone's mind.

"Perhaps the Gypsies can help," Merissa said suddenly. It was as if the solution had been staring her in the face all along. "Maybe they would be willing to let him travel with them until he could get to the coast."

"Oh, yes, Papa!" Harry jumped in. "They'll be heading south as soon as the harvest is finished. Who would ever think to look for him with them? Merrie, 'tis inspired!"

"We've already put it about that he is a Gypsy," Juliana contributed. "It would fit with the story."

"What you say has merit," Sir Barry said. "The Gypsies have no great love for our laws, and no strong allegiance to either Britain or France. They go their own ways. They try to steer clear of trouble, so they might be reluctant to accept the task. But they do have a strong sense of justice, having suffered unjustly so often themselves, and they can be influenced for a price. They might do it."

"Oh, Papa, could you arrange it?"

"I will speak to Mr. Glasson to see if any Gypsies are working in our fields this year. Otherwise, I might have to ride up to Wittering to seek out their camps." He sighed, and looked at Alex. "I will see what I can do."

"I am grateful, but I cannot allow it," the Frenchman said. "If something were to go wrong, the arrangement could be traced back to you. Better to let me make my own arrangements, so you are not involved. It is a very wonderful idea."

"The Gypsies are very wary of strangers. Even if you found them before you were caught, they might not talk to you. We will take our chances, *Monsieur le Comte, Capitaine Valmont*. After all, we *are* involved. Our safest course now is to see this project through to a successful conclusion."

Amen, thought Merissa. She would have felt more triumphant but for the pain in her heart. She suspected she had just felt its first crack.

By the end of the week, the wagonloads of harvested grain were beginning to come into the barn. Merissa and her sisters gathered up all the finished decorations for the fair and piled them in baskets in one corner of the barn. With Alex's help, they had made enough, and it was their duty not to get in the way of any work related to the harvest. So far, they and their neighbors had been lucky, for there had been little rain aside from the storm the night the Pritchards had stayed with Francine at Chetwood. The harvest was progressing rapidly, and would soon be done.

Alex had to retreat to the hayloft, where his confinement weighed on him heavily. He had grown used to the pleasant diversion of the young women's company, and now he had too much time alone to spend thinking. When the three Pritchard sisters came to him rejoicing with the news that their father had decided to allow him to move to quarters in the house, he had mixed feelings, however.

"Papa says he thinks it best to keep you out of sight as much as possible, and to limit the number who are aware of your presence here," Merissa explained. "Just now there are so many extra hands helping with the harvest, and he says all those hands have ears and tongues that go home with them to the village at night."

Alex was thrilled at the prospect of sleeping in something resembling a real bed, even if it was a cot in the servants' quarters. To move into the house meant he could live like a man again instead of an animal, for however short a time he would be there. He was in such dire need of a bath, he felt as if he might shed his skin like a snake.

The prospect of being nearer to Merissa was a problem, however. His friendship with her continued to deepen, and with it his desire for her continued to grow. Moving into the house would mean more chances to be with her. While he craved that, he knew it was a formula for disaster.

There was no solution. She was English! Their nations were at war; their paths led in different directions. He was naught but a temporary and unwilling visitor in this country. He knew he should stay away from her, but they had reached a point now where she would be hurt if he did so. Soon he would have to leave, and he suspected they would both feel pain enough when that time came.

Have to leave? He was startled to catch himself thinking in such terms, as if he had not freely chosen this course for himself. Of course, he wanted to leave, the sooner the better. No matter what messages he heard in his heart, he had always been ruled by his head. If only he had never met his blue-eyed Merissa. . . .

Alex looked around the hayloft, cursing his own weakness. Disastrous as the move inside might be, Sir Barry clearly believed Alex was at greater risk out in the barn. What would the servants think when the "Gypsy" moved into the house with them? Alex was not convinced that he should move, but he would. Servants be damned along with himself!

A few days later, Alex luxuriated in a hot bath, something he had enjoyed so infrequently in the last few years that the pure hedonistic pleasure of it temporarily drove all of his concerns from his head. Bean, whose quarters he was now sharing, and Backhouse, whose charge he had now become, had significantly altered their reactions to him after being informed that he was not a Gypsy, but none other than a French count. He supposed they thought he was an émigré in some small spot of trouble.

Alex cupped water in his hand and poured it down his shoulder and chest. He leaned back against the metal side of the portable bath, reveling in the feel of the water against his skin. He could happily have stayed right there until the water turned as cold as stone. However, the Pritchards had invited him to join them for dinner in the absence of any other guests.

It felt strange to dress for dinner in unfamiliar and ill-fitting clothes, but he was grateful to have them. Lady Pritchard had sent them downstairs the day before. He fussed over his collar-points and the tying of his one cravat like the most fastidious valet. He slid his arms carefully into the claret-colored coat he had been given and tugged at the sleeve ends, but they came no closer to reaching his wrists than they had during the previous day. After attempting to comb his unruly hair into some sort of order, he was forced to admit that there was nothing more he could do to try to improve his appearance. He would have to do as he was.

The dinner was exhilarating. Even if the food had been objectionable, the simple experience of sitting at table in a dining room with civilized people engaged in polite conversation was something he would never again take for granted. When had he last been so blessed? There had been a dinner for the officers the night before Busaco and Alcoba—three years ago. Little had they suspected then that most would never meet again!

Having Merissa at this dinner put it almost in the range of fantasy. If he had not been so hungry, he might have forgotten to eat altogether. Just watching her gave him great pleasure. He noticed that she was unusually quiet, however. Was it because he was there?

The conversation flowed easily enough. He was interested in the history of Pie Hill, as the great hall the Pritchards used for their dining room was obviously of much greater age than the other rooms he had seen. There was talk about the harvest, and the upcoming fair, and speculation over what the weather would do, and when ploughing would begin. There was even a little talk about what Sir Barry had seen and done in London besides tending to his business concerns.

"I am told that London rivals Paris in size and greatness," Alex said.

"Your Corsican with all his monuments and boulevards cannot outshine our theaters and opera, the gas lamps on

our streets, the great buildings and sheer size of London,"
Sir Barry answered proudly.

The food, as it happened, was surprisingly good. Alex
had heard daunting reports of how the English ate at home,
and had expected something like beef steamed to death,
served with cabbage. Instead, an excellent chestnut soup
had been served to start the meal, and what followed had
included an imaginatively seasoned roast beef with
Madeira sauce, and grilled trout that, while it could not
rival trout from the mountain streams near his grandfather's
estate, still tasted like heaven to one who had been deprived
for so long.

There were joking comments he did not understand
about an egg sauce that he did not try, but he did not mind.
Merissa had looked over at him at that point in the meal
and had given him what he thought was an apologetic
smile. It was the only time during the meal that she had actually acknowledged him. He hoped he would have a
chance to speak with her later, to learn what was wrong.

They adjourned from dinner to yet another room Alex
had not seen before, the salon that the Pritchards used as a
music room. Offered the choice of music or cards, Alex did
not hesitate. Music was a passion he had found little time
for in his military life, and he missed it. His heart lightened
at the mere sight of the Pritchards' pianoforte, a beautiful
instrument of mahogany inlaid with satinwood and gaily
painted with garlands of flowers. He remembered then that
he had heard the light, melodious sound of a flute playing
when, discovered and escorted at gunpoint by Bean, he had
first set foot in this house. It had struck him as highly ironic
at the time.

"You are our guest for the evening," Lady Pritchard said,
seating him in a comfortable armchair upholstered in gold
satin and fluttering around him like a fussy sparrow. "We
are going to give you a little concert."

Harriet seated herself at the pianoforte, and Merissa,
standing beside it, opened a case and took out a handsome
flute of ebony and silver. So, she had been the one he'd
heard playing that day. Somehow it made the juxtaposition
seem even more ironic.

"I'm pleased to be able to treat you the way you de-

serve," Lady Pritchard was continuing. "I simply did not
dare to accommodate you in a guest room, but please know
it galls me to think I have had to put a member of the
French nobility in our servants' quarters!"

"Madame, please do not be concerned. A fugitive such
as I am at present does not deserve to be so comfortable
and well fixed as I am. You have my eternal gratitude and
greatest esteem."

He was surprised to see the dignified Lady Pritchard
blush just like Merissa. How he would have liked to see
Merissa blush that way—from pleasure instead of embarrassment! Such a thing was not likely to be, however. The
conversation at dinner had made it very clear how little
time was left before the harvest would be completed. After
the fair, the Gypsies would leave, and he with them, if all
went as planned.

Lady Pritchard took a seat beside Harry on the bench of
the keyboard instrument, and to Alex's surprise, Sir Barry
came to join his wife and daughters with a violin and bow
in his hand. Alex began to feel excited. The violin had been
his instrument. Perhaps he might be allowed a chance to
play? *Could* he still play? Mayhap if he asked Sir Barry pri-
vately, at another time. Merissa whispered something to Juliana as she stood beside her, and there followed a shuffling
of sheet music as one choice was apparently exchanged for
another.

The little concert began with a current popular song, a
comic piece about a beleaguered husband and his shrewish
wife. Juliana sang the words in a sweet soprano voice with
great style, while Merissa and her father embellished the
melody with ornaments apparently of their own devising.
They followed this with some well-executed selections
from Mozart and a concerto by Beethoven that Alex had
known quite well.

The Pritchards were talented. Their efforts did justice to
the music, and Alex found his cares dropping away as the
music entered into him and filled his mind. He soared with
the notes of Merissa's flute, closing his eyes to aid the illu-
sion. The urge to take Sir Barry's violin in his own hands
grew stronger as he listened, not because of any fault in the

playing, but simply through his own need and desire to become a part of the music.

At the end of the piece he opened his eyes and found Merissa's blue ones regarding him intently. He smiled.

"Do you play, Captain?" she asked.

Lady Pritchard turned to him from the pianoforte. "Indeed, monsieur, would you care to join in? You seemed to enjoy it so much."

Alex shook his head. "I played the violin, but I have not so much as held one in my hands for a long time. I'm certain that all my skill has left me. Please continue."

Once he admitted that he had played, however, the Pritchards would not be satisfied until he took the bow from Sir Barry and tucked the instrument between his chin and his collarbone, cushioned on a lamb's wool pad.

It was a fine violin, light in weight and built with a narrow neck. He played a few notes, testing the tone of the instrument, getting the feel of the bow in his hand, adjusting to the feel of the instrument. A long time had passed since he had lost his own violin to a flooded Spanish river. He had never found a way to replace the solace it had given him after days of struggle, or the pleasure it had provided during endless stretches of inactivity. His men had missed the music until one of them had found a Spanish guitar . . .

Hesitantly, he began to play a simple exercise to test his old skill. The effort did not seem to bother his arm.

Encouraged, he chose another piece from his memory, one that was a little harder. As he concentrated on the music, he forgot about the Pritchards. He forgot everything until he came to the end of the piece, and they applauded. Embarrassed, he moved to return the instrument to Sir Barry. "*Merci*—thank you," he said soberly. "I cannot remember when I have had such pleasure! I shall remember this night always. I did not know that I would be able to play at all."

"I want you to play as much and whenever you wish, for as long as you are here," Sir Barry said. "It is barbaric for a man to be separated from his muse."

Chapter 13

Was his life barbaric? Alex had never stopped to consider such a possibility before. He had always accepted that forgoing certain aspects of civilian life was part of the price of a military career—a price he was willing to pay.

Until his capture, he had been accounted a promising young officer. Through hard work and talent, he had built an exemplary reputation for honesty, skill, and intelligence that rumor said had reached the notice of the highest circles, perhaps even Bonaparte himself. He had learned to handle his men, to identify and navigate around other people's ambitions and jealousies, and to be as alert off the battlefield as on it. He had also enjoyed extraordinary luck, that intangible protection that had seemed always to hover over him when he was most at risk. He had achieved much, and had planned to achieve more, as long as he survived.

Perhaps he had used up more than his share of luck. Since the loss of his parole and the charge of impersonation against him, his only plan was to clear himself—to regain his name and all that he had lost with it. If he were to change his life, what would he do?

He had plenty of time to ask himself such questions during the two days following the dinner. Sir Barry was out much of the time, observing the final days of harvest in his fields, and the Pritchard women seemed to be very occupied with preparations for the harvest fair. Merissa, in particular, seemed to have no time to spend with him. He had watched her go out to ride earlier this morning with a young man who was familiar enough to address her by her first name. Alex had not spoken to her alone since he had moved into the house.

He confessed that it was for the best. He knew it was.

Yet he had become addicted to her presence. A dozen times in an hour he would think of things he wished to say to her—questions he wanted to ask her, thoughts he wanted to share. To fill the emptiness, both yesterday and today he had yielded to the temptation to go into the salon and pick up Sir Barry's violin, seeking solace in the way he had done for so many years.

He found that his fingers seemed to have a memory of their own. If he stopped thinking and simply let the music wash over him, the bow seemed to draw the notes from the strings by itself, and his hands instinctively knew what to do.

Like making love came the thought, entirely unbidden.

He paused, trying to bury the thought back into whatever part of his mind it had come from. Merissa's sweet image had come to him with it, along with an intense stab of desire. *Impossible, impossible, impossible,* he railed at himself. Anger replaced the desire—anger at himself and at the circumstances in which he found himself. He channeled the anger into his music, first a Beethoven sonata newly published since his captivity, then a concerto by Vivaldi that admitted the full range of his emotion.

He was so lost in the music that he failed to notice when Merissa first slipped into the room a short while later. The musical phrases were building upon each other, one after the other, crescendoing and taking with them all his anguish, fear, doubt, and joy—for there was joy in his soul, too. He released them all into the music.

The effect was cathartic; when he reached the end of the piece, he was shaking. He let his hand with the bow fall limply to his side.

Merissa went to him and retrieved the bow from his fingers. "Never have I heard anyone play with such passion!" she exclaimed quietly. "Where did you learn to play like that?"

Alex looked at her intently, drinking in the welcome sight of her like a parched man. He must have let his gaze linger too long, for suddenly she looked down and fidgeted with the bow in her hands.

He could have gone on looking at her for days, he thought, without so much as saying a word. He wanted to commit her to memory—every inch of her creamy skin, the exact color of her lips, the graceful arch of her brows. Her scent, her hair, her eyes were his already and had been almost from the first time he had met her in the windmill. But now he wanted all—he wanted memories to last a lifetime without her. He was so glad to see her there, he wanted to sweep her into his arms. With a supreme effort, he called back all the control he had cast off while he had been playing. He must not touch her. Besides, she seemed unaccountably flustered. Was it only due to his music?

"I learned to play as a boy," he said, trying to study her without being obvious. "When I went away to school, I continued to play, and even as a student at the Polytechnic, I played and found others to play with. When I entered the military, it brought me much pleasure."

"But you said that you had not played in a long time," she pointed out.

"*Oui.* My violin was lost on campaign. I was not able to replace it."

"Why not?"

Why not? He realized that somehow, he had lost the heart for it. He had not replaced it when he might have, for he was certain some similar disaster would befall the replacement. His pay as a captain was not sufficient to finance multiple replacements of something as valuable as a fine violin. There was no place in his life for a violin, just as there was no place for a woman or a family. Startled, he glanced down at the instrument in his hands. He had never thought of it in quite that way before.

"Why not?" she asked again softly.

He placed Sir Barry's violin carefully on the pianoforte. Turning to Merissa, he held out his hand for the bow. Her gloved fingers brushed his bare ones as she gave it to him, and they both pulled back like frightened deer.

"Too great an expense, too little opportunity, too rough a life," he said brusquely. "Pick a reason. *Ça ne fait rien.* It does not matter." He busied himself collecting the sheets of music Sir Barry had given him into a neat pile.

"Here is one of yours," he said with surprise a moment later. He handed her the pages marked "flute solo" in a neat hand across the top. He wondered if it was her own writing.

He paused and then added, "You play very well yourself, Miss Pritchard. I enjoyed hearing you the other night."

He realized that her hair was disarrayed. He knew she had gone riding—the removal of her hat might have been the simple cause. But an unreasoning part of his mind whispered jealously that the cause might have been the young man she had gone with. He should be glad that there was someone else in her life, he knew.

"What made you decide to choose the flute as your instrument?" he asked. She was not looking at him now, and he decided that, yes, she definitely seemed distracted. She did not usually fidget.

Still, she answered him. "I chose it because I liked the sound, and because it was relatively small and portable." She gave a derisive little laugh. "I had some foolishly romantic idea that I would take it out of doors and play it in the fields like some version of Pan. Of course, I have never done so."

"Why not?" It was his turn to ask.

She seemed surprised by the question. "Well, I just—I never felt comfortable enough. I suppose it seemed an unconventional and idiotic thing to do, and I don't really play that well. . . . People think I'm flighty enough as it is."

"Is that what they think?" He took a step nearer to her. God help him, there she stood, looking beautiful and distraught and very unsure of herself. "Then they don't understand you, do they? You should have more faith in yourself, be more accepting of your own nature."

Another step, closer to her, closer to hell. "When you want to be unconventional, you should simply be so. Are you afraid to be free? I never thought an Englishwoman would be." He reached out and took her hand between his. It was trembling. He looked into her eyes and saw tears beginning to pool there.

"What is it, Merissa? What is wrong? Can you tell me?"

Merissa shook her head, hoping to shake off the tears at the same time. How foolish she felt, trembling and weeping in front of him! How could she possibly explain what it was like to leave Harlan, who had behaved like a boor and a bully on the ride with her this morning, to come home to find him, pouring out his passion into music and talking

about understanding? She felt that they must be star-
crossed lovers, kindred souls kept apart by Fate. Harlan's
behavior had upset her, but this exchange between her and
Alex was unbearable. She had not realized she could feel
this much pain over parting with him before he had even
left.

"Is it something I said? Something I've done?"

She could see that he was truly concerned and puzzled.

"I thought that you might be intentionally avoiding me.
We have spent no time together since I moved into the
house, yet we shared many such moments when I was a
mere barn Gypsy."

She shook her head. He was trying to coax her into a
smile, she could tell. How she had missed him! She had
tried to stay away from him, to avoid just this kind of pain.
But she had realized that she would have a lifetime of missing him ahead of her, and that it was foolish to squander
these last precious days.

"Did you enjoy your ride this morning?"

He was looking at her intently, as if he suspected she had
not. Could she hide nothing from this man? How should
she answer? Harlan was her own problem, one she would
have to solve for herself. She shrugged, hoping a casual response would throw him off the scent. "It was unexceptional. Harlan Gatesby is a neighbor and an old friend. I
don't know what is the matter with me."

She reclaimed her hand and used the back of her glove to
wipe her eyes.

He spread his hands open, looking helpless. "I'm sorry, I
do not have any handkerchief."

The utter absurdity of it struck her, and she giggled. A
moment later they were both laughing.

"You are certainly the most poorly equipped gentleman I
have ever met, *Monsieur le Comte*. If you aspire to be more
than a mere barn Gypsy, perhaps we should work to rem-
edy that in the few days we have left!" She attempted to put
a bright expression on her face, to hide the pain she felt inside.

"As you wish, mademoiselle. I must admit, I would be
grateful."

*   *   *

Alex continued to indulge in playing Sir Barry's violin during the days that followed. The sweet strains filled the house and delighted the Pritchards and the servants who heard them. Enraptured, Merissa would sit and listen for as long as he would play. Alex was delighted simply to have her company once again, and gratified if his efforts brought her pleasure. He tried not to think about anything else.

What he missed most since coming to Pie Hill was exercise, fresh air, and the sun. Despite the comforts he now enjoyed, he found it difficult to be inside. He was an army officer, after all. His life had been spent in the saddle and out of doors. Even the prisoners in Norman Cross spent much of their time in the yards. The garden and the orchard close to Pie Hill beckoned to him, and at length he convinced Merissa that he would not be at risk to venture out.

"Who is likely to see me?" he questioned her. "All but your late fruit has been harvested from the orchard, and the garden is private and close to the house. Even if someone did notice, it would only be from a distance. They would have no way to know who I was. And, if they guessed, what harm in that? It is surely known by now that your family has been nursing an injured Gypsy."

Merissa thought his arguments made sense. She and Alex began to go for daily walks. When her mother protested that her sisters or Peggy should accompany them, Merissa tossed her head.

"Mama, we are never out of sight of the house," she pointed out. "Besides, we have Polly along for a chaperone."

On one particularly fine day, as they rested in the dappled sunlight under the trees on a blanket she had brought along, Merissa brought out the straw-covered box that contained her collection of Roman artifacts.

Alex examined the box critically. Polly was asleep with her head in his lap, and he was careful not to disturb her. "Many of the prisoners make marquetry boxes like this to sell in the market," he said. "This one is very well made, not crude like some I've seen."

He traced the intricate geometric designs with his finger, and she wondered if he was thinking about the year he had spent in the prison. In all the time they had spent together, he had never talked very much about it.

"Did you make such articles while you were there? I have seen how skilled you are." She thought of her "friendship bridge," as she called it, sitting proudly on the table beside her bed.

"I never did this type of straw work, but I made a few models," he admitted. "Officers receive a slightly higher allowance from your government than the regular men, but of course, I was not receiving an officer's allowance once I came to Norman Cross."

She held out her hand for the box, and he returned it to her. As she opened it and began taking out the little rolls of silk-wrapped treasures, she said, "You are so obviously a gentleman. How could they not have believed you to be an officer? It puzzles me."

He sighed. "When I was charged with impersonation, such a distinction no longer mattered. Gentleman, officer, or common soldier, I had broken the rules. To assume another's identity to gain parole or exchange is a very serious crime. All privileges of rank are forfeit. When I would not admit to being anyone but Captain Valmont, I think it angered them. They did not know what to put on the records."

"And now you have truly escaped." She unrolled the first parcel, which contained a handful of coins in three different sizes. "I wonder if any Roman prisoner ever had such a problem." She held the coins out to him and placed them in his upturned palm. How large his hands seemed compared to hers! She watched him sort the coins, turning them over with a fingertip, studying the designs and markings. His hands might be work-roughened, but they were sensitive and graceful. Those same hands coaxed the most beautiful music from her father's violin.

She leaned over to point out one small coin. "Look, you can see this one has Romulus and Remus being suckled by the wolf. I've always thought that wolf looked suspiciously like a horse."

He chuckled, and the sound deep in his chest made her suddenly aware of how close to him she was. She pulled back nervously.

He glanced at her but said nothing, handing back the coins.

She unrolled the next group of items into his palm, and he studied these fragments of glass and pottery with equal interest, admiring their fragility and great age. "It is amazing to me that even these small bits should have survived for so long."

"These are my greatest prizes," she said finally, unrolling a piece of silk that contained a round brooch, a gaming piece, and a spindle whorl. She held them out for him to see. "These are the ones, along with the buckles, that seem to me to bridge the centuries—they are so like anything we might use today. I think about the woman who lost this brooch—did she grieve over losing it? Who had given it to her—her husband?"

"Or perhaps her lover?"

Startled by the intensity in his voice, she glanced up at him, only to be trapped in the darkness of his eyes. Unable to look away, she felt his hand slip gently underneath hers. Her heart raced as if she was suddenly afraid, although that was not at all how she was feeling. What was he doing? But he simply took the gaming piece from her palm and held it up.

"This is the piece that catches a man's imagination. I have seen pieces almost exactly like it made out of bone by the prisoners now to help pass the time. I wonder if they had a prison in your—what was the name of the town?"

"Dubro Vitae. And they probably did, as it was supposed to have been a very large town."

She paused, and for a moment only the noise of two blackbirds fighting over windfall apples at the other end of the orchard broke the silence that hung over them. "You have never said how you escaped from Norman Cross," she ventured to say. "I can't help being curious."

He looked up at her, his brown eyes unfathomable. "It was nothing at all gallant or romantic—I suspect you will be disgusted if I tell you."

"Will you tell me if I promise not to comment?"

He laughed. "I have never met a woman who could refrain from making comments! But then, I know you are special."

What did he mean by that? She did not dare to ponder it.

"The guards at the prison always watched us for escape attempts. Once in the early years of the prison five hundred prisoners broke down a section of the wooden walls! That was when they built the brick enclosure and dug the trenches inside it.

"Because of my engineering skills many in the prison pressed me to build a tunnel and offered their labor. But a tunnel would have been like an open drain of desperate prisoners running out into your countryside, and it would have taken a long time to build, besides. I knew I had to go out through the main gate."

Still he hesitated. "I suppose it may help you to understand how desperate a man can become if I tell you. The guards search all the vehicles that go in or out. The only wagons they did not search were the soil carts that go out every morning. I am certain they thought the smell alone would deter any right-minded person from such a scheme as to hide in one, but that is what Guillaume and I did. The daughter of the prison's baker obtained a set of clothes for me and hid them outside the prison where I could find them after we were free. We had to wash ourselves in the nearest ditch we could find."

Merissa stifled her reply by putting her hand over her mouth. She had promised, after all. Her eyes met his, and he began to chuckle.

"You see? I warned you that it was not at all elegant."

She could not help laughing when he phrased it in such terms. He laughed with her. The laughter felt so good that once she started, she could not stop. They laughed together until her sides hurt and tears spilled down her cheeks.

"Oh, I cannot stop!" she cried, gasping for breath. She dabbed at her eyes with her hand.

"And why should you have to?" he asked, managing to subdue his own laughter to a chuckle.

"So I do not injure myself!"

"Ah. We must not have that." He reached into his coat pocket and produced a handkerchief which he waved with a flourish. "Here, you see? Today I can accommodate a lady."

Chapter 14

With the passing of New Michaelmas, September's quiet reign came to an end and only ten days remained until the fair. The harvest at Pie Hill was nearly completed. Only a few other neighboring farms had yet to finish. Everyone prayed that the rains would hold off.

Although October had barely begun, there was a noticeable change in the air, and it was not just the cooling breezes stirring the damp leaves. Time was growing short, and so were tempers among the three Pritchard sisters.

It seemed that the cushion covers for the church were not finished. Juliana complained bitterly about this and about Lord Rupert's inattention. Both she and Harry complained about and criticized the amount of time Merissa was spending with "their" Frenchman. Harry had taken to temperamental outbursts quite unlike her usual behavior, generally over some petty jealousy, to the point where even Alex remarked upon it.

Merissa thought she understood the trouble. Her family was suffering from tension due not only to the late harvest but even more to the captain's imminent departure. Harry had developed a full-scale infatuation with him, and now felt that no one's heart stood in greater danger of breaking than her own. Juliana's relationship with Lord Rupert had been deteriorating, leaving her cranky over her vanishing prospects. And as yet there had been no report from their father about arrangements for Alex to travel with the Gypsies. Time was running out on their plan. The days leading up to the Harvest Fair began to have a certain desperate quality about them.

The fact that Alex might disappear from her life in mere days haunted Merissa's every waking moment. She craved his company, and awoke every morning listening for the first notes of the violin in the music room to let her know that he was up and about. She stayed close to home, refusing to go into the village on errands or to go riding with Harlan. There would be time for all that soon enough, after her Frenchman was gone.

For his sake, she tried to present a brave, cheerful front. After all, barring disaster, he would soon be on his way home, headed for justice and the restoration of his old life. It was what he wanted, and no less than what he deserved, no matter how much she might wish otherwise. She tried not to worry about what they would do if the Gypsies chose not to risk taking him with them.

There was one thing Alex wanted before he left, and that was to see Dubro Vitae. They had talked of it several times. She wished that she had never told him of its existence.

"It calls to me," he told her, "beckoning like the ripest apple at the top of the tree, or like an inviting woman glimpsed in the window of a tower that has no door."

She had recognized the spark of desire in his dark eyes, and for an unreasoning moment felt jealous of the place.

He had questioned her about its location, and she had tried to discourage him. "You must not try to go there, Captain! It is too far, and the chance that someone would see you or question you is too great. Please promise me you would not take such a risk just to see it. There is nothing there but fields."

He had tossed her own words back at her. "You told me yourself that one can see where the outer walls stood, where the gates were, and how the main road passed through the town. I have never had the chance to see anything like that, despite all my travels through my own country and Spain."

One morning as they strolled in the garden, he began to press her again about going to the Roman site. "There is so little time left to us," he pointed out, striking the one argument where she was most vulnerable. "If we rode there together, who would make note of it? Is it not a place where you go often?"

She looked down at the dew wetting the toe of her slipper. "Does it mean so much to you?" she asked.

"Yes," he answered firmly. He turned to face her with a sigh, his brown eyes searching hers. "You must try to understand. The Romans were master engineers. Everywhere they went, they built roads and bridges that have withstood time itself. Too often it has been my job, my challenge, to destroy them in the name of war.

"So many centuries these roads and bridges stood—where did they lead? The Romans were settled people, not like me. The road is my life, but these Romans had destinations. Never have I seen where the roads and bridges were leading. Just once I would like to see such a place, where these masters set roots."

She could imagine that in his deepest soul, it had hurt him to destroy what he so much admired. If he escaped from England safely, he would be returning to that life—was one visit to Dubro Vitae so much to ask?

Risk aside, there was a more basic question she had to answer. Did she really want to take him there? Long after he was gone, she would still be here, riding out to her usual destinations. Did she want his presence to haunt her there, as it would in every other place they had spent time together? Dubro Vitae was very special to her.

Yes, came the answer. *Oh Lord, yes.* She knew instinctively that she had met the one man who could understand the magic of the place and share it with her. This one time might be the only time she would ever have someone to share that with.

"All right," she said at last. "If the weather holds, we'll go tomorrow." She studied him, taking in the handsome planes of his face and the boyish delight expressed there. How could she deny him anything? How would she learn to go on without him?

That night they learned at last that her father had not only made contact with the Gypsies but had received an answer. . . .

"I had to explain the whole story to them," Sir Barry said as they sat at dinner. Since Alex's move into the house, the Pritchards had tended to dine *en famille* so that the young Frenchman could join them.

"They were reluctant. They are feeling nervous and anx-

ious to finish the last fields and be on their way. There have
been bad omens, they say. They have agreed to take Captain Valmont with them, for a price, but he must join them
on the night of the fair. The next morning they will be
gone."

"What do they mean by bad omens?" Merissa asked,
speaking for everyone.

Sir Barry shrugged as if the superstitions were of no consequence. "Oh, something about the number of pied wag-
tails flocking in the fields being worked—too many, or not
enough, or something. You know how the Gypsies are. If
they see two goldfinches fighting over a thistle, or a field-
fare choking on a hawthorn berry, they think it is a sign. I
guess what really got them started was that apparently
when the workers were cutting Tom Sibley's last field, the
last sheaf was felled by mistake."

This information was greeted by a moment of appreciative silence around the table. Country people all over
Britain held various superstitions about cutting the last
sheaf.

"How did it happen?" Lady Pritchard asked.

"They had a young one working his first harvest in the
cutting crew, and instead of putting him in the middle of
the line, had him at the end. I suppose he simply misjudged
his swing. One moment the stalks were still standing, the
next thing they were down."

"What does it mean?" Alex asked, clearly thoroughly
confused.

" 'Tis thought bad luck to cut the last sheaf. Usually
they'll tie it and then all the workers together will throw
their sickles at it. Sometimes the women even plait it into a
corn dolly before it is cut!" Merissa answered.

"Why is it bad luck?"

"In the old days, people thought the spirit of the corn fled
before the sickles, taking refuge in the last stalks. Later
they thought it might be the devil, so no one wanted to be
the one who cut the last sheaf. On some farms they make a
parade with it, to celebrate the end of the reaping, or even
dress it in clothes and set it up to ride on the wagons, or to
sit in honor at the harvest dinner. You see, 'tis not even the
Gypsies' own superstition, but one of ours."

"Well, it shouldn't affect us," said Sir Barry, obviously trying to lighten the somber mood that had come over the table. "It was not one of our fields, and not our crew. Our corn dolly is hanging in the barn even as we speak, and our corn has almost all been gathered in. We have much to celebrate, including the good news for the captain. We will pray that his coming days as a Gypsy will see him safely to the coast. In fact, I propose a toast. To Captain Valmont, future count of Montiere—may your journey be safe, and your good name restored to you."

"And may our countries learn to be at peace with one another," added Lady Pritchard.

Merissa raised her glass with everyone else, but the sound of the rims touching rang hollow in her ears, and a shiver ran down her spine.

In the morning, Merissa dressed in her blue riding habit with ceremonial care, submitting to her abigail's fussing with unusual patience. Taking Alex to Dubro Vitae had something both joyful and solemn about it, like a sacred ritual that marked beginnings and endings. As Peggy brushed her hair, Merissa glanced at the little straw bridge that Alex had made for her, and thought of the strange friendship that had blossomed between them.

Outside, the sun poured down with summerlike brightness, auguring well for the proposed expedition. Harry had wanted to come, but Merissa had managed to dissuade her.

"We must all find our own ways to say good-bye to the captain, Harry," Merissa had counseled. "This is my way— my one special gift. You must think of something for yourself to do that you think would please him."

When she was ready, Merissa went downstairs to find Alex awaiting her in the hall. Even in his ill-fitting claret coat, he looked extremely handsome. The tight shoulders and too-short sleeves only emphasized his powerful form. How strange it seemed to be going out riding with him! Strange simply because it was such a normal thing to do. She realized that she had never so much as seen him on a horse.

"Miss Pritchard." He gave her a broad grin that lit up his entire face and complimented her better than any words he might have said. "You are *magnifique*." Then he looked down at his own attire and chuckled. "I, on the other hand, must take care not to split my seams with a sudden move of the reins."

Jackson and Collins had Godiva and Sir Barry's bay gelding, Orestes, ready when Merissa and Alex arrived at the stables. If the grooms had any opinion about her going off with the Frenchman with no other escort, they gave no sign of it, nor should they have. Merissa suspected that her mother might have something to say on the matter when she returned, but she absolutely did not care—not this time, this one special time.

As she and Alex set off together, he looked over at her with an engaging smile.

"You seem so very solemn and serious this morning, Miss Pritchard. Unless I am much mistaken, I believe the sun is shining upon us, is it not? May I not be permitted to see you smile?"

Embarrassed, she looked down, feeling the telltale blush tingle in her cheeks. Of course she could not help smiling when he teased her. On this day she was not sure she could deny him anything at all that he wanted.

"Ah, that is much better. You are very obliging." He gave her a long, speculative look. "Should I press my luck? But no, it is too much to ask."

She giggled. "What is?"

"That. There it is! Now I shall be in heaven, surely. You laughed."

This, of course, brought a full-fledged laugh from her, in which he joined.

Merissa felt her sadness melt away in his presence. If this day was to be treasured and remembered for a lifetime, if it was to be a parting gift from her to him, surely it should be a day of joy. She threw back her head and let the warmth of the sun bathe her face for a moment, as she breathed in the fruity October scent of the air.

She knew he was watching her. After a moment, she straightened and gave him a level look. "Would you care to offer these beasts a bit of exercise, monsieur?"

They had allowed the horses to saunter down the farm lane at a leisurely walk and had now come to a gate that opened onto a grassy pasture. She inclined her head toward the field and let a raised eyebrow convey her meaning.

Alex knew perfectly well that she meant the horses, although that was not the first thought that had come into his mind. Did she know how enticing she was when she lifted her face to the sun like that, exposing the long column of her neck? He knew professional courtesans who practiced to make that move so gracefully.

He nodded, knowing she was waiting for his answer. *I know a better use for the soft grass in this field,* he wanted to say. Instead, he bit his lip, willing the pounding blood in his veins to be calm. He must not allow himself to be seduced, whether it was her intent or not.

"To the end and back again, a race," he offered as he watched her lean down to lift the gate latch. The gate was too low to be pushed open from horseback, so in the end he dismounted to open and close it while she rode through, leading his own mount.

When he was back in his saddle, she said, "To the end and back, on a count of three."

He found needed release in the exhilarating sensation of speed. The raw power of the animal beneath him, pounding the length of the field and then circling to pound back up the length again, filled him with playful exuberance. Merissa, too, seemed to find freedom in it, for when they came to a halt she was breathless and laughing, her cares seemingly forgotten.

He hoped it was so—he wanted the day to be one of enjoyment for both of them. She had so clearly been reluctant to bring him to the Roman site she prized, but he had not been able to discern how much of her reluctance stemmed from her concern over his own safety and the risk of discovery, and how much was from a reluctance to share her private, personal pleasure.

"I believe you won," she declared, gulping in air and releasing it in a huge breath.

He was certain she could not know how perfectly her skillfully fitted riding habit followed every movement of her body. He had always been able to appreciate fine tailoring.

"What is my prize?" he asked.

"Whatever you wish," she answered innocently.

A kiss, his mind said, but he managed to bite back the words. *No, far too dangerous.* "A token," he said instead, warming to the idea as he thought of it. "I gave you a little bridge of friendship, poor as it is—I would ask you for a small token in return."

She nodded thoughtfully. "You do not have to win that as a prize. I would give you one willingly. But what should it be?"

"That you must choose. Now, where is this Roman town of yours?"

She smiled and brought Godiva alongside his own mount. "It is not more than a mile from here, although we will have to walk the last little part of the way. There is only a footbridge to cross the river near there." She pointed to the southwest.

The full glory of early autumn was in evidence everywhere as they rode toward Dubro Vitae. The hedges were bursting with colorful hips, haws, and berries of every variety, and alive with birds feasting upon them. The sun glittered off spiders' webs in the bushes and stubble-covered fields. Although the leaves had not yet turned colors, bright yellow butterflies fluttered like precursors of those to come, searching the countryside for Michaelmas daisies.

When Merissa and Alex reached the river, they tethered their horses. "They won't mind if it's just for a little while," Merissa said, rubbing Godiva's nose apologetically. "We can give them a good run on the way home."

There were actually two wooden footbridges connecting the banks of the opposing water meadows to a small grassy island that stood in between.

"This is the most hazardous part of the route," Merissa said with a laugh, waving her hand over the diminutive expanse of grass. "There are some aggressive swans who sometimes decide that this is their exclusive property, and will actually chase people off of it."

She and Alex stayed on the well-worn path. As they crossed the second footbridge, Merissa stopped to admire the beautiful colors of several ducks cruising the river there.

"You see beauty in things other people take for granted," Alex said admiringly.

Merissa was thinking of the day she had first met him in the windmill. "Ducks always look as though they know something we don't. I think it is the way they cock their heads, with those bright beady eyes." She glanced at Alex. "Did you ever stop to wonder . . . No, never mind."

What would he think of a woman who pondered the happiness of ducks! Of course he would never have questioned any such thing, living the life he was used to. How thoroughly bored he must be by now, after so much idle time in the countryside! He was a man of action, a warrior. She could understand his interest in the Romans. She should not expect him to share an interest in ducks, or for that matter, in her.

Smiling brightly, she set off again. "Farther up the river is the place where Ermine Street must have once had a bridge, though it is long gone. If you look up ahead you can see the embankment that runs around the site of the town."

Alex quickened his pace, and she had to lengthen her strides to keep up with him. "The best way to approach it is from the north end—this way," she said. "There was a gate at each end."

Alex stopped completely when they reached the spot.

"This was the road," he said a look of utter pleasure coming across his features. "You can see the raised surface. The gate would have been just there, I think."

Slowly he advanced through the imaginary gate, looking about him intently. Merissa was certain he was visualizing the town.

"What do you see?" she asked softly, coming up beside him.

"It is not what I see, so much as what I feel, what I sense, what I know must have been."

She nodded. Hadn't she known he would understand? The seeing could not be done with the eyes.

"I had no idea it would be so large! I had envisioned a small village." He looked about in amazement. "This must spread out for some twenty hectares—forty or fifty of your acres! It must have been a large town indeed!"

He was excited, and that made her smile. She moved

ahead of him, walking along the raised ridge that ran through the middle of the site. All around them were open green pastures, and in one distant field small fluffs of white dotted the grass, the faint bleating of sheep carrying on the breeze. "I like to think that along this road there were shops, like the main street of any town," Merissa said.

"Shops, a marketplace, buildings for official business," he enumerated, following behind her and nodding his head at the empty space as if he could see them. "The space is so regular, I suspect the cross streets were laid out at consistent intervals in a pattern."

She laughed. "Now you sound like an engineer."

"Engineers have always been scientists and builders. The Romans were the greatest ones of all—they were true artists. Come," he commanded. "Walk with me." He took her hand and tucked it under his elbow, where it seemed to Merissa it entirely belonged.

They walked together over the open pastureland, reconstructing Dubro Vitae in their imaginations. They might have been lost in time, walking there, but in some part of her mind, Merissa was still very aware of the warm, attractive man close beside her. She was not imagining the strong, invisible current running between them.

"Why would they choose this place to settle?" Alex asked, looking out over the landscape.

She glanced at him. "Why does anyone settle where they do? They have loved ones there, or something that gives their life meaning."

"Is love such a powerful force in life, do you think?"

She sighed. Did he not think so? "I suppose the Great Road and the pottery industry here had something to do with it, too," she admitted.

"Ah, yes, I remember your shards." He chuckled. "You sound disappointed that something practical might have played a role in it." He had stopped walking, and turned suddenly to face her with eyes as dark as mahogany. "Is it love that gives meaning to your life?"

Merissa caught her breath. His question had caught her by surprise, with no response ready. Now as she opened her lips to reply, he just as suddenly put his arms around her and lowered his mouth to hers.

Merissa felt like a bonfire suddenly ignited when all the torches were thrown in at once. This was what she knew she had wanted from the beginning. His kiss was seeking, testing, and she responded, giving back passion for his passion. She looked into his eyes and saw fire there to match her own. The kiss turned into another kiss, longer and more demanding. His arms pulled her closer, and her body fit against his as if it belonged there.

"God help me, I cannot resist you. You are so beautiful, so alive," he whispered into her hair.

She could not form words to answer. She turned up her face to invite another kiss.

"I have wanted to do this for so long," he confessed, surprising her more.

This time his kiss was long and drugging. Merissa clung to him, knowing that if he laid her in the grass at that moment she would have given anything he asked.

He held her, supporting her, and buried his face against her neck. He seemed to do nothing for a moment but breathe in her scent. Merissa was very aware of every inch of her body pressed against his.

Finally he spoke. "I have asked God why he would put us together on this path, when we must only part," he said in a voice filled with anguish. "It is too sweet a torment! There is no room in my life for a woman. If I were a free man, if I were not a soldier, not a Frenchman—there are so many 'if's' that could have made this all be different. I ask, why? But I get no answer—only pain." He pulled back from her to look into her eyes. "I did not know if you felt it, too."

Silently she nodded. She did not know how she could explain all the turmoil she had felt since he had come into her life. "If only there was some way you did not have to go," she whispered.

"A man cannot live his life in hiding," he said gently. "I can go as an escapee or I can go as a prisoner, but either way, I still must go."

"And what if the war ended tomorrow?"

He shook his head sadly. "I would still have to go. My country is on the edge of great changes. I need to be there. My skills can play a part in building something new and great there. France is my home—my past and my future. I suppose it is what gives my life meaning," he added with an uncertain smile.

"It must be, since you are so willing to risk your life to regain it." She slipped out of his embrace and moved away from him. "Perhaps it is only we foolish women who believe in love."

She looked up at the wide expanse of sky above them, noticing that thin swirls of clouds, nearly transparent, had overlaid the clear blue of the earlier morning. The sun still shone, but somehow the day seemed cooler now.

The corner of her eye caught a movement at the other end of the field. Turning to see what it was, she inhaled sharply.

"What is it?"

"Someone's coming. Look."

"Can we not simply appear to be casual strollers? Is it someone you know?"

It was. As the figure came closer, Merissa could see that it was Harlan. A moment later, Alex recognized him, too.

"Ah. It is the neighbor friend with whom you went riding," he said in an odd voice, particularly emphasizing the words "neighbor friend."

Merissa felt panic fluttering through her heart. "He mustn't discover who you are. I'm not sure what he would do." As Harlan approached she could see that the expression on his face was as black as a moonless night.

Chapter 15

What wretched luck! Merissa couldn't imagine how Harlan had happened to come to this particular place, at just this particular time. She did not have to wait long to find out.

"Merissa! I was on my way to Pie Hill when I saw Godiva and Orestes tethered down by the edge of the river." She saw his eyes flick toward the captain, but he continued to address only her.

"I thought it odd, since you have been refusing my invitations to go riding, but I at least expected to find you with your father!" Now he turned to inspect Alex quite openly, his lip curling in undisguised disgust. "Instead I find you here with this . . . ! I suppose he is the Gypsy fellow I've been hearing about."

He grasped Merissa's elbow and forced her to take several steps away from Alex. "Does Sir Barry know you are out here with this rough fellow, this stranger? Unescorted? Does he know a Gypsy is riding Orestes? I think you have overstepped yourself too far this time, Merissa. I shall escort you back to Pie Hill myself, and I will make certain that your father knows about this. Thank God I was the one who found you here like this. Suppose it had been somebody else? What would people say? Do you never think, Merissa? It is shocking beyond words."

Merissa glared angrily. "Harlan, how dare you lecture me—" she began, trying to pull her elbow out of his hands.

Harlan would not release her. "Someone needs to lecture you, obviously. We are not children anymore, Merissa, to misbehave and miraculously escape the consequences."

"No, Harlan, I agree—we are not children anymore. I'm a grown woman who can make her own decisions. Whether you happen to agree with them or not is a different question altogether. Let go of my arm."

"Not until I know you are returning with me now."

"Let her go." Alex had been silently observing them. Now his deep voice had a dangerous undertone.

Merissa turned toward him quickly, shaking her head. *He must not speak!* If Harlan had failed to notice Alex's accent in those first three words, certainly he could not help but notice if the Frenchman said anything more. The way the two men were glaring at each other, she feared that words would not be the only thing they exchanged.

Harlan was clearly incensed. "You dare speak so to me?"

"Perhaps it is time we went back," she said in a conciliatory tone, burying her own anger hastily. "We can all go together. Why were you heading to Pie Hill, Harlan?" She turned and began to walk back toward the north end of Dubro Vitae. As Harlan was still holding her elbow, he had no choice but to go with her.

"As you have not been willing to ride with me for so many days, I finally asked Juliana. No doubt she is beginning to wonder where I am."

He paused and looked back over his shoulder at Alex, who was following slowly behind them. Lowering his voice, he said, "I have heard strange reports about your Gypsy, Merrie."

She felt a prickle of alarm run along her skin. "What have you heard?"

"That he has the run of your house and garden, that he plays the violin and acts the part of a gentleman. Of course, I found such things hard to credit, until now I find him socializing with you and riding your father's horse like an honored guest."

Merissa was aware of Harlan's intense scrutiny. She must make certain to seem unconcerned, despite the hammering of her heart. She shrugged as if the report quite mystified her. "He does seem to be an exceptional Gypsy. Clean, well-mannered, respectful, to say the least. My father has taken a liking to him. My father, you may recall, plays the violin."

She hoped Harlan would draw his own conclusions.

"He does not strike me as respectful, I must say! Surly is more like."

Merissa actually managed a light laugh. "Really, Harlan, can you blame him? You were not acting particularly respectful yourself, especially toward me."

"I don't see where that's any concern of his," Harlan answered.

She sighed. Had she actually expected an apology? "Well, you needn't be concerned about him for much longer," she pointed out. "He will be gone after the fair tomorrow."

At least Harlan was obviously not at all inclined to engage the captain in conversation. Perhaps they would come out of this unexpected coil unscathed. Merissa did not think that mere suspicion on Harlan's part could harm them with so little time left. As they continued to walk along in silence, she thought ahead to the footbridge and the swans on the island. What she wouldn't give to see those fierce birds give Harlan a good chase!

Alex walked behind them, fists clenched to the point of pain, exercising every ounce of control he could summon to keep his seething rage in check. This was the man in Merissa's life? Never! The man was a sanctimonious, insensitive clod; he had no understanding and no respect. Merissa deserved so much better! She had said there was no man whom she found interesting, and indeed, she clearly had not welcomed this one. What had transpired between them the day he had seen them go riding? Her disinterest notwithstanding, he could recognize in Harlan the proprietary signals that said the man staked his claim on her. He obviously wanted someone he could bully and control, and he wanted it to be Merissa. A future subject to this man would be a living death for her.

Yet what could Alex do about it? He was leaving tomorrow. The prospect that should have lightened his step with joy and hope at this moment only choked him with anger and heart-wrenching regret.

He had never meant to touch Merissa. He had known the danger of indulging their mutual attraction, but even so he had been unprepared for the force of his reaction to her.

Kissing her had gone far beyond the experience of pure physical pleasure—it had felt more like the mating of souls. Ah, he had known it would be a grave error! So carefully had he restrained himself until this day, this hour. He did not know how he had lost control, but he had. Now he felt as though the future held only misery, no matter what happened.

It was illogical, he knew. The events of the past few weeks should not have altered anything; both he and Merissa faced the same future now as that which had awaited them before they met. Reason and cold logic could not prevail against the intensity of his feelings, however— they dashed against his helpless rage like waves against the base of a dark cliff.

By local tradition, the fair was held on the date of Old Michaelmas at the farm that was last to finish its harvest. This year the honor had fallen to Tom Sibley, whose last load of corn had been brought in only four days before October 10. Booths and the huge tables for the harvest supper had seemingly sprung up overnight. A crisp breeze hurried clouds across the blue sky and made the ribbons on the booth decorations flutter and snap.

The events of the day had begun in church, for this year the date fell on a Sunday. The pew cushion covers, hastily completed at Pie Hill in the last few days, were presented to the vicar of St. Gilda's by Lady Pritchard. Later, as the good reverend read the story of St. Michael casting the devil out of heaven from the Book of Revelations, Merissa remembered that St. Michael was supposed to be the patron saint of soldiers, and she prayed that he would watch over her Frenchman in the hazardous days that lay ahead.

When the Pritchards arrived at the Sibley farm, the annual ploughing match, held in a field of the host farm owner's choice, was already underway. The ploughmen were hard at it, and the spectators were as full of comments about the equipment and the men's respective skill as they were of the cider and ale that was made available in bountiful supply for the entire day.

Merissa could not match the high spirits of the celebrants around her, although she tried mightily. Her heart had been slowly turning into lead since Harlan's appearance yesterday, and during the night it had somehow become so heavy that it seemed to weigh down her entire body.

Alex, of course, was not with them. There was too much risk in exposing him to conversations with so many people. It had been agreed that he should not come until after dark when the bonfire had been lit and he could slip through the shadows to join and blend in with the other Gypsies.

The afternoon was filled with games and contests and buying and selling; workers sought new positions while farmers grudgingly admired prized stock on exhibit. There was a procession that carried scaled models of the Spanish Armada, ships made of sticks and straw to be placed on the bonfire; later these would be burned amid the huzzas and great celebration yet to come with nightfall.

The mixed sounds of honking geese, squealing pigs, fiddle and drum, laughter, and shouts of glee washed over Merissa without effect; she moved through it all in a daze. These rituals were as familiar to her as the cycle of the seasons, yet this time the gaiety seemed forced, brittle, as if it could be shattered in an instant.

Harlan did not seek out her company until late in the afternoon.

"I very nearly beat Henry Dawes in the last footrace," he said, approaching her with the eagerness of a young pup. "Were you watching? I did not see you, but I had little time to look."

She nodded without enthusiasm. Harlan either did not notice, or chose to ignore the fact, falling into step with her as she trailed behind Harry and Juliana.

"You will be my partner for the supper, will you not, Merrie? You are not still angry with me for what happened yesterday, are you?"

Merissa stopped walking. She turned to face Harlan, studying his features for a moment before she replied. Here was her old childhood friend, the eager-to-please boy who never held a grudge and never expected anyone else to do so. How had he grown into the kind of man he had become? She had to blame his domineering father. Unable to extricate himself from his father's control, Harlan now sought to prove himself by exercising a similar control over others.

Did she forgive him? She knew he meant well, as aggravating as he could be. It was not his fault that she had impulsively rescued a man she should never even have met, or that she had fallen in love with that man, impossible as such a thing should have been. She had come to realize that she did love Alexandre Valmont. After he left, she would have to come to terms with her grief. For now, she needs must hide it.

"All right, Harlan, I will sit with you at supper," she agreed, but a cheerful smile was quite beyond her.

At least Harlan seemed quite sober compared to many of the other men, who had been drinking since early afternoon. There would be the bonfire and dancing after the meal, and then gradually the mixed company would begin to dissipate, some disappearing discreetly into the woods and fields, it was true, but most of the respectable folk heading home before fights broke out. The remaining men would trade boasts around the fire until the embers died or they passed into a blissful state of drunken senselessness.

Merissa struggled through the supper, paying scant attention to the conversations around her and barely tasting the traditional roast goose. The table of mixed company that was set up for the gentry stood between two rows of separate tables for the many men and women laborers. She could not keep her eyes from straying to those workers' tables, where she tried to discern the Gypsies among the rest.

Alex's future would depend entirely upon these people with their odd way of life. Would he be safe with them? She liked their liveliness and the quick smiles that would suddenly flash against their dark skin. Would any of the women form a *tendre* for him, as she had almost from their first meeting? He was so handsome and gallant, how could they not?

Her hand slipped down under the table to feel the reticule that hung from the belt of her silk pelisse. The lumps inside it reassured her that at least she would see her Frenchman one more time. She had promised him a token. She did not want him to leave without it—somehow she thought it might bring him luck.

The supper seemed interminable, but finally the rounds of toasts that signaled the conclusion began, starting with the highest-ranking gentleman, Lord FitzHarmon, the earl who owned Foxhall and was Lord Rupert's host. Despite her own misery, Merissa had noticed that Juliana had stayed close to Harry all day and that Lord Rupert had not been in evidence until just before the dinner. He and Juliana were sitting together now, but they did not look well pleased with the arrangement. Every so often when Merissa glanced at Harlan, she would notice that he was watching the young couple.

Finally the vicar rose to give the benediction, and the firelighters were dismissed with enthusiastic whoops to go and get their torches lit. It was not quite dark, but once the bonfire was burning brightly it would render everything around it dark by contrast to its flames.

As Merissa waited for the firelighting with everyone else, Harlan came to stand close beside her. He claimed one of her hands and, covering it with his own, brought it to hang between them by his side. When she glanced at him dubiously, he smiled.

"I know I may not have all the dances with you, Merrie, but surely I may have the first one?"

Actually, it was what Merissa preferred. She did not want to be dancing with Harlan later when she would need to slip off to meet Alex in the shadows. She accepted with something that almost could have passed for enthusiasm.

With great ceremony and an equal measure of glee, the torches were applied to the bonfire, and in a satisfactory roar of flames the Spanish Armada went up in smoke for another year. The fiddler began to pick out fragments of dance tunes, and the tables were quickly cleared and removed to make a space for the dancers.

The light from the bonfire cast a glow over the celebrants as they formed a large circle to begin the first dance. The shadows seemed to lead a dance of their own as the couples advanced and retreated, skipped and whirled. The sparks and smoke from the bonfire whipped in the breeze in what seemed almost an imitation of their movements. After three lively country dances in succession with Harlan, however, Merissa began to doubt his intentions. Despite his remark, was he planning to keep her with him all evening? What should she do? She was certain that Alex had arrived by now, but she was not free to seek him out.

Glancing at the other dancers thoughtfully, Merissa saw Juliana and Lord Rupert in another set and knew what she should do. If only she could catch Julie's eye! She did not think either of them would mind switching off to other partners, notably Harlan and herself. After that, she thought it should not be hard to find yet one more partner, and then temporarily disappear.

Her plan was complicated by the choice of dances, and she could not slip away until she was certain that the next dance was not one where she should have come into contact with Harlan during the progression of the moves. If he questioned her disappearance later, she would say she had become tired and sought out her parents, but it was essential that he should not notice her defection too soon.

Excusing herself from her last partner, who was almost too drunk to notice, she scouted the edges of the darkness. She went cautiously, knowing that after so many hours the temper of the event tended to change from one of simple celebration to one of less innocent revelry. A young woman alone in the darkness was easy prey.

To her intense relief, Alex quite suddenly materialized beside her. *He must have been watching,* she realized. Such joy and pain filled her at the sight of him, tears sprang into her eyes. *Oh, no. I will not cry,* she vowed. She wanted their parting to be dignified and calm. It would be so much easier for both of them.

Silently he beckoned her to follow him deeper into the darkness after a quick glance around them. Merissa looked, too, but saw no one likely to notice them. How precious were these few stolen moments! She suddenly regretted with all her heart who she was and where she was—she was filled with envy for the serving maids and village girls who could sneak off with their lovers this night to lie in the fields.

She loved this man! Those girls would see their loves again, but she was not so blessed. How could she let him go without ever knowing how it would be to lie beside him and hold him and let him know her? Was the darkness so deep that he could not see the naked yearning that must surely show in her eyes?

Alex took her gloved hand and kissed it. "I saw you dancing," he said, his deep voice sounding unbearably warm and dear to her. "You are as graceful and light as a leaf in the wind."

"I—I would have liked to be dancing with you," she said softly, her voice breaking despite her determination to control it. She noticed that he had not released her hand.

"Do I dance?" he teased her. "How do you know?" The beloved sound of his deep chuckle nearly caused her tears to brim over. She could make out the flash of his grin even in the darkness.

"Of course you do," she managed to answer in a muffled voice. "You are an officer and a gentleman."

"And a Frenchman," he added. The reminder sobered them both.

"We have only a few minutes," she said hurriedly. Reluctantly reclaiming her hand, she stripped off her gloves and tucked them into her belt. She opened her reticule and grasped the little silk-wrapped packet that lay in the bottom.

"I promised you a token yesterday, and I always keep my promises." She placed the packet into his open bare hand, catching her breath at the touch of his skin. How large his hands were! How she craved the feel of them in her hair, against the softness of her face, on her body, as she had felt them so very briefly at Dubro Vitae!

He unwrapped the little parcel with utmost care. She heard his intake of breath when her token lay at last in his palm.

"The Roman brooch. *Ma chère,* you must not give this to me. It is what you prize the most in all your collection."

"Please, take it. I want you to have it." *Do not reject the only thing I can give you, not when there is so much more I would willingly give!* "Please," she repeated, "I hope that it will bring you luck."

His hesitation pushed her tears over the brink. Surely he would not be so cruel as to reject her parting gift. Did he not know that her heart went with it?

Her tears seemed to dissolve his so-proper reserve. Lapsing into French, he took her into his arms, murmuring soft words of comfort. "*Ma belle, ma précieuse, ne pleure pas.* I will accept your gift, since it means so much. I will carry it with me, and when I have achieved my mission, I will send it back to you, so that you will know that I am safe."

Merissa clung to him, inhaling his scent, desperately seeking to memorize the strong feel of his body. She could not settle for a token someday returned to her. She could not let him go. Yet, he could not stay. She could not ask it of him, for one way or another, it would surely mean his death.

"Please," she said in an agonized whisper, "please, love me. Let me go with you. I will go with you, now, tonight."

He did not push her away, nor even release her, but she could tell by the slight stiffening of his body that she had shocked him.

"*Ma chère,*" he said gently, "you cannot. It is far too dangerous, what I must do. Besides, I cannot marry you. I am a lost soul—I have no name, no honor, no hope to offer any woman. You must forget about me."

"Someday you will have your name again. You have never lost your honor, despite what you say. And I don't care if we are not married," she said passionately, recklessly. "I would go anywhere and be happy just to be with you."

For a moment longer he hugged her, and then he did put her from him. "No," he said firmly. "I would care that we should be married. I will not allow you to risk your life just to ruin it, and as an army officer's mistress, you would be ruined indeed. Seldom would you be with me, yet you would be scorned by your true equals. If I fell in battle, which is likely, you would have no recourse but to give yourself to the next protector you could find. That is, if we even reached my country safely, and if I won my case against my cousin, so I could rejoin my regiment."

Her tears fell faster at the black picture he painted. She put a fist against her lips to try to stop their trembling and stifle the sobs behind them.

"Even if I married you here, in your country, my own country would not recognize the marriage as legal. If we managed to cross the Channel safely, you would be turned back."

He sighed. "Things were not always so. My grandmother was English—said to have been very beautiful. Like you, my dear." He cradled her face in his hands and with a touch as gentle as a breath, brushed the tears from her cheeks with his thumbs.

"Perhaps one day things will change again," he said, trying to joke with her in the darkness. "Shall I return for you someday, when I am grown old and bent and gray? As I recall, my grandfather was very handsome for an old man."

How could he joke? Filled with anguish, Merissa suddenly pulled back her arm and struck Alex full in the chest with her fist. When the impact seemed to have no effect, she pulled back, ready to do it again. But somehow, it was not her fist but her whole body she flung at him the second time, and he caught her in his arms and began kissing her fiercely.

"I would wait my whole life for you," she whispered softly, seriously, between fevered kisses.

"*Ma belle Merissa*. If only it would do any good."

Merissa closed her eyes, abandoning herself to these few moments of lovemaking, all that she would ever have with him.

An instant later, they were interrupted by shouts and cries of alarm. "Fire!"

Chapter 16

The Sibley stables were on fire. The wind apparently had carried a few sparks from the bonfire farther aloft and afield than anyone had anticipated. Nestled into the thatch roof of the stone stables, the sparks had smoldered there unnoticed until they'd burst out into a full-fledged blaze.

Now those revelers who were sober enough to rally their senses and be useful were hurrying about, struggling to help rescue the panicky animals from the burning building and to find water to throw on the adjoining sheds and barns. Those who were not sober enough seemed inevitably to be in the way.

"I must go and help them," Alex said. "I cannot simply stand by."

"No!" protested Merissa. "It is too dangerous. What if you are discovered?"

"I must risk it. I shall be one of the Gypsies—I will speak to no one, if possible. I will tell any suggestions I have to your father, and the instructions will seem to come from him." With that small reassurance, he pulled himself from her arms and ran toward the flaming stable block.

Those who were not helping had been herded to one side, where they stood clustered in little groups, watching the destruction with horror. The wind picked up sparks from the new conflagration and carried them off toward other roofs in the farmyard, while flaming bits of thatch rained down inside and around the stables themselves.

Merissa tried to follow Alex's movements. She saw him talking to her father, hauling buckets, and pointing and pushing as her father began to call out orders in a suspiciously military manner. Miraculously, the task of saving the buildings began to become organized. Men were stationed on the neighboring roofs with blankets, alert to the capricious wind and ready to snuff out any live sparks that landed. Two teams were organized on the ground, one to work fighting against the fire, and one to rescue animals, harness, equipment, and anything else they could salvage or move from the stables and adjoining spaces. Shovels as well as buckets were put into use, and the earth became a resource against the fire along with water.

Merissa had found her sisters and mother among the crowd, and the Pritchard women formed a little knot by themselves, their worried faces reflecting the shifting light from the fire. Loyal Backhouse, too frail to take an active part in the fire fighting, came to watch over them, and Bessie joined them, too, as Jackson, Bean, and the other able menservants helped to battle the blaze.

Suddenly a cry went up, "Jarrod Garvey's still in the stables!"

Harry whispered, "Who's Jarrod Garvey?"

"One of the Sibleys' young grooms, miss," Bessie answered, shaking her head.

Someone yelled, "The roof's going to go!" and even as the horrible realization was still dawning on most of the crowd, Merissa saw Alex dash a bucket of water over himself and dart into the inferno.

Her mother must have seen him, too, for as Merissa started to move, Lady Pritchard threw her arms around her.

"No, Merrie, there is nothing you can do!"

"Mama, please!"

"What would you do, go in after him? 'Tis in his own hands now and God's. We can only pray and wait."

Merissa struggled at first and then became still as an ominous cracking sound came from the charred roof timbers. For one awful moment the entire mass of burning thatch seemed to quiver like a live thing resisting death; then with one great roar what had once been the stable roof collapsed inside the walls. A massive wave of heat and smoke and flying embers drove the crowd back.

"Oh, God!" Merissa cried, thinking that to lose Alex in this way was a hundred times worse than the agony of losing him in the way she already had. She prayed, promising to let him go gracefully without a struggle, and to be grate-

ful all her life for simply having known him, if only God
would let him live.

Alex went into the burning stables with a very clear idea
of what he was about. The young groom, trapped or overcome by the smoke, had only one chance for survival, and
that was if someone swooped in quickly, snatched him, and
got out equally fast—someone like Alex.

He had not spent his day drinking. He was sharper and
faster than most of the men here. But more than that, what
had he to lose? Far less than any other man here present,
from the lowliest worker to the great earl himself. Merissa
and the kind of life she represented were something he
could never have. He was already gambling on an uncertain
future, and the stakes, ultimately, were the same as at this
moment—his life might be forfeit at any time in the days to
come. He was used to gambling with Death. If this gamble
saved another's life, how much more worthwhile!

The heat inside the stable was even more intense than
Alex expected. He heard the cracking of the roof beams
above the hayloft over his head, and somehow increased his
speed, scrambling past heaps of burning straw and skirting
the outline of burning stalls that helped him keep track of
where he was in the thick smoke. Alex prayed that the lad
was still conscious or at least somewhere near the back—
there would be no chance to turn around, and only one
chance to call his name.

"Jarrod!" he yelled, pulling his loosened cravat up to
cover his face. Once his own lungs filled with smoke, he
would never reach the wooden door at the back, which was
his destination. He heard the boy moan, still ahead of him
somewhere. Necessity had tuned his senses to the finest
possible pitch. Seconds—he had only seconds left.

Above the roar of the fire, he could hear the unmistakable sounds of the roof starting to give way. The hayloft
would only delay total collapse for a few extra moments, for
the support beams were already burning. He could not flat-
ten himself against the walls, although he knew they would
stand—the stone was hotter than the hottest oven and
would burn him alive as fast as the flames. The door was
their only hope.

As fast as he could, Alex heaved the cross bar aside and pulled the door open. Its ancient thick wood had withstood the onslaught of heat until now, and Alex was betting that it would hold up part of the descending roof long enough for him and the lad to slip out beneath it. The rush of fresh air fanned the blaze behind him, as he had known it would, but for a moment it also pushed back the smoke around him. He looked to his right and saw the boy on his knees, dazed and terrified with flames all around him.

"Jarrod, jump!" Alex commanded in his sharpest officer's voice. "To me, now!" He held out his arms, praying that the young groom would not hesitate. Such hesitation would kill them both.

Lady Pritchard had moved her little group away from the crowd, where Merissa's distress would be less noticeable. Thus it happened that when a blackened, coughing figure stumbled miraculously from the back of the burning stables half carrying another, the Pritchard women and their two servants were the first to see them.

No power on earth could have stopped Merissa from going to Alex then. Even as she rushed to him, he dropped to his knees, depositing Jarrod Garvey upon the ground.

"Tend him," Alex said, coughing and pushing the hair out of his own smoke-smudged face. "I am all right, just *un peu charbonné*." He coughed some more and added, "The boy was trapped there much longer than my half a minute."

Half a minute? Was that all it had been? To Merissa it had been an eternity in hell. Her eyes must have said so, for as the others began to minister to Jarrod, Alex got to his feet and drew her aside by the hand.

"I'm sorry you were frightened."

"Are you certain that you are truly all right?" she questioned, touching and inspecting him in the light of the fire.

She was only reassured when he gave her a rueful grin. "I will do. Once again I have won the toss. However, I'm afraid that I have ruined these clothes."

She wanted to laugh aloud and throw herself at him to hug him until the sun came up, but she remembered the promise in her prayer.

"You Gypsies don't know how to keep clean, do you?"

she scolded, determined to keep her tone light. "Never mind. Those clothes never did fit you properly."

"I'm grateful that your mother purchased me an extra set."

Taking his hand, Merissa pulled him farther away from the light and noise and growing numbers of people. Others had come to help with Jarrod. The darkness was protection against questions or discovery. They skirted the stable paddock and found refuge in the lea of the carriage shed.

"Perhaps these will wash," she said, brushing black ash from the sleeve of his coat. "Those other clothes are for when you reach the coast, so you may look respectable and not arouse suspicion. If you begin to wear them now, how respectable do you think they will appear in a few weeks?" she whispered.

"I do not doubt that I can procure some from the Gypsies, and I will look all the more authentic," he replied.

"Have you enough money?"

He nodded. "I shall manage. I accepted the loan of a small sum from your father."

"Do you know where to meet with your Gypsies?"

Again he nodded.

She hated to say the words that came next, but they were the most important of what she had to tell him. "If you go now, this minute, we can simply say that Jarrod was rescued by one of the Gypsies, we don't know which one. Later, if anyone specifically remembers seeing you go into the stable, we can deny that we ever saw you come out. Should the authorities come looking for you, we could make them think that you died in the fire! They would have no reason to continue the hunt. You would be free to make your way home."

"And you and your family would no longer be in jeopardy. Thank you, Merissa. I owe you a debt that can never be repaid."

His voice was gruff in the darkness. She peered into his face, trying to discern the expression in his eyes. The night under the open sky was not as dark as inside the windmill where they had first met, yet she was reminded of that meeting. How well she had come to know that face, those dark eyes, which had been hidden from her that first time!

She knew he must go, yet seemingly of their own will, her arms went up around his neck and her lips sought his. *Just one good-bye kiss,* she thought, one small last taste of him. For luck, and to say "God be with you."

He did not respond at all for a moment. Then with a groan of surrender, he crushed her to him, claiming her mouth with all his passion.

Merissa's heart and very soul went with it. *I love you!* she wanted to shout, or at least whisper, but she did not dare. It would only make their parting harder, and might make him feel as if somehow he was at fault. She had done this to herself—she had invited this joy and pain from the beginning, had chosen her course against all his warnings. She would have no choice now but to live with it.

"After yesterday, somehow this little scene does not surprise me," came a voice, its tone as cold and sharp as ice.

Merissa and Alex broke apart as if they had been doused with water. It was Harlan.

"Oh, God, not now," Merissa cried. "Please, Harlan—" she started, but as she turned to look at her old friend, she saw the pistol in his hand.

"What are you doing?" she exclaimed.

"I am charging your so-called Gypsy friend with being an escaped French war prisoner, and I fully intend to turn him in."

"But he's not—you can't—"

"I believe it is time you stopped deceiving me, Merissa. I have done a great deal of thinking since yesterday, and put a few things together. Your behavior this evening confirmed my suspicions, or did you think I would not notice?"

"You have no idea what you're talking about, Harlan," she said angrily. "Put that gun away, before you hurt someone." She glanced around, but there was no one else nearby.

"I would not look about for help if I were you," Harlan said in a particularly cutting voice. "The last thing you should want is for anyone else to make this discovery. You and your whole family could be arrested, Merrie, if anyone learned of your part in all this! I'm willing to overlook it, and will simply say I discovered this fellow myself. Please step away from him."

"No!" Merissa stepped closer to Alex and put her arms back around him.

"*Ma chère,* he has a gun," Alex said gently. Turning to Harlan, he said, "The pistol is not necessary, *monsieur*— you are endangering Miss Pritchard. I will surrender voluntarily."

"No!"

"Hush, Merissa," he whispered. "Perhaps it is for the best, after all."

"How can you say that? Harlan, please—listen to me. He has done nothing wrong; he has harmed no one. He is leaving this minute—it is all arranged. Let him go! Why would you do this?"

Harlan actually laughed. "You do not see it, Merrie, do you, even now! He has used you! By God, I'd like to kill him. If I ever suspected that you might have gone so far as to give yourself to him, I *would* kill him! He has taken advantage of your soft heart and impulsive nature. He has used you to get what he needed—assistance and shelter and who knows what else? Has he claimed to be in love with you? He is our enemy! He has turned you into a traitor against your own country! Do you not wonder how many other women he has used thusly before you? How many more would he use so to make good his escape? What if they were less virtuous or gently bred than you, Merissa? They might offer more than stolen kisses. Do you think he would care if he left a dozen French bastards behind him on our shores?"

Merissa had put her hands over her ears. "He is not like that! You are wrong, Harlan. If you do this I will never forgive you!"

"Look at him now, Merrie. He would like to kill me, I'll warrant. He did not expect to be exposed."

"He did not expect to be vilified and subjected to such terrible lies by a man who is already taking away his chance for freedom! What is the matter with you, Harlan? You never used to be so cruel and unreasonable!"

"What is the matter with you, Merissa? You never used to be so blind! I'm trying to protect you. Do you think he cares if your reputation is ruined, or if you are arrested and imprisoned for helping him? He would be gone! It would mean nothing to him! Step away now. I will not put up this pistol until he is delivered to the constable, and maybe not even then. We will make certain he reaches the hands of the militia and is returned to the prison where he belongs, not left roaming the country preying on our women."

"I'm not moving. If you have such a great desire to deliver him to the constable, you shall have to deliver me with him." Merissa stared at Harlan defiantly.

Finally it was Alex who intervened. Ever so gently he pushed Merissa away from him, his hands lingering on her shoulders for only a fraction of a moment. "There is no point to such a sacrifice, Miss Pritchard. Think of your family! I will deny that I have ever seen you before. Listen—you can hear others coming now. I must face the consequences. Alone."

Chapter 17

"My dear Merissa," said Sir Barry, "you cannot go on refusing to see young Gatesby forever, you know. How much longer do you plan to continue this?"

Merissa was in her father's library, sitting in his favorite wing chair with Polly at her feet, while he paced in front of the fire and occasionally made forays over to look out the window. The warm days of St. Luke's little summer had quickly given way to gusty October showers in the weeks since the Harvest Fair, and on this day, like so many others, the wind-driven rain was running in streams down windows and through fields.

Despite the weather, Harlan Gatesby had come to Pie Hall to call on Merissa every single day since the fair. Every day she had refused to see him.

"Why can I not, Papa? I warned him that night that I would never forgive him if he turned in Captain Valmont. How can you be so ready to forget what he did?"

"Captain Valmont knew very well the risks he was facing, as did we, my dear. It could easily have been someone else who discovered him and turned him in. We were most fortunate, in fact, that it was Harlan that night and not someone else, who might have turned all of us in along with the captain if they had put facts together. Then where would we be?"

In Peterborough Gaol, or some worse place. Merissa knew the answer perfectly well, for she and her father had covered this part of the conversation before. But thinking of the destinations she and her family had been spared only made her think of Alex, who was a prisoner once again at Norman Cross.

She sighed. "Do you think that the rains have made the

prison yards terribly muddy, Papa? What do the men do there when it rains every day?"

Sir Barry returned from the window and bent to stir the fire with the poker before he answered. "I wish you would not torture yourself so with thinking, Merrie. It only makes matters worse."

She paused, listening to the hiss of the logs and the ticking of the clock that filled the silence. Then she said, "I am not to think, Papa?"

Her father let out a sigh that rivaled her own. "You know quite well what I mean. Not about *him*. You would do so much better to forget him, my dear."

"As you have, no doubt," she said dryly. "I notice you have not once touched your violin in these weeks since he's been gone."

She had to smile when her father turned a somewhat guilty-looking face toward her. "He did play handsomely, did he not? I had thought of giving it to him, but there was no point, considering his situation."

Merissa thought of her own gift to the captain, the brooch she had so prized in her collection. Had he been able to keep it? Or had it met the same fate she imagined had befallen it originally—exchanged between lovers, then lost? Was he lost to her as well? So much had happened in such a short time.

It was all very well for her father to say not to think of her Frenchman. She had hardly been able to put her mind to anything else in the weeks that had passed in his absence. Did he stare out at the rain and think of his lost opportunity? Did he ever think of her?

The little bridge he had given her was the last thing she looked at every night when she went to sleep and the first thing she saw every morning, not counting Polly. She would wonder where he was, what he was doing. Any room in the house that he had been in was likely to trigger her thoughts of him. She had known better than to set foot in the barn, and the rain had helped keep her away from Dubro Vitae.

"It is so nearly time for dinner, I think we should go and join your mother in the salon," said Sir Barry.

He was not very comfortable dealing with matters of the

heart, Merissa knew. *Retreat and seek reinforcements?* She winced as the military turn of her thoughts led to Alex yet again. How long would she suffer this consuming grief?

In the salon the pianoforte stood silent; no one had wanted to play music in recent days. Lady Pritchard smiled bravely as Merissa entered the room, trailed by the faithful Polly. The spaniel followed Merissa more closely than ever now, as if afraid that her mistress, like the captain, would disappear. Although Lady Pritchard spoke of the matter very little, Merissa suspected that she also felt the loss of the charming Frenchman's company.

Harry and Juliana were far less circumspect—they complained and reminisced and wrangled loudly over which of them missed the captain more. Lord Rupert had reportedly ended his visit to the earl and returned to London, with the effect that Julie suddenly was spending more time with her sisters and acted more like the schoolroom miss she had been until so recently.

"Merissa has no plans to forgive Harlan for his sins, ever," announced Sir Barry as he took a seat by his wife.

"That does seem a bit extreme, my dear," Lady Pritchard responded.

Of course. Her father had deliberately made it sound that way. But Merissa's parents had not witnessed the confrontation between Harlan and Alex, and had not heard the awful things that Harlan had said.

He has used you . . . turned you into a traitor . . . taken advantage . . . Has he claimed to be in love with you? Alex had never made any such claim—he was too honorable, too honest. Merissa had known that his heart belonged to his country, and had made her own choices. She had only to recall Harlan's cruel words to instantly rekindle her anger.

"Let us remember that Harlan was only upholding the law, doing his duty as he saw fit," Lady Pritchard continued. "We were the ones who chose to ignore it, and I suppose we are paying the price, after a fashion."

"Our price is nothing compared to what Captain Valmont must be suffering," Harry said.

Merissa was certain that Alex would indeed be suffering, given all he had lost. He had kept himself so utterly under control when Harlan held him at gunpoint—had he been controlled or simply resigned? Would her gallant French-man admit defeat? Would he despair? He had seemed to take their failure in stride, yet all the Pritchards knew how much had been at stake in his escape attempt.

"I wish we knew how long he will remain at Norman Cross," she said aloud, although they had discussed this more than once since his recapture.

"There is no way to predict. If he is lucky, it could take months for the paperwork to be processed before they ship him down to Chatham," Sir Barry said soberly. "The best thing that could happen would be for the paperwork to get lost. By all reports, the hulks are a living hell."

"It isn't fair! He doesn't deserve to be sent there," Merissa said bitterly. "He is not—what did you say they called it, 'criminally inclined'?"

"By their rules he is, as he knew very well. The impersonation charge, and then his escape, put a double mark against his account."

"At least he's alive," said Juliana abruptly.

Everyone turned to look at her.

"If he had succeeded in leaving with the Gypsies the night of the Harvest Fair, what would we know now of his ultimate fate? Would we know where he was, or how he was faring? Would we have had any assurance that he had not been killed or recaptured? At least where he is now, he is safe and alive." She looked at the rest of them as if she dared them to contradict her.

Safe and alive, living under the shadow of a crime he did not commit, with no name and no honor, no comfort, no freedom, nothing to live for, thought Merissa. Was knowing such unpleasant certainties preferable to the doubts and worries they might have had? "We don't really know how he is faring at the prison," she pointed out.

"Papa, why could we not go to see him?" Harry suddenly sounded excited. "Do they not allow the prisoners to have visitors?"

"How would we explain how we happened to know him?" Merissa replied discouragingly. "Don't you think I have already pondered such a thing at length, Harry? At best we could only claim to have met him the night of the Harvest Fair, and I do not think the prison officials would find that sufficient acquaintance to warrant our visiting him."

"There might be another way, one that would still avoid suspicion," Lady Pritchard said quietly, fixing a steady eye upon her husband. "What if we were to visit the prison market? Perhaps we might catch a glimpse of him or find some way to get word of him while we were there."

"No, my dears." Sir Barry shook his head. "I know you miss him, but the prison is no place for refined ladies."

"But Papa! All sorts of people go to the market."

"Tobacco merchants and farmers with eggs to sell, not the genteel ladies of the neighborhood." He hesitated, which told Merissa that his resistance might be overcome. "Perhaps I could go, and report back to you."

A chorus of negatives met this offer.

Four determined Pritchard ladies ranged against one baronet were formidable odds, especially given their tenacity. Over the next few days Merissa and her mother and sisters waged a campaign worthy of Wellington himself to change Sir Barry's mind. Bribes, threats, and rash promises were all offered at various times along with a continuous recital of newly discovered examples of "genteel ladies" who had personally visited the prison market to purchase workboxes, parlor pictures, model toys, or trinket boxes made by the prisoners. The fact that Sir Barry was himself concerned over the captain no doubt worked in their favor, as did his definite desire to preserve his sanity.

The mere possibility of seeing Alex at the prison lightened Merissa's step considerably. Her mind became occupied with possible ways to ease his physical suffering in confinement. Could she bring him food? Clothing? Books? If she brought him candles, would he be allowed to keep them? Would the other prisoners steal them? She did not know of any way to ease the anguish that must be in his heart, but she hoped that such small tokens of caring might help in some fashion.

If only there was some way to prove that Alex should be spared from going to the hulks! Almost as soon as Merissa thought that, a possible answer popped into her head. Alex had been a hero on the night of the fire. His courage and selflessness were not the traits of a criminal. Did the authorities know? Would Harlan have mentioned the circumstances under which he had been able to capture the captain? Merissa doubted it. If the Pritchards could find a way to make that information known, surely it would weigh in Alex's favor.

When she shared her ideas with her mother and sisters, they adopted her project with enthusiasm. The brightening of their mood was not lost on Sir Barry. When Merissa approached him with her ideas for helping Alex, he was finally ready to agree to escort them to the market at Norman Cross.

Anyone who traveled the Great North Road between Cambridge and Stamford passed the western gate of the barracks and prison at Norman Cross. The complex was situated at the intersection where the road to Peterborough split off from the main route; thus it was bound on two sides by well-traveled roads filled with coach traffic and commerce. Merissa had always been saddened by the grim prospect of the long wooden palisade that stretched along the highway, broken only by the gate that offered a glimpse of the militia barracks. Beyond these, the red-tiled roofs of the tall caserns that housed the prisoners could just be seen, along with the chimneys of numerous other buildings. Never had she expected or desired to see more than that brief view; it seemed strange indeed to be sent around to the south front and actually enter inside the walls.

A second, more imposing wall of brick masonry enclosed the prison itself. The Pritchards passed between this and the numerous buildings of the East Barracks until they arrived at the prison's east gate. There the soldiers on duty determined the purpose of their visit and instructed them to leave their carriage in the open area outside the wall where they could already see vehicles of every class and description.

Nothing could have prepared Merissa for the utter contrast of the bustling prison market and the dismal setting surrounding it once she and her family entered the fenced-off space used for the market. The atmosphere of the market itself seemed almost festive; booths and stalls set up by the local merchants offered the prisoners everything from soap and needles to small tools and craft supplies, while from small tables and barrel tops selected prisoners hawked the crafts made in their endless idle hours. The mix of English and French voices sounded like incoherent babbling until Merissa's ears became used to the noise and individual voices began to stand out.

The scene might have passed for a normal weekly market in a town if one could overlook the ever-present guards on duty with their bayonets fixed in place and the ragged appearance of a number of the prisoners. Some wore the remains of their own uniforms while others were dressed in the ill-fitting yellow coats and trousers issued by the Transport Office. The walls—the high brick wall with a deep trench along one side, and opposite it the wooden stockade that enclosed one of the quadrangles where the prisoners lived—were somewhat obscured by all the booths and activity of the market. What nothing could obscure were the forbidding shapes of the four caserns ranged one behind the other within that quadrangle, looming tall and peculiar with their small, high windows—higher by far than a man could reach to see out.

Merissa shuddered. How many men shared the cramped quarters of those dark, gloomy buildings? Four more just like them stood within another stockade to the other side of the market gate, and there were said to be two more quadrangles directly behind these. Where was Alex in this vast complex, and how would they ever get word of him, let alone manage to see him?

She wandered along close to her parents and sisters, looking at the wares being offered for sale and ignoring the occasional comments in French that three pretty young Englishwomen were bound to inspire. She hoped her bonnet hid her blushes. She was beginning to see why her father had discouraged them from coming—she was finding the experience truly disheartening. How could these other people come here to trade so cheerfully? Did they give no thought to the men who lived here day after day, year after year, with so little comfort and so little to occupy them during the rest of each week? She supposed that by purchasing the prisoners' products they were at least providing them with some monetary support.

A knot of men and women were crowded around one table that displayed a variety of models fashioned from bone. There were mechanical toys with exposed wheels and gears that turned by a crank and, what was drawing the most attention, a large model of a guillotine. Merissa shivered as she peered between the other onlookers. The model was exquisitely beautiful and gruesome at the same time. It stood nearly two feet tall and had three levels connected by stairways, each level crowded with little bone figures of people and surrounded by carved railings of almost lacelike delicacy. The top level was a smaller platform with soldiers and the tower containing the blade. . . .

Merissa did not look to see if there was a kneeling figure of a doomed victim—she hurried on to the next table. Why would a prisoner choose such a depressing subject upon which to lavish long months of work?

The next table displayed a number of models made both from wood and straw, and here she found something that captured her attention. Someone had made a model of what she would swear was meant to be a Roman villa. It was exquisitely fashioned, with wooden columns and walls, and a carefully detailed roof of tiny wooden tiles. The open courtyard in the center had a floor of straw marquetry that mimicked perfectly the look of mosaic.

Her heart began to beat faster. She was certain that Alex had not been here long enough to have made this model, and yet, could there be another prisoner with his engineering skills and his love of the ancient Romans? The model was perfect in every respect. Her father would be very interested. She looked up to discover she had lagged far behind her family.

"Please, who made this model?" she asked quickly in French, addressing the prisoner who sat behind the table.

"Ah, the mademoiselle has a discerning eye," the man answered also in French, obviously pleased to be addressed in his own language. His face was gaunt, and his smile seemed only to emphasize it. "This model, it costs only seven pounds, a bargain for such a large and intricate piece of work. You will agree that it is very special."

"Yes, I agree. But please, can you tell me who made it?"

"The names are on it, with the price, there."

A small slip of paper was attached to the side of the small house. Merissa peered at it, trying to make out the scribbled writing. The price was prominent, but the names were small.

"*Fait par S. Laloup, Jean Redoute, et A. de la Porte*," she read. She swallowed. Had she really expected the tag to say "Valmont"? The captain was not likely to be entered here under his own name, because of the impersonation charge. She had no idea how he would be identified.

Her disappointment must have shown. "For such a beautiful mademoiselle, perhaps the price could be six pounds," offered the prisoner.

As she looked up, she saw Harry and Juliana returning to find her. "Look what I have found," she said. "Can one of you please fetch Papa?"

Harry dashed off and Juliana turned to inspect Merissa's discovery. "It's beautiful!" she exclaimed. Narrowing her eyes, she looked at Merissa. "You're thinking he may have made it, aren't you? But how could he? Think of the time it must have taken!"

"His name is not on it," Merissa admitted, "but then, we do not know what name they are using for him." She lowered her voice. "Suppose he had begun this before he decided to escape? Perhaps he gave it to someone else to finish, or they took it?"

Before Juliana could answer, their father's voice interrupted. "Well, what have we here?" Sir Barry maneuvered himself between browsers to reach the front of the table where his daughters stood.

"Papa, look at this model," Merissa said. She whispered the rest of her theory into his ear.

"Hmm, yes, I see."

The thin-faced prisoner looked particularly hopeful in Sir Barry's presence. "A fine piece of work, monsieur—only seven pounds."

"I wish to question the makers," Sir Barry said firmly in French. "Are you one of the men?"

The prisoner shook his head. "Sulpice!" he called. "You have customers!"

From behind the next table emerged a young boy who could not have been much older than Harry. Merissa supposed she was hopelessly naive, but the thought of him in such a place as this shocked her.

The lad positively beamed when he saw which model they were looking at—Merissa had never before seen a grin that seemed to reach so literally from ear to ear.

"Sir? Ladies? You wish to buy?" Merissa was astonished that he spoke to them in passable English.

"You are very young to have made such a skilled model," Sir Barry said skeptically. The boy's blank look showed that he had not understood, so Sir Barry switched to French.

"I work with my friends," the young man answered in English, pointing to the slip of paper. "We sell—you buy?"

"Are your friends here? We would like to meet them," Sir Barry said.

Merissa was bitterly disappointed when the lad said, "No, only I, Sulpice Laloup."

"Where are the others?" she put in softly, speaking to him in French.

"Ah. De la Porte is around somewhere, and Jean—he is not allowed."

Merissa turned to her father. "Papa, let me speak to him for a moment." She signaled to the boy and he followed her to a spot a little removed from the bustle at the table, but most significantly for Merissa's purposes, away from the ears of the nearest guards.

"You must tell me about your friend Jean," she said, speaking in a low voice. "Is that really his name? Why is he not allowed to be in the market?"

She had been thinking about the name Redoute, how it meant a part of a fortress, and how appropriate such a name might be for someone who was a military engineer. When she learned that he "was not allowed," she had begun to hope again.

"I have a friend, too," she added, "a captain named Valmont. He was recently caught after escaping."

The boy's eyes seemed to grow to twice their size. In a hurried spate of rapid French, he told Merissa how in the past year Captain Valmont had befriended him and hired him as his servant so that the lad could live with him in the less crowded officers' casern. The captain had been teach-

ing him English and reading and writing, and had told him
all about the ancient Romans. They had been working on
this model for months, and de la Porte had contributed the
beautiful straw work. Another officer had wanted to hire
Sulpice as a servant after the captain escaped, but he had
not trusted the man and moved back to the regular quarters.

"Now it is the captain who needs the money," Sulpice
confided. "Will the monsieur buy our model?"

Merissa nodded, but before she could speak another
word they were interrupted by a soldier.

"Here now, boy, get along! You are not to be bothering
the young lady."

"Oh, it is all right, officer," she said as sweetly as possible, turning to him with what she hoped was a pretty smile.
Sulpice wisely retreated back to his former post, leaving
her to deal with the guard. "It was I who approached him
with a question. Tell me, to whom would one apply for information about a prisoner? My father, Sir Barriemore
Pritchard, would like to make inquiries. . . ."

She glanced at the fellow in a coquettish manner not at
all natural to her and tipped her head in the direction of her
father. "I'm certain he would be most grateful if you could
direct us."

Chapter 18

Alex was making his way across the muddy airing ground of his quadrangle, deep in conversation with a man who had been a private in the 14th Regiment, when another prisoner hailed him from the paved area around the edge of the open yard. It seemed the turnkey wanted a word with him. Alex turned and trudged wearily toward the gate. He would be lucky if this deep mud did not ruin his boots, his only pair.

"Some people are wanting to talk to you about a model, Redoute," the turnkey informed him. "Wait here and go with the guard when he comes to get you."

Alex nodded. The turnkeys generally treated him well, because he could speak English and this made their jobs easier. He supposed he would be manacled and escorted into the agent's office, a short walk across the small court on the outer edge of the quadrangle. It was degrading that he could not be trusted even to walk such a little way without fetters and an armed guard, but those were the rules under which he lived now.

Rather than make himself miserable chafing over something he could not change, he resigned himself to wait, wondering instead about the turnkey's terse message. What could someone want to discuss about his models? The Roman villa was the only one available. He desperately hoped it would sell. He and Sulpice would split the remaining money after they paid de la Porte his share.

Merissa would have liked it, said the little voice in his mind. Instantly he tried to suppress the thought. It was just the sort that plagued him with surprising frequency despite the fact that weeks had passed since the fateful night of the fair. The time he had spent at Pie Hill seemed little more than a dream to him now, while the present was reality.

Alex could not afford to live in a dream. He tried to banish all thoughts of beautiful, vibrant Merissa from his mind, at least during the day, as if he did not want the vileness of his surroundings to contaminate those thoughts. In the daylight hours he occupied himself with the welfare of his fellow prisoners, falling back into old patterns of teaching, counseling, and mediating disputes. The prison and the routines, even some of the faces, were the same, despite the fact that he was back among the regular prisoners now instead of the officers. The boredom was the same, the wretchedness and crowding were worse, and the fights more frequent.

It was at night, when he could finally crawl into his hammock and lie awake in the privacy of darkness, that he allowed himself to conjure Merissa's image and to draw what comfort he could from his small store of memories. Had he loved her? He sensed that something in him had changed. His exposure to the Pritchards' peaceful, domestic country life had left him questioning and restless, subject to a yearning he could not identify. At night he would wrestle with it as well as his thoughts of Merissa, staring sleeplessly into a darkness that looked remarkably like his future.

Alex had detached the Pritchards from his present so firmly, he was momentarily confounded when the guard at last delivered him to the bare little room used for the agent's office and he stood facing Merissa and Sir Barry in the flesh. They were seated in a pair of hard wooden chairs, but the baronet rose as Alex came in. The only other person in the room was Mr. Rice, one of the prison clerks.

"This is the man we call Jean Redoute, although that is not his real name," Mr. Rice said. "He is the one who made the model you purchased."

"Why does he not use his real name?" Merissa asked sweetly.

Mr. Rice stared at her as if he could not believe she had the effrontery to speak after having been permitted so great an irregularity as to accompany her father.

She is actually here! Alex thought, struggling to grasp

the concept at the musical sound of her voice. There she sat, real and breathing, resplendent in a sky-blue pelisse. He wanted to touch her to be certain she was real. Hell, he wanted to sweep her into his arms and never let go. He shook his head to clear it of delusions. She and Sir Barry had actually come. How had they managed to find him? Had they done so without raising suspicion about themselves? He did not know how he should react. At the same time that he rejoiced at seeing her, he wished she had not come, to see him standing here degraded like a whipped dog in such a dismal place. This was nothing like the time he had stood in Lady Pritchard's parlor.

"He is charged with assuming the name and identity of an officer in order to gain parole, and his real identity has not been established," the clerk said in an icy tone, fidgeting impatiently. He spoke with exaggerated formality, as if he only practiced the style of speech on what he deemed necessary occasions. He turned to Sir Barry in appeal. "Sir, if you don't mind? We must keep the interview as short as possible. You are fortunate that Captain Hansell has allowed it at all, and if the brigade-major should get wind of it, well, I must simply say it would not do."

"I think I know this prisoner," Sir Barry said with a creditable imitation of curious amazement. "When was he brought in?"

"A few weeks ago. I would have to check our records to ascertain exactly when."

"Three weeks ago almost exactly, a French prisoner who had escaped from here was recaptured near Eastholme," Sir Barry continued. "I would almost swear that this is the same man. He helped to fight a fire there and courageously rescued a young lad from the flames!"

"Well, now, I don't know anything about that," Mr. Rice replied cautiously. His gaze flicked to Alex and back to the baronet.

"But you could check, could you not? This model we have purchased is not the work of only a few weeks. The fellow must have been here before."

"Redoute escaped and was recaptured—that I can confirm. His stay here is temporary. I would advise you not to commission any model that is too complicated—he might not have time to finish it for you."

Alex had hardly taken his eyes off Merissa from the moment he had walked in. He knew he must appear a miserable wretch in her eyes—the past three weeks had been none too easy on him. Still, she seemed unwilling to take her eyes off him, and he saw only too plainly the distress that passed across her face at the clerk's frank words. Fortunately, the clerk himself was too occupied with Sir Barry's conversation to notice.

"I want to know if this is the same man," Sir Barry said in a firm voice. "The man we saw that night in Eastholme might never have been taken if not for his heroism. I want to be sure it is on his record."

Mr. Rice appeared dubious. "I would have to go into the next room to look in the records . . . I suppose I could call in one of the guards from outside. . . ."

Sir Barry took a step toward the clerk, seeming to draw himself up to the fullest height possible for one of his modest stature. "I'm certain it only takes a moment to look in your files," he said. "With guards at the door and the poor fellow in fetters, I doubt we will be in any danger. We will discuss the model I wish to commission while we await your information."

He raised his eyebrows as if he dared the clerk to contradict him, and the little man vanished through the connecting door to the next room.

Alex took a step uncertainly toward the Pritchards. Now that they were blessedly alone for a moment or two, he still did not know quite how to act.

Merissa stood up, and Sir Barry came forward with hand outstretched.

"It is good indeed to see you, Captain," the baronet said warmly, his voice low. He grasped Alex's hand despite the manacles. "We were extraordinarily lucky to run across your model villa in the marketplace, or we might never have got word of you." He glanced back at Merissa, who seemed to be hovering behind him, as uncertain of how to behave as Alex was. "It was Merissa who put it all together, and who got the story from your young friend Sulpice."

At that Alex broke into a smile. "So, you have met young Sulpice. He has a bit of the devil in him, that one." More soberly he added, "It will help him to survive all this."

Merissa stepped forward at last. "How are *you* surviving?" she asked, placing her hand on his arm. Even shadowed by her bonnet brim, her eyes showed him the weeks of worry and concern she had suffered.

No, he was not about to burden her with the truth. "I am well," he lied. "I have settled back into my old routines, and as you see, reconnected with my friends here. I cannot complain."

Was it disappointment he saw flicker across her face? Should he have said how much he missed her? But that would only bring her more pain in the end. If she could tell he was lying, surely she must know he only did so to protect her tender sensibilities.

"Is there nothing that you need?" Her blue eyes searched his face, as if they could ferret out the truth he was hiding.

My life, my freedom, you, answered the voice in his head. Dear God, how he wanted to kiss her! He tried to make his mind blank, like a slate wiped clean.

"Harry, Julie, Mama, and I—we were trying to think of things that might bring you some comfort—books, extra food, perhaps candles?"

He shook his head, smiling. "And how did you think you would get those things to me, if I said yes?" He kept his voice light, teasing her. She did not need to know that such luxuries only caused trouble, arousing jealousy, greed, and sometimes violence between the prisoners. "You must not betray our prior acquaintance," he reminded her in a whisper.

He took a step back as they heard a rustling of papers and the sound of a drawer scraping shut in the other room.

"I will provide you with the mahogany and any other materials you will need for the model," said Sir Barry loudly, steering Merissa back toward her chair and clearing his throat. "You'll have to draw up a list. Ten pounds seems a bit steep, considering that we just paid eight for the one we bought today. However, as it is a special commission and your work is so fine, I agree to it."

They had repositioned themselves none too soon. A moment later Mr. Rice came back into the room, looking puzzled.

"You appear to be right about the date of his recapture. It was just three weeks ago, in or near Eastholme. The bounty was paid to someone named Harlan Gatesby. There is nothing about a fire or any rescue, however."

Of course not, thought Alex derisively. *Why would Harlan trouble himself to mention anything like that?*

"If what you say is true, Captain Hansell will want to know about it," Mr. Rice continued. "If I send word to him and he can see you now, would you be willing to give him such information as you know?"

Sir Barry did not pause. "My wife and other daughters are awaiting us in the market, but I'm certain they would forgive the further delay for such a worthy reason."

"Let me send word to Captain Hansell right away, then, sir. The market closes at three o'clock."

Mr. Rice had dispatched one of the guards from outside the door to take a message to the agent, while the other took Alex back into his custody. Merissa watched as her Frenchman was marched away.

This is not going to be the last time I ever see him, she vowed. How much pain and despair could one broken heart suffer? In the last few weeks she thought she must have exhausted her capacity. Seeing Alex like this had awakened different feelings in the depth of her heart—anger and determination.

That he was not "well" had been more than obvious to her, and not merely from seeing him manacled and marched in under guard. That he had lied to her about it had only made her more suspicious and concerned. In three weeks he had lost enough weight for her to notice. His clothes, the same ones he'd been wearing the night of the fire, were even more soiled and shabby now. Most telling of all, the spark was gone from his eyes, even when he smiled and tried to tease her. She could only begin to imagine what effect a place like this would have on the spirit of a man like Alex, but if he had thought to spare her feelings by his reticence, he had utterly failed.

Now she hoped that the agent, Captain Hansell, might prove to be an ally. Alex had said the former agent had interested himself in his case, and that this new man had had conversations with him as well. How would the agent be disposed toward Alex now, since his escape?

She did not have to wait long to find out. Less than half an hour after he had been dispatched, the guard returned from Captain Hansell requesting to escort Sir Barriemore Pritchard and his family to call upon the agent at his residence.

First they had to retrace their steps to the prison market to find Lady Pritchard and Merissa's sisters. The ladies saw them coming and greeted them eagerly.

"Papa, see what we bought!" cried Harry, who was lugging a large picture of what appeared to be Peterborough Cathedral done in straw marquetry. Juliana was carrying a box made of bonework. Their expressions changed to puzzlement when they noticed the guard escort.

"We have been invited to have a word with the prison superintendent," Sir Barry explained, inclining his head slightly toward the guard. "We were astonished by the most amazing coincidence—it seems the prisoner who made the Roman villa model is the same one we saw recaptured on Michaelmas eve! But they knew nothing about his fighting the fire or rescuing that poor young groom."

Lady Pritchard knew how to recognize a cue. "That gallant young man? I'm so glad! I never saw such a courageous act in all my life. By all means, they should be made aware of it!"

As their route led outside the brick prison wall and past the place where the Pritchards' carriage stood waiting, it was a simple matter to deposit their purchases there, including the Roman villa. Their soldier escort managed admirably despite being burdened with packages in addition to his musket.

Captain Hansell lived in a large house the Pritchards had passed upon first entering the prison grounds in their carriage. It stood just outside the prison itself, in its own walled garden.

A soldier received them at the door and led them into a perfectly ordinary, slightly old-fashioned parlor whose cream-colored walls were hung with paintings of ships. Merissa did not know why this appearance of normality surprised her, but it did. She supposed it was simply the enormous incongruity of it, with four of the tall dark prison caserns visible right outside the windows. A maid appeared bearing a loaded tea tray, and after she had finished arranging it, Captain Hansell himself appeared.

Merissa took stock of him while the introductions were being made. He was taller than her father and sported a splendid crop of white hair. While he had the air of one accustomed to command, he moved like a grizzled old sea dog. No one would doubt for a minute that he was Royal Navy. She half expected him to refer to the prison as his ship and the prisoners in it as his seamen.

"Well now, Sir Barry—I may call you Sir Barry? I have more than six thousand men under my care here. Most, I confess, are faceless and nameless to me, simply by fact of the sheer numbers of them. Leek wanted to send some of their overflow to us here, but I refused them. No room. That this damned war had better end soon is all I can say, sir—beg pardon, ladies.

"As it happens, I'm aware of the case you are here to discuss, and on my way over here to meet you I took the liberty to refresh my memory with the records. The prisoner Jean Redoute, or Captain Valmont as he may one day prove to be, is an interesting and challenging case, I must say." The agent peered at Sir Barry in a way that struck Merissa as distressingly speculative. "No one has any idea where he was for the seven weeks he was at large. One might have thought he would have gotten farther away from the area."

"He is certainly a skilled model maker," Sir Barry said carefully. "We purchased a marvelous model of a Roman villa today in the market—it was that which brought him to our attention."

Merissa stared down at her gloved hands folded demurely in her lap, listening to the conversation intently. Her father was no fool—she did not think he would make any mistakes to betray a former connection to Alex. But she guessed that Captain Hansell was an astute judge of human character. Would he suspect any connection between three young ladies in his parlor and the fact that the prisoner in question was more than ordinarily handsome?

"He—or the man he is supposed to have been impersonating—is a highly skilled engineer," the agent said. "Those are not skills one can merely pretend to possess. That is in part what led my predecessor to believe his claim of innocence. If what he claims is true, he has been dealt a terrible injustice—to be charged with impersonating oneself! Can you imagine?"

"How terrible indeed," agreed Sir Barry, as if he was slightly bewildered by the whole thing. Perhaps he was, Merissa reflected, or else he must surely be the source of Harry's fine theatrical talents.

"It is regrettable that he tried to escape and was recaptured," Captain Hansell continued, leaving it quite unclear whether it was Alex's attempt to escape or failure to succeed that he regretted. "With that added to the charges against him, there is nothing I can do for him now short of small things like delaying paperwork or seeing that the brigade-major cannot keep him locked in the black hole for too long at a time."

"The black hole—what is that?" asked Sir Barry sharply.

Captain Hansell sighed. "There is a cellblock that is used to punish troublemakers, and the brigade-major seems to have taken it into his head that Captain Valmont—that is, Jean Redoute—is one of those. The man does have two criminal charges against him now, and he did take another prisoner with him when he escaped. He was in the black hole for five days after they brought him in before it came to my attention."

"Dear God."

"Indeed. I must confess that the major and I have our differences regarding the prisoners. I'm afraid each of us believes that disciplining them falls under our own separate jurisdictions, and we seem to approach it with quite different philosophies. For instance, when that other prisoner who escaped with the captain was retaken, he was in terrible condition. He should have gone straight into our hospital, but Major was all for the black hole. We had quite a go-round over that. Ah, but I digress. About Valmont/Redoute. I believe you told Mr. Reed you had some information?"

Sir Barry launched into a description of the Harvest Fair and the fire that followed, detailing Alex's organization of the fire-fighting effort and his rescue of the young groom. Merissa knew that she must remain silent, and tried to judge the agent's reaction as her father talked. She thought the signs were positive; the navy man's lined face became more animated and his continuous pacing increased in speed. When Sir Barry finished his narrative, Captain Hansell hastened to him and shook his hand.

"Sir Barry, you may have done a very good thing for this young man today. This sort of thing can make a tremendous difference in how a case is viewed from higher up. Valmont/Redoute—that is how I think of him—is in a very precarious position, kind of like those trick riders at Astley's in London—have you ever seen them?—who ride two horses at once, standing with one foot on each. In his case, one horse is the process of investigating his impersonation case, which has proceeded so slowly he felt pushed into risking his neck to escape. The other is the process now in motion to send him down to Chatham as a result of the other. My hope has been that the attention his escape has drawn to his case may speed up the first horse, while I may do whatever is in my power to slow down the second one. The information you have just given me is bound to act as a prod on the former, and may even help to stop the progress of the latter."

Merissa could not help smiling at the agent's use of metaphor and the growing excitement that became apparent as he talked. She had her answer—Captain Hansell was every bit as much on Alex's side as could be hoped. The man obviously believed in his innocence, but lacked the power to right the wrong.

"I will see that this information goes to London by the next post," promised the captain. "You have been very kind to take an interest—not everyone would have bothered."

He raised an eyebrow and surveyed the ladies decorating his parlor, suddenly giving Merissa the feeling that they had never fooled him at all.

"If you should wish to interest yourself any further on his

behalf . . ." he began, "but no, you have done so much already."

"What?" asked Harry and Lady Pritchard in unison, obviously unaware that they might be falling into a trap. Merissa and Juliana exchanged despairing looks.

"Well, it's just that I have no power to exempt him from the rules. The price of the bounty paid for returned escapees is deducted from their daily ration allowance until it is paid off. It tends to leave most of them in pretty reduced circumstances—sometimes so desperate they cannot afford soap or adequate food. . . ."

Small wonder that Alex had looked so terrible! The black hole, this deprivation, the guards, the manacles, and who knew what other indignities were dealt to him each day! Merissa balled her fists, willing herself to stay silent. Surely her father would not let this go unredressed!

Sir Barry pulled out his purse. "How much was the bloody bounty?" he asked.

It was very unusual for Merissa's father to curse.

Chapter 19

The day after the visit to Norman Cross, Merissa sat silently at the table in the breakfast room of Pie Hill, pushing the food around on her plate while she listened to Harry and Juliana argue about Alex. A soft gray fog shrouded the fields outside the house and seemed to have dampened the spirits inside it as well.

"I would much prefer not to know with such certainty that he is facing total misery day after day," Harry declared with typical dramatic flair, gesturing in the air with a piece of toast. "If he had gotten away, we might not know what became of him, but at least we would be able to hope for the best."

"We can still hope, even if his situation is not very good at this moment," Julie countered defensively. She sipped her hot chocolate, peering at Harry over the rim of the cup.

"Oh, yes, of course! We can hope the war will end before he dies of illness in the dark bowels of a prison ship. We can hope his cousin won't already have disposed of every sou that rightfully belongs to him if he ever gets back to his country. We can—"

"Harry!" Merissa interrupted, setting down her fork. "Things may seem grim, but there is no need for us to give in to despair, never mind wallowing in it. If you wish to wallow, go out to the pigsty with Annie and the rest of them."

"Hmm," said Harry, pretending to think. "Do you have any better suggestions?"

Indeed, Merissa did. She had given herself the same lecture earlier and had pushed herself beyond the state of reaction that Harry was now in. "I think we should hope and pray that the government will establish his innocence or at least spare him being sent down to Chatham. There are many things that could happen. In the meantime, I know I plan to do whatever I can to keep his spirits up." She gave a small chuckle. "Papa and I have no idea at all what sort of model the captain is going to make for us, but as we have commissioned *something*, Papa has an excuse to remain in touch with him, and even to send him packets of materials and tools. We may be able to include other small items as well."

"Like letters? We could write to him!"

"No, Harry, I don't think so. The prison officials would read them, I'm certain, and it would look very suspicious at any rate. We aren't supposed to know him, remember? However, I spoke to Papa yesterday about going into Peterborough to try to buy him some books."

"Why go into Peterborough?" asked Juliana.

"Why would books not seem suspicious?"

"These are special. I want a copy of Tacitus's *Histories* or maybe some poetry by Catullus or Virgil. Roman authors could be explained as having to do with the model—at least, with the one we already bought."

"I should think you'd have to find those in London," Harry said dubiously.

"If I can't get them in Peterborough, we could all go down to Cambridge to visit Rodney. I'm certain we would find them there. Wouldn't Rodney think this all a great lark? Someday he'll feel terribly deprived to have missed it all while away at school. Say you'll go with me and help me look."

Merissa found that keeping busy seemed to be the key to warding off the depression of spirit that threatened to overtake her when she failed to guard against it. She found herself volunteering for tasks that would never normally have fallen to her, like checking the mousetraps and turning the apples in the apple loft, or helping Bessie to make quince jelly, a project far too mundane for Melders.

Harlan Gatesby continued to call on her every day, and she continued to refuse to see him. Unfortunately, she could not avoid attending the Guy Fawkes service at St. Gilda's with her family on the fifth of November. She saw

Harlan in his family's pew, but she refused to speak to him after the service. That night when the rest of the Pritchards went into Eastholme for the annual celebration and bonfire, Merissa pleaded a headache and stayed home.

She thought Harlan should have been banished from Pie Hill, and had hoped that her father might consider such a step after paying for the bounty money Harlan had received. The only change that she could perceive, however, was a lessening of the pressure from her parents for her to consider Harlan's suit.

She could never marry Harlan. Especially now. Any chance he might once have had had disappeared the day she met Alex. But if she was honest with herself, she had to admit that she should have realized long before that day that she and Harlan would never suit.

Why did he persist in riding over to Pie Hill every day? After weeks of her refusing to see him, did he not sense a message? Perhaps she was being cowardly, hoping he would come to see the truth without a confrontation.

It was the bleak prospect of never marrying that had loomed like a dark specter over her future and made her hesitate to acknowledge that truth. Her parents would make her go to London again in the spring, and she would be another year older and no richer than before. Why should her chances be any better this time? How could marrying a stranger she liked no better than Harlan be better than marrying him?

That she had never been cowardly in her life would be attested by everyone who knew her including her mother, who would have liked to see her show some sense of natural caution. Merissa decided that if Harlan was so stubborn or so obtuse as not to perceive her message by now, she had no choice but to see him and state it flatly to his face.

A cold drizzle filled the morning of the following day, but by afternoon the sun was shining. Harlan arrived to pay his usual call and appeared to be thoroughly stunned by Merissa's consent to see him.

"Would you be pleased to ride out to Dubro Vitae?" he asked.

"No, thank you," Merissa replied coldly, thinking she'd

rather ride there with the devil than go there with him. Harlan was too obtuse to realize what a poor choice he'd made. "Let us simply go walk in the garden."

Of course, even walking in the garden was not safe from memories. There was no place that Merissa liked to go that she had not been with Alex except under her willow tree down by the river or out walking in the fields. She realized with something like dismay that she had come to trust Harlan so little, she did not want to be out of sight of the house with him, even though what she needed to say wanted privacy. She no longer felt that she could predict how he would react.

"I never would have believed you could stay angry with me for so long, Merrie," he began once they had gone through the salon and stepped out onto the flagstone terrace. "I'm glad that at last you are starting to see sense."

Merissa stopped walking and turned to face him. "It is not I who needs to see sense, Harlan, but you. Do you think it is sensible to have come to call here every day for four weeks when I have made it clear you were not welcome?"

Harlan seemed to pause to consider this. "You are not the only one who lives here, Merissa, and besides that, how else was I to wear you down? I know you were very angry with me that night at the Harvest Fair, but I only did what I had to do. I had to protect you, even if you didn't want me to, and I had to uphold the law. I never thought it would take so long for you to come out of the cloud that fellow spun around you, once he was gone."

He did not spin any cloud around me, Merissa thought. *I spun my own, all by myself.*

She sighed as Harlan chose a path and they began to walk along it. "Despite what you think, Harlan, Captain Valmont never tried to deceive me or use me, and he never pretended he loved me. He was just an unfortunate man who was the victim of a terrible injustice . . . a conspiracy, actually. . . ." She stopped, aware of how ludicrous her words must sound. "He was a courageous and conscientious man. Why did you say nothing to the authorities about the fire or his rescue of Jarrod Garvey?"

"Was it he that rescued Jarrod?"

"You know very well it was."

"Well, suppose the authorities decided to investigate that incident? What if their questions led them to you and your family? After all, how did this supposed Gypsy come to be at the fair in the first place? I thought it too dangerous to report it, Merrie. I was thinking of you."

That seemed to be Harlan's answer to everything. Merissa frowned. "What happened cannot be undone, and I suppose there is no point in our wrangling over it, for we will never agree," she said finally.

"You cannot blame me for thinking you were deceived, Merrie. I can hardly believe you would flaunt the laws of our country and put your entire family at such terrible risk quite knowingly."

"You have always held far too high an opinion of me, Harlan. It is better that you should learn now that I have feet of clay."

Harlan reached for her hand and tucked it under his elbow. He began to walk slowly along the garden path again, chuckling.

"No, Merrie. If that were true, you would not be so humble and honest as to admit it. I have always known that you were exceptional. Difficult and sometimes misguided, but exceptional."

Merissa wanted to scream in frustration. She had hoped to make Harlan see that she was not the perfect wife for him. What did one do with a man who stubbornly wished to stay blind?

She halted, forcing him to a stop as well. The progress of their walk was beginning to feel like a tug-of-war between moving and stopping. "Harlan, I know that I have kept you waiting all summer and now into the autumn while I pondered the possibility of being your wife. I wanted to be certain that I would not make a mistake I would regret for the rest of my life. I should have known by the length of time I needed, however, that the answer was no. Do you not sense it also? We should never suit."

She saw the stricken look pass over his face, to be replaced by one of desperate pleading.

"How can you say that? Of course we should suit. We always have, Merrie. No one understands me so well as you do."

He released her hand from his side, only to face her and take both of her hands in his.

She stood very still. "Harlan, I do *not* understand you. Perhaps I did at one time, but not anymore." *And you have never come close to understanding me,* she reflected.

Yet, at this moment, she did feel almost a kinship with him, for in his pleading face she saw a reflection of herself pleading with Alex that last night, when she had begged to go with him and swore that she did not care if they could not marry. Would Harlan demean himself as she had that night, begging and casting all semblance of decency into the flames? What must Alex have thought of her then, offering to be his whore?

He had not betrayed the disgust of her he must have felt. Small wonder he had been so cool when she saw him at the prison! Perhaps he would not be heartened by the gifts she planned to send him. Perhaps he already wondered instead how he would ever rid himself of her attentions!

"You are still angry and confused over this episode with the Frenchman," Harlan said, his choice of words showing at least a little more respect than usual. "Now is not the time to finally make your decision, Merrie. I want you for my wife more than ever. You need someone to guide and protect you. I once thought that perhaps Francine and I . . . Of course, once she had set her cap for Chetwood, there was no chance for me. But I soon realized that you and I were far better suited. We need each other, you and I. We have so much we can give to each other. Please don't say no to me now. I love you, Merissa, with all my heart."

What Merissa wouldn't have given to hear such a declaration from someone else! As it was, she cursed the tears that welled into her eyes, knowing full well that Harlan would misinterpret them. Why couldn't her Frenchman have uttered such words? Her tears were as much for the love that could never be between them as for the frustration of having Harlan's unending devotion.

"Please, Harlan, it can never be. I must say no. We have been friends for so long, I cannot allow you to see hope where there is none. Please accept my answer—I have thought about it long enough. I cannot marry you. You are a good-hearted man. You will find someone else."

As she feared, Harlan saw the tears. "Ah, sweet Merissa, do not cry. I will not accept your answer now. When all of this business since Michaelmas has had enough time to heal, when you have forgotten his kisses and truly know your own heart, then I will hear your answer. I will give you more time."

I will never forget his kisses, thought Merissa angrily, *and I know my own heart right now.* "I don't want mo—" she started to say, but Harlan moved more swiftly than she had ever thought possible. Pulling her against him, he pressed a quick, hard kiss on her lips.

"I know you need more time, Merrie, but I promise I can make you forget him. I can make you happy." Harlan released her and headed for the garden gate. "I will see you again soon, but not too soon."

Merissa stared after him, fuming. Leave it to Harlan to completely ignore an answer that wasn't the one he wanted to hear! She should have known that he would never beg. He could never even imagine that he might not get what he wanted. . . .

At the prison, each day passed as much like the one before it as the one to follow. Only the ever-shortening hours of daylight and the increasing frequency of rain and wind showed the progress of the autumn, for there were no trees to turn colors or shed their leaves, only grass trampled into mud in the airing yards.

The tension and excitement stirred up among the prisoners by Alex's recapture and return died down slowly, as "escape season" passed. There would be little pressure on Alex to help engineer escapes for other prisoners now until spring. And by then, he thought grimly, he would no doubt be at Chatham.

Alex kept busy, teaching mathematics, English, reading, writing, and even the rudiments of engineering and mechanics. Idle hours were a torment for him, for he could not then keep his thoughts at bay. He only saw the drummer boy Sulpice on the days when they could be outside, for they lived in different caserns. The poor weather kept the prisoners inside too much of the time, and the dark days and short hours made it difficult to work on projects with so little light. Some prisoners slept, some prisoners fought. There was nothing else to do.

One day when the precious sun was shining and Alex and Sulpice were sitting on the paved edge of the airing ground trying to work on the model for Sir Barry, Alex was summoned to meet with Captain Hansell. Unsure of what to expect, he turned quickly to Sulpice, addressing him in hurried French.

"If it is my transfer to Chatham, I may have no chance to say good-bye, my friend. Hush, listen to me. You must finish the model yourself, and be sure to keep in communication with Sir Barry. He is a good Englishman, and would give you any help that he could, I believe. May God watch over you and see you home safely someday to your family."

"Come on, Redoute. It don't do to keep the captain waiting," muttered the guard, who shook his bayoneted musket impatiently.

Alex nodded and rose to go with him. He could see the turnkey waiting at the gate to put the irons on him. When he glanced back at Sulpice, he saw that the young drummer was crying.

He sighed. There was no comfort he could offer the boy. There never was any comfort, he reflected as the guard marched him away. He had not been able to offer comfort to Merissa, either, although he had offered warnings at the beginning of their friendship. That was just why he tried so hard not to form attachments—why he had tried so hard not to fall in love with her. His life had no permanence. What was happening to him now was hardly different from what had happened so often before. He was always separated from those he cared about. And he admitted now that he had loved Merissa. As an adult, he had never allowed himself to love anyone—how could he have fallen in love with an English girl?

Filled with sudden anger, Alex felt an overwhelming urge to bolt as he walked toward the gate. The guard beside him could not possibly fire upon him at a moment's notice, and the reach of his bayonet could be outrun in seconds.

The turnkey was foolishly holding the manacles in both hands in front of him, and could easily be fouled in them and thrust in the way of the guard.

Of course, there was no point in it. A sentry and another turnkey were on duty in the small office court. If Alex actually made it past them, there was no chance he would get any farther.

He thought of Sulpice, already distressed over their parting, and he thought of Merissa. How would she feel if she learned he had been shot down in such an ignominious and obviously suicidal manner? Chances were good that he would not even be killed, and he might be shipped off to Chatham with his wounds.

Alex had reason to thank his good sense in resisting that urge when he faced Captain Hansell a few minutes later. They met in the same bare little office where Alex had so recently seen the Pritchards.

"I have the best possible news to give you," said the agent, astonishing Alex with his barely contained excitement. He rose from behind the small desk and directed his beneficent smile at the two guards flanking Alex. "Take those hand irons off him, gentlemen. This man has been paroled."

Alex stared at Captain Hansell, trying to understand what he meant. How could he possibly have been paroled? Was it some kind of cruel joke?

"Congratulations, Captain Valmont. It is possible that even as we speak, your cousin and the witnesses he paid to swear to your death are being placed under arrest in France, although governments seldom move so quickly. While you are not a free man, at least your name has been restored to you, and along with it your *parole d' honneur*."

Alex felt the manacles drop away from his wrists, but he did not take his eyes off the prison agent. "How can this be? What has happened?" he asked, too overwhelmed by the news to begin to think of the hundreds of other questions he must ask.

Captain Hansell stepped up to him and shook his hand. "I want you to know how glad I am that this case has finally been sorted out, Captain. Perhaps you would like to sit down? I will read you the two letters I have received, one from our Admiralty Office and the other a copy of one from your government. Then we will have to get busy making arrangements."

Chapter 20

At Pie Hill a few days later, Sir Barry stood in his library also reading a letter, one that had just come in the post brought up from the village. As he finished, the baronet grunted in satisfaction and grinned. Without so much as refolding or setting down the letter, he went to the door of the room and, opening it, yelled into the passage beyond.

"Backhouse! Find Lady Pritchard and my daughters! I want them assembled in here immediately!" He remained in the doorway, fingering the letter and letting his eyes roam back over the words on the page, as if he wanted to make sure of its contents.

Within remarkably few minutes, Lady Pritchard, Harry, Juliana, Merissa, and Polly all arrived at the library from the various parts of the house where the aged butler had found them.

"Goodness, my dear, what is all this fuss?" asked Lady Pritchard.

Merissa's curiosity had been aroused immediately by the jubilant expression on her father's face. "Something good has happened, Papa? Hurry and tell us!"

"Sit, sit, everyone," he said, ushering them in and waving his hand vaguely at the assorted chairs. Merissa settled herself into the wing chair, since her father had taken up a position by the fireplace like a lecturer waiting to begin. Polly stationed herself beside Merissa in close enough range to have her ears scratched, and the rest of the family took seats also.

"I have received a letter from Captain Hansell at the prison," Sir Barry began.

Merissa's pulse leaped before her father said another word. *News about Alex—good news, and so soon!*

"Our friend Captain Valmont has been reprieved from going to Chatham."

Merissa wanted to shout and cheer, but her father was holding up his hand, signaling to the women that they should not interrupt him.

"He has been moved from Norman Cross Prison, but not to some worse place. His case has at last been resolved by the Admiralty Office! He has been released under his own name, on parole. It means that he is clear now to be exchanged, or at least to go home when the war ends, and to rightfully claim his inheritance."

"How wonderful!"

"At last!"

All four of the Pritchard women were aflutter at the news, jumping up from their chairs and hugging one another and Sir Barry. The pitch of excitement in the room set Polly to barking, which of course only added to the confusion. After several moments, Sir Barry was finally able to get in a word between laughing.

"I quite agree that the news is exciting, but could we possibly have any less commotion?"

The ladies retreated to their former positions and Merissa tried to quiet her spaniel as she spoke. "Where is he, Papa? Where have they sent him?"

Her tremendous initial joy and relief had quickly become shadowed by the thought that Alex might already be far away, and she would surely never see him again. Somehow, while he was still so near at Norman Cross, she had not come to terms with that inevitable reality.

But instead of explaining, Sir Barry chuckled. "How would you ladies like to get dressed to go visiting in Swaleford?"

"Swaleford? But why?"

"Who would we be visiting there?"

"Is that where he is, Papa?" Merissa hardly dared to hope such a thing. Swaleford was only three miles distant from Eastholme.

Sir Barry closed up the letter. "I think I'll let you see for yourselves."

Merissa could not fathom what mischief had gotten into her father. She had imagined that good news from the prison meant that Alex was saved from the hulks at Chatham, but she never would have dared to dream for so much more. To have him paroled, and at Swaleford! It was too much to believe, yet what else could this mysterious visit signify? Her father was playing a game with them all, but instead of enjoying it, she felt annoyed and a little bit frightened, lest she hope for too much. She hurried to her room to change her gown.

With Peggy's assistance she quickly dressed in a carriage dress of deep rose kerseymere and found a silk bonnet to match it. In her haste and distraction, she would have forgotten her blue wool cloak without her abigail's reminder. Slipping the garment around her shoulders, she hurried to join her family downstairs.

All four Pritchard women were ready in less than an hour, which said something about their impatience with the mystery Sir Barry had set for them. Once they had settled themselves on the leather squabs in the family's landau and were on the way to Swaleford, they pestered him with questions. When he was not forthcoming after repeated efforts, they gave up and rode in silence, listening to the creak of the carriage and the jingle of the harness as the horses drummed along the road.

The way to Swaleford ran between open grassy pastures and fields newly turned dark brown from ploughing. A cold November wind swept across them, rattling the closed top of the carriage. The Pritchards came into the town from the north, crossing the ancient stone bridge over the Nene and passing the famed Swan Inn, where they attended local assemblies. The ladies exchanged puzzled looks as the carriage continued down the road to finally halt before a singularly modest old village house of the usual Barnack stone.

"I think we may have arrived," announced Sir Barry, opening the carriage door and climbing down. After a word with their coachman, he returned to assist his wife and daughters from the carriage.

"Where are we? We don't know anyone who lives here!"

"On the contrary, my dears, you do." He ushered them up to the door.

Merissa hung back, tugging on his sleeve. "Please, Papa,

you must tell me. Is it the captain?" She was suddenly filled with trepidation, thinking of the goose she had made of herself on the night of the fire, and wondering how Alex would act now that he was no longer a fugitive with "no name and no honor."

Sir Barry nodded his head and winked.

A ruddy-faced matron answered their knock and admitted them into her small parlor when Sir Barry said they had come to see her new lodger. There were not enough chairs for all five of them to be seated, but Merissa did not feel like sitting, anyway. Her father stood in front of the fire, and she stood by the window overlooking the street, fidgeting with her reticule. After what seemed to her scarcely a moment, she heard hurried steps descending the stairs.

"My friends," said Alex, standing in the parlor doorway with his head brushing the top of the frame.

To Merissa he looked more magnificent than ever. He dominated the small room even from the doorway, exuding a presence of authority she had never sensed in him before. Was it only because he was dressed in what appeared to be his full regimental uniform?

It shocked her to see him standing there, resplendent in the trappings of his military life. The high-collared blue coat with its gold epaulets and braid was buttoned over a white waistcoat that fit his form perfectly. Gleaming brass buttons graced not only the wide white lapels of his coat but also emphasized the fine shape of his calves as they ran in a vertical row down his black gaiters. Despite a few missing buttons and the obvious fraying and wear on his uniform, Merissa thought he looked splendid—vital and healthy, as if he had gained back the weight he had lost. But more, he looked proud and confident in a way that seemed different from the Alex she knew. Had the accusations against him taken such a toll, then? Would he act differently, too? He seemed transformed. She realized she had never fully understood to what an extent this man was really a military officer, devoted to his career and his country.

Alex came into the room with his hands outstretched, a huge smile lighting his face. His gaze seemed to take them all in eagerly. Merissa was not certain if it lingered on her for an extra moment—perhaps she only imagined so, or wished it.

"My friends, I owe you all so much, I have no words to express my gratitude," he said. "I thank you, thank you, for all you have done. That I should be here, standing before you, is to me nothing less than a miracle—one I never thought possible even four days ago. I still think I will wake up and find myself in my hammock at the prison, surrounded by darkness and the snoring of five hundred other men!"

Sir Barry stepped forward to shake his hand. "We are delighted for you, Captain. But you must realize that we had little to do with it. As you told us yourself, our government has been investigating the case against you for more than a year. It is appalling that it took so long to document your innocence, especially with so many letters and so much information provided to them. But I suppose we should not be surprised, since our two countries are at war."

"My dearest, will you not tell the rest of us how this has all come about? We have not read the letter," Lady Pritchard reminded her husband.

"Oh? Oh, yes," Sir Barry said, moving back to his place by the hearth, where he could address all the assembled company. "Apparently the captain's escape back in August helped to refocus attention on his case. At least in that sense it did you some good, *Capitaine*. Also, the letters you sent to France must have helped at that end to establish your cousin's deception."

"Ah, yes, but such a way to have had to attract attention!" Alex said ruefully. "Captain Hansell told me that the complication of my escape set up another entire case against me. It was only the help and the information you gave, my friends, both at great risk to yourselves, that saved me from the consequences of my desperation."

"You give us too much credit," Sir Barry replied modestly. "With the Transport Office, the Admiralty, and the War Office involved, it is probably a miracle that any decision was made, but it seems the ruling not to send you to Chatham was already determined by the time they received our account of your actions on the night of the fire. That is how the results have seemed to come so quickly. Captain

Hansell wrote in my letter that what your heroism and our information did do was give the authorities grounds for the restoration of your parole. Despite the justification for it, your escape had made that impossible."

"It seems the least they could do," Merissa exclaimed, unable to stay silent as she had resolved to do. "After all, he never did break his original parole."

"I agree. Our government has exchanged or simply sent home other prisoners for similar heroic acts. But I don't believe any of them had also tried to escape. We must be grateful for what the authorities have allowed."

"And how has he come to be at Swaleford, Papa? You still have not explained that," Harry prompted her father.

"I'm getting to that. In the course of my communications with Captain Hansell over the commissioning of the 'mystery model,' I indicated to him that I would be happy to serve as sponsor to Captain Valmont if such a thing as a restoration of his parole ever became possible. The main purport of the letter I received today was to inform me that this has happened, and they have taken me at my word. I now stand before you, ladies, as Captain Valmont's sponsor. His lodgings have been arranged here in Swaleford because it is our nearest parole town."

"Papa, that is famous!" cried Harry, leaping up and dancing about. "May we come to visit whenever we wish?"

"Harry!" hissed Juliana, ever conscious of her sister's lack of propriety.

Sir Barry smiled and looked at Alex. "That is entirely up to the captain, my dear. His life is now his own again, at least within the limits permitted by the terms of his parole."

Alex looked chagrined. One by one he searched their faces, ending with Merissa. "How could you possibly think I might not wish for you to come? I hope you will come as often and whenever you wish!"

"You will begin to have something of a social life, Captain Valmont, for there are other officers on parole here."

Alex grinned. "Last night they called on me and took me to dinner with them at the Wheatsheaf. It is on the main road and just inside the one-mile limit that we are allowed beyond the village. I felt like a true human being again for the first time since I left the sanctuary of your home. I can never, never thank you enough."

"What will happen to the model you were making for Papa?" asked Juliana.

"Ah. I have left it in very capable hands, Miss Pritchard, and I have hopes that your father will still want it. You met my friend Sulpice Laloup, the young drummer from the Eighty-ninth? He could use the money very well."

After a few more minutes of talk, the Pritchards gathered themselves to depart. Merissa was aware of Alex's eyes on her, but she took little part in the conversation. Such an on-slaught of feelings had attacked her all at once, she felt numb.

Alex walked with them as they filed out to their waiting carriage. He put a hand on Merissa's arm as she tried to brush past him to catch up with the others.

"You have been very quiet, Mademoiselle Merissa."

He spoke in a low voice that made her heart triple its speed. The touch of his hand burned through all the layers between their flesh—his glove, her cloak, her dress sleeve. Unsure of her own voice, she simply nodded.

"May I hope that you will come sometimes to see me?"

Would she? It was frustrating to be with him and not say or ask the things she would most like to—the things that would reassure her that he was still the man she loved. In the company of her family, they had not the freedom to talk as they wished. Yet even if she cared nothing for her own reputation, she could not disgrace her family by calling on him at his lodgings without them. And Alex could not come to Pie Hill, for it was well beyond the one-mile limit.

"I—I don't know," she stammered, pulling away. Perhaps it was too painful to be with him under any conditions. The same specter of eventual separation hung over them now as always. Was there any reason to suppose that their relationship would change? "I will think about it."

Knowing that her words must hurt him, she turned back for just a moment. "I'm happy for you that this has happened," she said in a shaky voice, waving her hand vaguely at the lodging house behind them. "I hope that it will not be long before you find yourself ho—back in your country."

She could not use the word "home." He had told her himself that it did not have any meaning in his life.

It took only a few days for Merissa to make up her mind. She did not go with her family when they next drove into Swaleford, but she asked Harry to deliver a note to the captain.

"Within the confines of the village there is a path along the river that leads to the mill," she had written, "and there is a footbridge over the old flashlock by the mill. Unless it rains, I will be there tomorrow in the early afternoon, should you choose to walk out that way."

She had found that she could not bear to stay away from him, knowing that he was there and that she had a choice. Just as before, when he had been at Pie Hill, his presence drew her like a magnet, even from the distance of Swaleford. So she threw the choice to him. She would go, and she would try to show him that she was strong enough simply to be friends, for as long a time as was given to them. If he did not come, she would find a way to make herself accept that.

The following day began cold and foggy, without a trace of wind, as if the very universe held its breath in suspense along with Merissa. The scent of fallen leaves hung in the air, and pools of color stood in the road under the half-bare trees. By the time Merissa called for the pony cart and she and her abigail, Peggy, set off for Swaleford, the day had warmed slightly and the fog had retreated to the gently rolling fields in the distance.

The road, flat with only occasional dips, followed the gradual curve of the river, and eventually Merissa was able to look across the water meadows to her destination. Someone was sitting on a small bench by the mill across the river, his figure still difficult to distinguish in the distance. She squinted. Was he wearing a blue coat? She could not tell. Surely it must be him—who else would be waiting there at just this hour?

As she turned the pony onto the track that led across the meadow to the footbridge, she could see that it was indeed the captain, wearing his officer's bicorn and a dark brown

cloak over his uniform. When she approached close enough
for him to recognize her, he broke into that wonderful grin
that lit up his whole face. Her hand trembled on the reins.
Could she do this? Had she made a foolish decision? Perhaps resuming their friendship would bring her more pain
than she could bear.

She halted the cart, and after she and Peggy climbed
down, Merissa tethered Mignon and hurried across the narrow wooden bridge. Alex came over and doffed his hat to
the two women, tucking it under his arm as an apparent af-
terthought.

"Peggy, do you care to walk a bit under the trees, or
would you prefer to sit here by the bridge?" Merissa asked.

"I'll sit, miss. Don't get much chance to rest my feet
most days."

Merissa and Alex turned to walk along the riverbank in
the shadow of the old brick and weatherboard mill. Wil-
lows and alders grew near the bank and their leaves car-
peted the path. The captain took Merissa's small hand in
his large one and tucked it neatly under his elbow beneath
his open cloak.

"So. Here we are," he said, glancing at her.

Merissa felt suddenly tongue-tied and awkward. She had
summoned him, he had come, and now she had no idea
what she wanted to say to him.

She needn't have worried. As if he realized her distress,
Alex took command of the conversation.

"I was disconsolate when your family called on me yesterday without you, Miss Merissa Pritchard. Of course,
your note quickly remedied that. I thank you for honoring
me with the pleasure of your company."

She nodded. "I was not sure if you would come."

"Not come, *moi*?? Not come, when a beautiful woman
summons me?" His mock tone of shock made her giggle.

"I thought perhaps you would begin to be busy with your
new friends and your new freedom. Or perhaps you would
think I was too forward."

"Ah, I see how it is," he said. "First of all, allow me to
assure you that my new friends, while likable enough,
spend most of their hours drinking, eating, and playing
cards. There is not a great deal for us to do with this 'free-

dom,' as you call it. We cannot stray beyond the village more than a mile, and only then if we stay on the main road. While we have the privilege of privacy in our own quarters—and after sharing space with five hundred others, this is no small thing—we still cannot escape the greatest curse, which is idleness."

Merissa could not help thinking that she had spent several months in London pursuing such idleness with the fashionable members of the *ton*, but she did not say so.

"Your father has given me the greatest gift imaginable—the gift of innumerable hours of creative pleasure—for he has lent me his precious violin. No doubt my landlady and neighbors will soon be fully sick of the sweet sound of the strings. But I think, *ma chère,* that you have forgotten what we have been through together and what friendship we share, if you are worrying that I will think you are forward."

They had moved out of Peggy's earshot, although not out of her sight, and now Alex stopped walking and turned Merissa to face him. "I know how I would like to remind you, but there are a thousand reasons why I must not do it." His dark eyes were searching her face, roaming over it in the way she knew he would have trailed kisses had he dared.

This was her Frenchman. He had not changed. He might not love her, but he understood her and desired her, and if there had been any way they could be together, that would have been enough for her. Such sweet torture! She realized now that she had not really had any choice about seeing him. She could not help herself.

They walked a bit more, back and forth along the edge of the water, talking, and Merissa found her awkward feeling easing. She curled her hand into the crook of his arm a little more firmly, feeling the warmth and size and hardness of the muscled arm beneath his coat sleeve. She heard herself agreeing to meet him here on other days—in fact, on any day when the weather permitted.

Finally Alex said, "There is something I would like you to do for me. I will never ask anything else of you, dear Merissa, who has done so much for me already!"

"What, more?" she teased him, on familiar footing with him at last. "Is the man never satisfied?"

For a moment he gave her a dark, hungry look that sent fire racing through her veins right down to her toes, startling her. She felt the blush come up in her face, and her shock must have shown, for suddenly he smiled and laughed. How she loved that sound!

"I want you to bring your flute with you the next time," he said.

She was not sure she had heard him right. "My flute?"

"If the day is not too cold, yes."

"To play?"

"No, to admire as a work of art. Of course, to play!"

"Well, I—but I've never . . ."

"That is exactly why I am asking. Do you not remember telling me one day why you took up the flute in the first place? You play beautifully, but you have never moved beyond producing that beautiful sound you admired—you have never let the instrument set you free, Merissa. Sometimes the passions in our hearts need to be let out, free of the restrictions we create to protect them. If I can help you to dare to do that, to reach for that, it will be a gift that can serve you always, after I'm gone and for all of your life. Please, will you bring it?"

Merissa heard the unspoken message behind his words. Passion through music could one day save her soul from a bleak future without him, and it would also create a bond with him that could transcend time and place and separation.

Play her flute, for him, here, under the open sky? "All right," she said, nodding. She was grateful that at least there would still be a "next time."

Chapter 21

Merissa did bring her flute to her next meeting with Alex, for the day proved unseasonably bright and warm. After much coaxing on his part and hesitation on hers, she finally played for him, choosing some bits of a Bach sonata that she knew from memory. The music seemed to flow out of her more easily after that, and she soon became so caught up in it that she forgot where she was, who she was, and even why she was there. She knew only the music and the feeling it produced.

She brought the flute on most sunny days after that, sending the sweet, clear sound of her notes soaring over the countryside, sheltered from the wind by the trees on the colder days. Sometimes Alex would sit on the damp ground at the foot of one of the larger tree trunks, just listening. The look of utter contentment that would steal over his face at those times made her want to go on playing for him for hours, but her fingers would grow too cold, and their precious meeting time would run out.

She wondered how often they would manage to see each other when the winter truly began—that is, if Alex was still at Swaleford. The leaves were disappearing from the trees like the sand from an hour glass, and each day of wind and rain between meetings hurried the process. Any morning now she expected to awaken to find a hard frost had tumbled the last of them.

Preoccupied with such thoughts on her way to meet Alex one afternoon as she drove in the pony cart with Peggy, she scarcely noticed the sound of a lone horseman approaching until the rider drew abreast of them and slowed.

"Good day, Merissa," said a familiar voice.

Oh, Lord, it was Harlan! What wretched luck had sent

him along just now? "Good day yourself," she answered, slowing the pony. How was she going to be rid of him?

"I happened to notice you passing through Eastholme village. You wouldn't happen to be on your way to giving a concert, would you?"

"A—a concert? What do you mean?"

"There seems to have been flute music issuing from a certain copse by the Swaleford mill on several days recently. It has become the subject of a good deal of talk."

"What sort of talk?"

"The kind of gossip I have been doing my best to refute on your behalf, Merissa," he said darkly.

"I have done nothing that should occasion gossip."

"That is beside the point. The point is what people think, Merrie, and they always think the worst. I could scarcely believe it when I heard that you were meeting this Frenchie quite openly. I couldn't believe that your parents would allow it." Harlan's expression was growing darker as he spoke. "Then, when I came by on the road the other day to see for myself, there was your pony cart, and Peggy sitting by the footbridge bundled up like a frozen sparrow, and no sign of you at all!"

"If it was so cold, I was probably just around on the other side of the trees to get out of the wind."

"I also didn't hear any music, Merissa."

She could see that Harlan was truly angry now.

"I can't be playing every minute," she said in exasperation. "Sometimes we just talk. Some days it is too cold to bring my flute. The wood might crack, and anyway, the tone would be off."

"Unfortunately, I don't believe you," Harlan said harshly. "For your own sake and the sake of your misguided parents, I've come to put a stop to this. Today."

For the first time, Merissa felt a hint of alarm. "I don't give a fig about other people's opinions at this moment, Harlan—just what do *you* think is going on? If I were doing something wrong, would I bring my maid as a chaperone? Would I carry on my activities in such a publicly visible place as the Swaleford mill bridge?"

"I would not have thought so, Merissa, and I have sworn as much to other people, but I remember when you tried to tell me that you had feet of clay. Now I would say that is only too apparent. You have not been yourself since the day I found your bonnet down by the river near Pie Hill more than two months ago. What should I think?"

"Harlan, how can you believe that I would—that I—"

They had reached the point in the road where she could look across the river and see the mill. Alex was sitting on the bench, waiting as always. Merissa turned the pony onto the lane to the bridge.

"Someone must save you from yourself, Merrie," Harlan continued in a louder voice, his horse forced away by the movement of the cart. "You are headed for disaster. As the man who wants to wed you, I cannot simply stand by." He suddenly spurred his horse around the pony cart and pulled in front of Mignon. The little pony halted, her path blocked.

"What are you doing?" Merissa cried.

"Stopping you."

"You have no right!"

"I think I do."

"Well, you are wrong." Fully angered herself now, Merissa gathered her skirts and climbed out of the pony cart.

"Please, miss, what should I do?" whispered Peggy, looking frightened.

"You can see us?"

The maid nodded.

"Then stay there."

With her head high and her back rigid, Merissa marched purposefully towards the bridge, too proud to run. Alex had stood up, as if he sensed trouble.

Please stay where you are, Merissa begged silently, lengthening her strides. Harlan would be the first to make an issue of it if Alex stepped out of bounds by crossing the bridge.

"I'm not going to allow this, Merissa," Harlan said in a warning tone. He had followed along slowly behind her on his horse, but as she drew near the wall of the flashlock, he swung down from his saddle, letting the reins drop.

"Harlan, there is nothing you can do about it and no need for you to interfere." She tossed the words angrily over her shoulder as she started up the slight embankment.

"That's where you're wrong, Merrie, on both accounts."
Suiting action to word, Harlan suddenly threw his arms
around her from behind, pinning her against him with her
arms to her sides.

"What is the matter with you?" she cried.

"Nothing," he growled. "The matter is between you and
him."

"Take your hands off her," shouted Alex from across the
water, starting toward his end of the bridge.

"Make me, Frenchman!"

"No, Alex, stay back!" Merissa called. "Harlan, let go of
me."

"You have always underestimated me, Merrie. Now you
will see that I am more of a man than you thought," Harlan
said. "If you are going to make more than music out here,
by God, you're going to make it with me, not him."

Shifting her so he could take both of her wrists in one
hand, he used the other to fumble with the fastenings of her
cloak. Merissa squirmed and tried to get a hand free to stop
him. She sensed more than saw when he glanced up to
gauge the captain's reaction. Realization of exactly what
Harlan had in mind struck her like a dousing of ice water.

"Alex, stay back! He only *wants* you to step out of
bounds! You mustn't come across! Peggy, come help me!"

Merissa struggled against Harlan's strong grip, the sight
of Alex's furious expression fixed in her mind. "Harlan,
stop it! You're hurting me. I know you don't really mean
this."

Harlan replied in earnest, "You are hurting yourself,
Merrie, by struggling. Truly, if you stay still I will not hurt
you. And if your friend is the honorable fellow that you
claim he is, he will stop me."

"That isn't fair!" Merissa countered breathlessly, trying
to kick and jab at him. "Oh, Lord, Harlan, you will freeze
me!" she exclaimed as he wrenched open her cloak.

Peggy had already climbed from the cart when Merissa
called to her. Hesitantly, she tried to grab hold of Harlan's
free arm. "Please, sir, you mustn't do this!"

Harlan threw the little maid off onto the ground. "Run
and get help, Peggy, there's a good girl," he said mock-

ingly. "Go get some witnesses to this Frenchie breaking his parole."

Merissa cried, "No, Peggy, don't!"

The abigail burst into tears.

Taking Merissa's chin in his hand, Harlan taunted loudly, "Will your lover watch me do this? I'll make you mine right here and now. He must care more for his precious parole than he does for you, Merrie."

"Stop it!" Merissa was no longer certain that he was bluffing. "Harlan, you are being vile and cruel! Please do not do this," she begged. "Why must you ruin his life?"

"So I can have you, Merrie. I got rid of him once—this time I'll make certain they'll never let him out."

"No. Please. I—I will marry you, if only you will not do this."

Harlan crushed her body against his and lowered his mouth to her lips in a punishing kiss.

It was too much for Alex. "She will never be your wife, *cochon*!" he shouted.

In despair Merissa heard him charge across the wooden bridge.

"Alex, no!" she cried, pushing against Harlan suddenly and breaking off his kiss. She felt as if the whole world was collapsing around her.

Harlan shoved Merissa roughly to one side and rushed forward to meet the angry Frenchman. "How do you propose to stop me, parole-breaker? You've signed your own warrant now!"

Alex swung at Harlan's head and missed as the shorter man ducked under. Harlan brought Alex to the ground with the force of his charge.

"Stop it! Stop it! Oh, Alex, you could still go back before someone comes!" cried Merissa.

"Oh, miss, what should we do?" wailed Peggy between tears.

As Alex lay momentarily stunned, Harlan pinned his arms and pulled back his own arm to strike him.

"I said *stop it*!" Merissa shouted. She stepped in and pushed Harlan sideways with all her strength. As he toppled off of Alex, the Frenchman quickly rolled with him down the slope of the embankment and gained the upper position.

Harlan glared. "I don't suppose they'll keep you at Norman Cross this time, Frenchie, after all the trouble you caused before! Did you call me a swine?"

"Should I choose something worse? Do you want me to kill you now or wait?"

"Stop it, please!" cried Merissa. "You are like dogs fighting over a bone—brawling like ruffians!"

Behind them came the hollow sound of feet running over the bridge. Two burly men laid hands on Alex and pulled him off of Harlan. "What is all this fracas?"

"Ah, you would be the constable, I expect," said Harlan to the man who had spoken.

The fellow nodded. "You'd be the new parolee," he said, squinting at Alex. The other man was holding the captain with his arms pinioned behind him. "Didn't take you long to break your word, I see. Word of a Frenchie—hmph! Out of bounds, and brawling besides. Nothing but trouble!"

Merissa was staring at Harlan. "You knew he was coming, didn't you? You arranged it all."

There was still a chance for Alex, if she could only convince the constable. "You're making a terrible mistake," she said desperately, turning to him. "This man was goaded into breaking his parole—it was all a trick. You must listen to me! How did you know to come here?"

"Got a letter, gave me time and place, particulars."

"Doesn't that strike you as odd?"

"No, ma'am. Helpful, is all. This officer's out of bounds, and caught brutalizing an Englishman, besides." He turned to Alex. "Hit'll be the lockup for you, monsieur, and back to prison."

"You don't have all the information!" Merissa cried. After all they had been through, to lose it all now was too much to bear. "Harlan, I beg you! Please say something!"

Harlan was standing in the lane, brushing off his clothes. "This so-called officer tried to attack this woman," he said.

"No! That isn't true! He was trying to protect me."

Alex looked back at her, his eyes dark and unfathomable. "Promise me you will never marry him, Merissa," he said urgently. "You would die a little bit every day."

She knew Alex did not understand that without him, she would die a little bit every day no matter what her future held.

"Promise me—I will never ask anything more of you."

"You have told me that before," she answered, trying to smile bravely despite the tears welling into her eyes. How much she loved him! She did not think he realized the painful irony his words carried this time.

Unnoticed in all the commotion, a curricle had approached from the Eastholme road and now drew to a stop behind the pony cart. With dawning hope Merissa saw that it was her father's. "Papa!" she called, running toward it. "Oh, Papa, help!"

Sir Barry climbed down, obviously perplexed. "Exactly what is going on here? Merissa? Peggy? Are you all right?"

Peggy burst into a fresh bout of tears.

"Harlan forced the captain to break his parole, and now they are taking him away!" Merissa blurted out in one breath. "Harlan did it all on purpose—it isn't fair! I said I would marry him, but that still didn't stop him! Please, Papa, do something!"

"Well, I'm not certain who it is you have promised to marry, Merissa, or quite what has happened, but they can't take Captain Valmont in for breaking his parole. Hold up there!" In quick strides Sir Barry presented himself before the constable, who was walking up the embankment to cross the bridge. His assistant had already started across with Alex.

"I am Sir Barriemore Pritchard, of Pie Hill near Eastholme, this French officer's sponsor," he said authoritatively. "You cannot put him under arrest for breaking his parole. Beside some question of jurisdiction because you are on the Northamptonshire side of the river, as of this morning the captain was no longer a paroled officer subject to the terms."

His own was the only face that was not puzzled.

"Papa, explain," Merissa demanded, her heart in her throat.

"I have received a dispatch from London. Captain Valmont is a free man—I was just coming to you with the news. Lieutenant-Colonel David Merley of the Second Foot

Guards arrived in London yesterday in exchange for the captain's freedom. Our friend may do anything he pleases except bear arms again against our country."

"They exchanged a lieutenant-colonel for a captain?" Harlan said incredulously.

Sir Barry looked at him with an expression of intense disapproval. "Captain Valmont is a very highly regarded member of the *Corps du Génie*—so highly regarded, in fact, that when he gets home there is a promotion waiting for him, as well as the considerable estate he has inherited from his grandfather. My sources in London say there are rumors that Napoleon might reinstate his grandfather's title for him . . . of course, it would not come without strings attached."

"Of course," said Alex, looking more stunned than when Harlan's rush had knocked him to the ground.

Alex couldn't quite take it all in, so much had happened so quickly. Within the space of only a few minutes he had given up his freedom and his future, only to have them handed back to him shining more brightly than ever before.

He felt overwhelmed, certainly, but not by the joy that should accompany such good fortune. He had worked so hard to achieve recognition in his field, and now that long-coveted promotion awaited him. If his inheritance was so substantial, it could provide him with an income well beyond his army pay. A title would give him prestige among his peers and the entree to circles where he could truly make a difference in his country's future. It was what he'd always wanted and worked toward—a future most men could only dream of. But in the moment that he had come raging across the bridge, he had known that everything he had worked for and lost, everything he had gambled his life to regain, meant nothing to him without Merissa, the one thing that he could never have. It had suddenly been very easy to throw away his own future to ensure her happiness.

Had he succeeded at least in that? He was not sure. He had been enraged by Harlan's ungentlemanly behavior toward her. When he had heard her offer herself to Harlan, sacrificing herself for him, something inside him had snapped. Her words to Harlan and the kiss that followed them had tipped Alex beyond any rational thought save that he could not allow their union, no matter the cost to himself. Now he was not exactly certain of what she had said. Was she committed to marry Harlan?

She surprised him by coming over to him and very improperly throwing her arms around him in front of all the others. "I'm so happy for you. It is wonderful news, is it not?" she gushed. "You can go back to France!"

In the brief moment that he felt her body pressed against him, she seemed like the single stable point in a universe gone spinning. It took all of his control not to wrap his arms around her and hold her fast.

He noticed as she stepped back from him that her blue eyes were unnaturally bright, and wondered if the tears he saw in them were tears of joy, relief, or something else entirely. If he discovered that she was bound to Harlan by her rash promise, he knew that he would kill the man. He was free now. He could do as he wished. He would challenge Harlan and make sure that Merissa was free of him forever. If Alex survived the duel himself, at least he could cross the Channel knowing Merissa would not have to spend her life shackled to such a man as Harlan Gatesby.

"Will you try to arrange your passage right away?" Merissa asked him, cutting into his thoughts.

He shrugged. He knew he dared give no hint of what he was thinking. "I have not yet had time to consider it—this has happened so suddenly. I think I have not yet even taken it in."

Let them think I'm too overwhelmed to react, he told himself. How ungrateful he would seem after all their risk and efforts to help him if they knew how little it all meant to him now!

"What of you, *ma chère?*" he whispered, stealing the moment while he could. Sir Barry was still talking to the constable and Harlan. He could not predict what would happen in the hours ahead. "Will you have to marry Harlan? Can he hold you to your offer?"

Merissa smiled grimly. "Do not be concerned for me. He did not meet the conditions of my offer. After what he tried to do today, I could never marry him!"

Her assurance filled him with relief. "You are very spe-

cial, Mademoiselle Merissa Pritchard. Someday you will
meet a man who will love and cherish you and nurture your
spirit." *As I would have.* "I hope then you will marry that
man, Merissa. You deserve to be happy."

"Yes. We both deserve to be happy," she agreed, her
eyes glittering again with tears. He saw her lip tremble, and
she put her fist to her mouth to hide it.

He could not do it—he could not stand there without
touching her. For two people who deserved to be happy, he
had never seen anyone so miserable.

He opened his arms and she walked into them, burying
her face against his neck and shoulder. He let his chin rest
against the pale soft silk of her bonnet. How could he go
back to his old life now? After knowing her, he would
never be the same. He loved her. He knew that she loved
him—that had been clear on the night of the fire. But because he loved her, he could not marry her, and he would
have her no other way. Surely hell itself held no torment
worse than this.

Lost in his agony and the sheer bliss of holding Merissa,
Alex was startled by Sir Barry's voice.

"So is it you she has promised to marry, then?" the
baronet asked, clearly not missing a detail of their close
embrace. "I should think you would both look a bit hap-
pier."

The constable and his assistant were departing back
across the footbridge, and a defeated-looking Harlan was
mounting his horse. The maid was standing by the pony
cart, stroking the pony's nose.

Alex shook his head slowly without releasing his hold on
Merissa. "How can I offer for her?" he said, making no attempt to disguise his misery. "To marry her I would have to
give up the only prospects that would make me a fit husband for her. If I go back to my country, I will be a prominent man swept up in the changes there, and I do not think I
would be allowed to return here. Such marriages are not
legal in my country at this time. I love her, but if I remain
here, I will be a man with no wealth or position, no career,
no land, no country—nothing to offer to her or her children.
I could not bear to see her wed to such a man as I would
be."

"It is a dilemma," agreed Sir Barry ruefully. "In your own country you would be a man of considerable consequence. No doubt they would want to see you wed a woman from a highly placed family of your own nation."

Merissa stirred in Alex's arms. "In all this concern for my future, monsieur, have you no thought of consulting me? What do you say, Papa—have I any say in what my life should be?" She pulled back from Alex just enough to be able to look up into his face.

Hope bloomed in Alex's heart suddenly, like a bubble sending out ripples in ever-widening circles. "If I came to you with nothing but my name and my honor, a man without a country who would have to work for his living—no fortune, no place in society, no land, no prospects—how could you consider my suit? It is as unthinkable as you marrying Gatesby."

"Do you love me?" she asked, her eyes a more vivid blue than he had ever seen them.

He nodded. "I love you with all my heart."

"Did you not tell me that when I met a man who would love and cherish me and nurture my spirit, I should marry that man?"

Of course, he had. Again he nodded.

"How can you think that there would ever be any other man like that for me but you? I don't care if you would bring nothing to our marriage but yourself! It is you I love. I know that you could start a new life and you would be everything that is splendid and wonderful, simply because of who you are."

Alex turned to Sir Barry. "Would a French engineer be able to find work in your country?"

Sir Barry beamed. "Unquestionably. Just as in your own country, great changes are beginning here. You could teach! Our own engineers are still far behind you French in technical training. You could work as a civilian engineer in almost any capacity. You might not be allowed to or want to participate directly in a military capacity, but you could probably be an invaluable advisor. There are many influential people with whom I could put you in touch!"

"Would you consider my suit if I asked your permission to court Merissa?"

"My boy, I might consider the courtship completed at this point! There is a good chance I could insist on you marrying her, just for the sake of her reputation."

Merissa spoke again, in a smaller voice. "Would you sacrifice so much for me, *Capitaine*? You would give up all that you have strived for. I would never ask it of you."

Alex looked down into her eyes, his heart so full of love and joy he wondered that it did not burst. "Without you, it means nothing to me now. I never knew what love could be." *Or what choices the heart could demand.*

The answer to his dilemma was shining in her eyes. "If you think that I can make you happy—if you think that having my heart and my soul and enduring devotion can make up for what you are sacrificing for me, then there is nothing in the world I want more than to be your wife."

"If I have you, I will never need anything more," he declared. "I will strive to give you everything that you deserve. I love you, Merissa. Please be my wife."

As he bent to kiss her, she met his look with a brilliant, tearful, teasing smile. "If I have your love, I shall never ask anything more of you!"

Alex claimed her lips in a kiss that promised to last into eternity. This, at last, was surely heaven.